MURDER OF A SUICIDE

Elizabeth Ferrars

Constable . London

First published in Great Britain 1941
as *Death in Botanists Bay*
by Hodder and Stoughton Ltd
Copyright © 1941 by M. D. Brown
The right of Elizabeth Ferrars to be
identified as the author of this work
has been asserted by her in accordance
with the Copyright, Designs and
Patents Act 1988
Reprinted 1993
by Constable and Company Ltd
3 The Lanchesters, 162 Fulham Palace Road
London W6 9ER
ISBN 0 09 4731209
Set in Palatino 10/12 pt by
Pure Tech Corporation, Pondicherry, India
Printed and bound in Great Britain by
Hartnolls Limited, Bodmin, Cornwall

A CIP catalogue record for this book
is available from the British Library

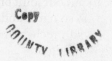

1

When the voice she wanted answered, Joanna Prees said into the telephone: 'Oh, is that you, Gerald? I'm so sorry to disturb you when you're probably working, but father hasn't come in yet. What d'you think I ought to do about it?'

Gerald Hyland's slightly grating, elderly voice replied: 'Not come in yet? Edgar not come in yet? Edgar late for his dinner? Goodness me!'

'No, Gerald,' she said, 'it isn't a joke. At least I think it isn't. I'm worried. I rang up the Haybox an hour ago, to find out if he was working late or something, and they said he'd left at the usual time.'

'But what about Miss Winnpole then? Hasn't she come back either? She always drives the car for him, doesn't she?'

'Not to-day. She didn't go to work this morning. She'd a headache, she said. She's been in her room all day.'

'Hum! Then Edgar was driving the car himself. Perhaps after all you've got something to worry about, and perhaps I'd better come round so that we can put our joint brains to the problem. If only it weren't raining quite so hard, and if only these damned camels weren't giving me so much bother at the moment.... I hate to leave them, even for Edgar.'

'*Camels?*'

'Yes, camels,' said Gerald Hyland. 'I'm trying to make some camels file round a sanddune with ineffable, Oriental dignity, but they're being very awkward about it – it's in Chapter Seven. Well, I'll be round in about five minutes. Don't get too worried, my child, I'm sure there's nothing wrong really.'

That was at a quarter to nine.

The storm had started about a quarter of an hour earlier.

As Joanna put down the telephone she gave a sharp little hiss of a sigh. Staying where she was, seated on the arm of a chair, staring across the room with wide, rather resentful eyes, she let her hands fall together in her lap. She made no other movement.

Joanna was twenty-three. She was a slim girl, very erect, with a conscious, nervous dignity. Her face was a narrow oval. There was no make-up on the white skin, but only on her mouth a warm, red splash of lipstick. Her eyes were brown, the kind of brown eyes that seem to be all iris, with a lustrous, slightly blank innocence in them. Above them she had strong, dark brows. But her hair was fair; its bright, smooth coils, rolled into a big knot on her neck, formed with her eyes and eyebrows a conspicuous, almost bizarre contrast. She was wearing shantung slacks, a silk shirt and sandals.

The room in which she had done her telephoning and in which she was sitting in that uneasy posture on the arm of a chair, was a big room, panelled in light wood, furnished with armchairs and bookshelves. It had big windows, the sort of windows which, on the placards of an estate-agent, change a sitting-room into a sun-parlour. There was a clock on the mantelpiece, a ridiculous yet graceful object in an old gilt case with smirking cupids supporting it. While Joanna watched, five slow minutes passed on its enamelled face.

Suddenly, when another three minutes had gone by, she jerked herself on to her feet. Going out into the hall, she flung the front door open.

Beyond the porch the rain made a dense, leaden curtain. But even when the lightning cut great gashes in the streaming twilight there was no one in sight. The chalk track beyond the garden gate, supposed to be the main thoroughfare of the building-estate, was a river of grey-white slime. A steamy smell of drenched grass and soil met her nostrils, together with the tang of the sea. Here and there in the windows of the few other occupied bungalows lights were shining, but their gleam through the rain was faint and watery. The sea, beyond the rim of the cliffs, was a black cup of darkness round which the thunder rolled.

A shudder went through Joanna's body, and with a quick gesture she slammed the door shut again.

The noise brought Mrs. Searle out of her kitchen.

'Oh,' she said, 'I thought that might be him.'

Joanna shook her head. 'But have your own dinner, Mrs. Searle, and I'll dish up ours later. I don't know how much later it'll be. I've just rung up Mr. Hyland and asked him to come round. He'll be here any minute now.'

'Well,' said Mrs. Searle, 'I reckon you're right, something must've happened.' She went back into the kitchen.

While another minute passed Joanna continued to stand in the tiled hall of the bungalow. Out of a round mirror on the wall her own eyes stared at her with a frowning look of apprehension. Meeting that look, the frown on her face grew deeper. She muttered something. For an instant she looked unspeakably depressed, almost as if she might cry in another moment. But she hardened the set of her mouth, so that eyes and mouth matched one another in resentment and exasperation. She turned to go back to the sitting-room.

On the threshold she changed her mind, went to another door and knocked softly upon it.

A voice answered indistinctly and Joanna pushed the door open.

With curtains drawn, the room inside was in complete darkness. The wave of stuffiness, soaked in eau de cologne, that met her as she took a step forward, was like a pad clamped stiflingly over her face. She could see nothing. But, as she hesitated, the bed-springs creaked and a deep sigh rustled in the gloom. Someone seemed to be sitting up on the bed and fumbling about on the bedside-table. Something was knocked onto the floor; from the light thud and rattle that accompanied it, it sounded like a bottle of aspirins.

Joanna asked of the darkness: 'How are you, Peggie?'

The husky voice of her father's assistant and secretary replied: 'I'm feeling rather better, thank you. I've been to sleep, I think. What time is it?'

'About a quarter to nine. Shall I turn on the light?'

But at that moment the hand that had been fumbling over the top of the bedside-table found the switch of the reading-lamp, and the light came on.

'A quarter to nine!' In the sudden light the woman on the bed

7

clutched both hands over her eyes. 'Then I've missed dinner. But how kind of you not to disturb me. This head of mine's been simply dreadful all day. I don't know how many aspirins I've taken. But my sleep's done me a great deal of good. It really was sweet of you to leave me sleeping.'

'We haven't had dinner,' said Joanna. 'Father hasn't come in yet.'

Peggie Winnpole went on rubbing her eyes. Aged about thirty, tall and slackly built, she had fair, fluffy hair and a dull, unhealthy skin. At the moment she was wearing a cotton kimono over an artificial silk slip. Her hair looked damp and crushed. She had been lying on top of the counterpane, which she had rucked into a mass of creases.

Rubbing away at her eyes, she said in a voice still stupid with sleep: 'Quarter to nine . . . not come in . . . ?'

'I suppose he didn't say anything to you about going anywhere after he'd finished working?' said Joanna. 'There wasn't anyone he had to go and see? He didn't give you any message you've forgotten to give me?'

'Certainly not!' Peggie groped for the spectacles that lay on the table. As she pushed them on over her eyes Joanna suddenly saw that it had not been only from a headache that Peggie had suffered that day; her eyelids were swollen and her cheeks were blotched with weeping.

'But I don't understand,' said Peggie. 'He *always* comes straight back.'

'I telephoned the Haybox,' said Joanna, 'and they told me he'd left at the usual time.'

'But then—'

Suddenly what Joanna was telling her seemed to penetrate the drowsiness, the aspirins and the heavy aftermath of tears. In the bleared eyes behind the spectacles something was sharp and clear; it was panic.

'He always comes straight home!' cried Peggie Winnpole. Her voice was high and harsh. 'You know he does. All this time I've been working under him – always. Something's happened, Joanna, something must've happened.'

'I'm rather afraid so myself,' said Joanna.

'Something's happened – oh, God, something's happened!'

8

Peggie floundered on to her feet. 'I know it has, it must have, something terrible's happened to him!'

'If you're feeling well enough, you might get dressed,' said Joanna. 'Mr. Hyland's coming round; we can talk over with him what we ought to do.'

'But I *know* something's happened . . .' On the last word Peggie's high voice wobbled uncertainly, and it was almost in a mutter that she went on: 'Something was bound to happen. I've had the most horrible feeling of foreboding, a dreadful sense of . . . Oh, God, I don't know, but . . .' Stopping, she pressed both hands to her forehead.

Joanna's cold stare was full of irritation at the hysteria that fanned the flame of her own anxiety. 'What d'you mean, you *knew* something was bound to happen?'

'Never mind,' said Peggie Winnpole. 'I know a lot more about your father than you do – and I understand him much better than you do.'

'That wouldn't be difficult.'

'And I'm so terribly sorry for him!' said Peggie in a low, tense voice.

After a pause, looking at the floor, turning away, Joanna said: 'All the same, I don't see the point of working ourselves up until we're certain something's wrong.'

'I'm not worked up in the least. I'm just facing the facts,' said Peggie.

'We haven't the faintest idea what the facts are.'

'Perhaps *you* haven't.' Picking up the crushed, cotton dress that had been hanging over the back of a chair, Peggie plunged head first into it.

Joanna watched her contortions inside its folds with frigid antagonism. As Peggie's head, with red face and touzled hair, came through the neck-opening of the dress, she remarked abruptly: 'You've been crying, haven't you?'

Peggie turned to the mirror and started fastening the depressed, muslin jabot at her neck.

'You *have* been crying,' said Joanna.

'It's just my nerves,' said Peggie. Her fingers were trembling slightly.

'But what's the matter?'

9

'Nothing, nothing. Don't you know anything about nerves? Don't you know what they do to you? No, you don't, you don't know anything. You went to a grand, expensive school, and you went to Oxford, and now you've just come home from wonderful travels abroad, but heaven knows what the point of it all was, because you don't know any more than a—'

But here a recurrence of tears stopped her. She opened a drawer, took out a handkerchief and dabbed with it at her eyes.

At the same moment there was a loud knock on the front door. Joanna went quickly to open it.

With lightning blazing behind him, with thunder shaking the air, with the torrential rain like a wall of steel behind him, Gerald Hyland stood on the doorstep under a dripping umbrella.

Certainly it was Gerald Hyland, although with the umbrella, the oilskins and gumboots, little of him but his gaunt height showed. But that was enough for recognition; not many men are six foot seven.

As he lowered his umbrella his blue eyes in their deep sockets became visible, and the thick, grizzled hair cropped close to his bony head; the lower part of his face was still hidden in the turned-up collar of his oilskins.

Joanna greeted him: 'You said you'd only be five minutes!'

'That's right, five minutes – five minutes precisely.' He stepped inside. Standing on the mat he extricated himself from gumboots and waterproof, then prodded about vaguely with his umbrella, looking for somewhere it could be left to drain in safety.

Joanna took it from him and carried it into the kitchen.

When she returned she found him tugging a pair of red leather slippers embroidered in gold thread and beads out of one pocket of the flannel suit that hung in loose folds on his spidery frame. He put the slippers on over the thick blue woollen socks that drooped in wrinkles round his ankles.

'Now,' he said, rubbing his damp hands together as he followed her into the sitting-room, 'what's it all about? What's Edgar done or not done? What's the trouble?'

She held out cigarettes to him, but he shook his head and took a pipe out of his pocket.

She took a cigarette herself and speaking round it as she lighted a match, told him: 'It's simply that father hasn't come in yet.'

'And you telephoned the Haybox, you say?'

She nodded. 'And it's nothing to do with his driving the car. The car's here; he went in by bus this morning.' Between quick puffs at her cigarette, she added: 'Am I being very stupid, Gerald, worrying because father's two hours late getting home?'

He took a look at the clock with the gilt cupids wantoning round its prim, enamelled face. 'Two and a half hours,' he corrected her, and frowned at the clock. 'I don't know, Joanna, I don't know. He may just have run across someone he knows, or suddenly plucked up courage to go to the dentist and have a tooth stopped, or gone to the library and got engrossed in something, or gone into a pub and got involved in a metaphysical argument, or—'

'Yes, Gerald,' she interrupted with a smile, 'if it was you it might be any of those things – and I shouldn't be worrying.'

'Hum, yes. Anyway,' he said, 'who told you he'd started for home at the usual time?'

'The caretaker, Barnes.'

'Well, are you sure he was taking the trouble to find out if Edgar was really there or not?'

'Oh, yes, he told me to hang on and he'd go and see, and he took several minutes about it, then he came back to the telephone and said no, that definitely father wasn't there still, and that the other porter said he'd seen him leave at the usual time, or a bit earlier if anything.'

'I see.' With an odd, folding-up movement Hyland lowered himself into a chair. His eyes dwelt thoughtfully on her face. Then he took the pipe out of his mouth and absent-mindedly wiped the mouthpiece against his flannel trousers.

'It's not only unreasonable, it's inconsiderate!' he exclaimed in his grating voice. 'I've always said so. No one should be like that. I've told Edgar a dozen times it wasn't fair on other people. I knew he'd never be influenced by being told how ridiculous it looked, but I did think he ought to listen if I explained how others were bound to suffer by it sooner or later.'

'By what, Gerald?'

'By the fantastic regularity of his habits, of course. As you said yourself, if it was I, who was two and a half hours late, you wouldn't be worrying. The whole point is, it's Edgar. And

Edgar's *never* late, or if he is he *always* telephones. But Edgar isn't God, in spite of an occasional delusion that way, and even Edgar's plans were bound to get upset by something or other sometime. I've tried to explain it to him. I've pointed out that the very smallest lapse on his part would cause untold anguish. But the pigheaded, self-satisfied old fool actually had the nerve to tell me that it was *I* who ought to improve my habits. The blundering, fat jackass!'

She laughed. 'I know all that. But what shall we *do*?'

'Ah, yes, what shall we do? Well—' He placed the tips of his bony brown hands together. 'Telephone the police, that's the first thing.'

'And if they don't know anything about him?'

'There are the hospitals, the lunatic-asylums—'

'Gerald!'

'Well, he might have lost his memory, mightn't he? Or suddenly decided he was a poached egg? I've always thought that about him myself, so I don't see why he shouldn't suddenly have come round to the same opinion. Or perhaps—' But he stopped and gave her a long stare with his grave, mild eyes. The facetious note was gone from his voice when he continued: 'Joanna, my child, tell me, is it simply because Edgar's late getting home that you're worried?'

She nodded.

He said insistently: 'Simply that and nothing more? Isn't there something at the back of your mind all the time?'

She frowned at the cigarette in her hand. 'No. Why should there be?'

He shrugged his gaunt shoulders. 'I suppose because I've been worrying about him a bit myself. There's been something wrong with Edgar this last year or two – I mean something that isn't his digestion, or his rheumatism, or his arthritis, or his catarrh, or his blood-pressure, or anything like that. It's somehow his nature that seems to have altered. D'you know what I mean?'

She did not answer. She strolled across the room and tugged at the cord that drew the wine-red curtains together across the windows.

Hyland was continuing: 'I suppose I might have done something about it – talked to him you know, taken him to concerts or something. That would have been a good idea, wouldn't it – classical concerts? There's nothing so soothing and inspiring as good music. Of course I've only just found that out for myself. Really if I hadn't seen that gramophone going cheap at Schmelzer's last month, music might never have come into my life. But I never can resist a bargain. However, what I was going to say was, I've been here living almost next door to Edgar for years, and the change in him seems to have come on pretty gradually, so that I've never concentrated much attention on it. But you've been away a lot; it's been different for you. I've thought once or twice during this fortnight you've been home that you looked as if things here had been a considerable shock.'

'Oh, I don't know,' she said vaguely.

Through the gap still left between the curtains the lightning gave her a dizzy glimpse of grass and road and desolate bungalows. She tugged at the cord again and the curtains swung together.

She went on: 'It's true that somehow I don't seem to know him any more. Perhaps it's my own fault. I've done a good bit of changing myself, I expect – only at my age that's more or less routine. But Gerald, he seems so bitter and impatient and suspicious – I don't think he used to be like that. And he seems so aggressively proud of all that he's done for me, and to need me to thank him for it over and over again. And at the same time he seems frantically disappointed in me.'

'I know he was disappointed that you didn't do better at Oxford. Failing your degree was a rather bitter blow to him. Incidentally,' – he looked at her curiously – 'why didn't you do better? I'd always thought you were a quite clever girl.'

She gave a flat little laugh. 'Wine, woman and song – me being the woman.'

'I see. And it was carrying on in that tradition, was it, that you got yourself engaged to be married twice and broke it off both times? You know, speaking dispassionately, you haven't made such a promising start to your young life.'

'But it seems to be on father's mind all the time,' she cried, 'that I've let him down, wasted everything he's given me! And having Peggie Winnpole here doesn't help things, because she resents all the things I've had and keeps hinting to father that I'm not

13

really grateful and don't really appreciate it. The thought that perhaps that's so – but it isn't, Gerald, it isn't! – but the thought that it might be seems to drive him right out of his mind. I can't understand it, I simply can't understand anything.'

He shook his head gravely. 'I ought to have looked into all this before. I've been criminally negligent.'

She said impatiently: 'We ought to be *doing* something.'

Abruptly Gerald Hyland unfolded himself on to his feet. 'True. And the first thing's the police, and if that's no good, the hospitals. And then I'm afraid there'll be nothing for it but going out into the rain and seeing if we can pick up a rumour. That's what a search party always has to search for – a rumour. How I wish this cursed storm would stop, it makes the whole business so infernally melodramatic. Would you like me to tackle the telephone?'

Without waiting for an answer he crossed to it, his red and gold slippers slapping on the floor.

Picking up the instrument, he said into it: 'Police.' Then he grinned at Joanna. 'You know, if the Winnpole woman weren't at home I'd say he'd eloped with her; he's got such a high opinion of that piece of chewed – Eh?' This was to the telephone. 'I said police. Po-lice. I want the police-station, and quickly for a change. *Quickly* – the house is on fire . . . What? . . . No, my dear fellow, I never said anything about the fire-station, I want the police-station.'

The sitting-room door opened. It was Mrs. Searle. 'Shan't I dish up now?' she said. 'The dinner won't keep for ever.'

But Joanna, with her gaze on Gerald Hyland, gestured to her not to interrupt. The housekeeper, with a shrug, was turning away, when the high voice of Peggie Winnpole broke in on them from the hall: 'Joanna – he's come! There's a car just stopped at the gate!'

The next moment, as the fireman in the fire-station in the neighbouring town of Asslington was picking up the telephone and saying Hullo to Gerald Hyland, there came a volley of knocks on the front door of the bungalow.

Peggie Winnpole was nearest to the door. She flung it open.

A young man stood there.

He was a slender young man of about twenty-seven, in clothes that were sodden and smeared with mud. He started to say something.

But Peggie, clutching at him, gasped in a hissing whisper: 'Oh, my God, Gordon, what have you done?'

'Shut up!' he said fiercely, and turned to speak to Joanna.

But Joanna pushed past him and ran straight out into the rain.

At the gate stood a small saloon car. Around its wheels eddied the swirling, grey-white mud, rain put a glossy finish on to its worn paint. Beside it, at one of its open doors, two men were gently levering out from the back seat the stout, limp form of Edgar Prees.

Joanna said: 'What's happened?'

Her voice was surprisingly calm.

One of the men replied: 'Suppose we finish getting him indoors and then explain. Kind of damp out here for explanations, that's what I think about it.'

He was a big man with wide shoulders and a powerful look to his body. He was no one Joanna had ever seen before. As she took a startled look into his face he grinned at her. His face was a long one, sallow as a gypsy's, with a gypsyish ferocity about its dark brows and beaked nose.

He said: 'He isn't really hurt, you know. It's only shock.'

Joanna turned and went swiftly back into the house. She gestured the others away from the doorway.

'Bring him in here,' she said.

As the two men came in after her with her father supported between them she led them into the sitting-room. Water dripped from their clothes as they trod across the carpet, and their feet ground chalky mud into the soft, grey pile.

As they laid her father down on a divan the tall man glanced at the track of their footsteps, and with the same sardonic, rather wolfish grin remarked: 'Lucky it isn't a crime we're committing, isn't it? Those footprints'd make it a lot too easy to reconstruct.'

Joanna had stood still in the middle of the room. She did not approach any closer to the divan. There was something peremptory and hard about her, as if she were more concerned with her own attitude in an emergency than in the emergency itself.

A bluish pallor covered her father's face. It was a fleshy face with pouchy eyelids and a small, precise mouth. He was of medium height but thick in the limb with a soft, shapeless fleshiness over his bones. Mud was smeared over his face and his clothing. There was mud on the bald top of his head. His pince-nez were missing.

The tall man said again: 'It's only shock. If you can get him to bed with hot-water bottles and things, and a nice cup of tea, he'll be all right in no time.'

'Mrs. Searle,' said Joanna. She looked over her shoulder at the others who crowded in at the door. 'Mrs. Searle, can you start seeing to that? And Gerald, can you help me getting father to bed? Or perhaps Gordon would help you while I telephone for a doctor.' She looked at the dark-faced stranger again. 'What happened?'

For an instant he hesitated. Then he said: 'It was a car-accident.'

'Where? How did it happen?'

At that point Gerald Hyland came forward. Holding out his hand first to one stranger, then to the other, he said in his harsh but genial voice: 'We can find out all the details presently, my dear. As you suggest, Gordon and I will get Edgar to bed, and you, I think, might get some whisky for these two very wet gentlemen. Details are never very important when everyone's so wet.' Stooping, he started to work an arm under his friend's shoulders. 'Come on, Gordon, lend a hand.' He looked up. 'Where's Gordon?'

Gordon Weedon was out in the hall, standing on the doormat, trying to wipe some of the heavy, white mud from his shoes. He said: 'I'm coming,' and went on wiping his shoes.

Hyland made clicking, impatient sounds with his tongue.

Gordon Weedon repeated: 'Coming – just coming.'

But before he reached the door of the sitting-room someone else plunged through it. Thrusting past Joanna, Peggie flung herself down on her knees beside the divan. She tried to speak, but what she said was lost in a violent gush of weeping.

With a blaze of fury on her face Joanna cried: 'Get out of the way – get out and keep quiet!'

'For God's sake, everyone keep quiet.' In a wheezy tone of disgust, the words came through the blue, pinched lips of the man on the couch.

Complete quiet descended on everyone in the room.

The thick eyelids had lifted a little. Between their wrinkled folds the eyes that showed were glazed with weariness. Their gaze shifted slowly from one face to another. Again a few words were squeezed through the blue lips. 'I am not a peepshow,' said Edgar Prees, 'and even in my present, no doubt comical condition, I resent being treated as such. I have no interest in any of you at the moment and should be grateful if you would attempt to veil your – momentary – intense interest in me. I've had enough of you all.' His eyes, with their dull, tired stare, fastened on Joanna. He added: 'I owe nothing to anyone.' Then he sighed with a sound of self-pity and the thick eyelids dropped again.

Gerald Hyland said explosively: 'Well, I'm damned, if that isn't exactly like Edgar!'

Peggie Winnpole, staggering to her feet, turned to Gordon Weedon and buried her face against him.

Gordon Weedon, who was engaged to be married to Peggie Winnpole, had stooping shoulders and moved in the heavy and clumsy way that goes with an unmuscular build. His face was pale, with a worried, self-absorbed look in the eyes. His ears were large and stood out at a wide angle from his head; his hair went back from his forehead in little ridged waves. He started patting Peggie's head with one hand, but his worried stare went past her to the face of the man on the couch. As Hyland made more clicking, impatient noises, he disentangled himself from Peggie's hold and came forward.

Between them he and Gerald Hyland removed the unco-operating form of Edgar Prees to his bedroom. Peggie disappeared into hers. Joanna went to the dining-room.

Returning in a few minutes with glasses and a decanter, she met the look of the tall, dark man. He and his companion were standing with their backs to the fireplace, as if that, in spite of the fact that no fire was even laid in the grate, were the best place to steam themselves dry.

Joanna set the tray down on a table. When she had poured out the drinks she remarked: 'I don't quite know whether to thank you, or – just to ask for the details.'

'Meaning,' said the dark man, 'was it us who ran him down?' He gave his wolfish grin again. 'It wasn't.'

17

'Then,' she said, 'thank you – thank you far more than I can possibly say. I'll never be able to make my thanks sound as earnestly meant as they are; they're always such difficult things to get across convincingly. But please believe I'm as grateful as a person can be.' She brought the glasses across to them. 'And now, if you don't mind, I'm going to telephone.'

'For a doctor?'

She nodded.

But she had not yet succeeded in drawing the attention of the man at the exchange when she put the instrument down again.

'I'd forgotten,' she said, 'Dr. Jones is away, and his partner's no good; he's always half-drunk. I wonder who else there is.' She stood frowning, then she picked up the small, local directory and began a search through its pages.

'Er –' It was the dark man again.

She glanced up at him questioningly.

'Er, the doctor.' He was shifting his feet; he seemed oddly uncomfortable. 'You say he's away, the one you usually have? That means that the one you're going to call up is someone you don't really know? I mean, you don't know much about what kind of a man he is?'

'What d'you mean?' she asked abruptly.

'Well,' he said uneasily, 'if you don't really know him, you can't tell, can you, whether he mightn't –? I mean, he might be the sort of chap who insists on making trouble – or something. That's to say, if you don't know him, you can't tell what he'll do. And,' – he swallowed some of the whisky – 'I don't believe there's anything really wrong with your father.'

She crossed the room and planted herself before him. 'What really happened?' Her voice was hard and sharp. 'It wasn't a car-accident, was it?'

He stroked a hand thoughtfully over his long chin and looked into her face.

She repeated: 'It wasn't a car-accident!'

He gave a sigh. 'No,' he said, 'it wasn't a car-accident.' Then he went on: 'Look here, sit down. Have some of that whisky yourself. I'll tell you all about it; I'm sure that's the best thing to do. That young fellow out there, Gordon Somebody, he suggested we should stick to the story it was a car-accident, and in some

18

circumstances it might have been a good idea. But having seen you, I should think you can stand the facts, and if you can it's far better for you to have them. They may always need acting upon.'

'What facts?'

'I'll tell you, I'll tell you the whole thing – that's to say, all we saw of it, because we didn't come into it till nearly the end. It's only from that young chap Gordon Whatsit that we heard the part about how your father started walking home from Asslington, and—'

'Walking home? Did you say my father started *walking* home from Asslington?'

'Yes,' he said, 'that's what we were told.'

'But it's five miles – and he never walks anywhere.'

'Well, it's what we were told. As I was saying, we only saw the end bit of it. You see, we were down on the beach. We were sitting down there, throwing pebbles at the sea, having a day in the country. Some work I'd been doing had been getting badly stuck, and I'd had the idea that some green grass and sea air might unstick the brain again – anyway, there we were. You see, not having any definite idea of where we wanted to go, we'd thought we'd see what Asslington was like. Well, as a matter of fact, we didn't think much of it; in spite of its Botanical Gardens, its charm, I think, is overrated, and so we'd pushed on a bit further, and there we were, about halfway between Asslington and here, down on the beach. So when we heard the voice yelling we had to scramble all the way up the cliffs, which wasn't easy with the storm coming on so suddenly – you know how it started this evening, bang out of nothing. Still, we were just in time, and it was lucky we were too, because I don't think that young man would have been able to hold out much longer; your father's a good weight.'

'But d'you mean —?' She stopped. She sat down in an armchair. 'I don't understand at all,' she said.

'Course you don't, miss.'

Joanna gave a slightly surprised glance at the second stranger. It was the first time he had spoken since he had come into the room. A small man, two inches shorter at least than she was herself, with a resilient-looking plumpness and a round, pink face that had been only indecisively moulded into features, he

19

wore a shabby blue suit, pointed patent leather shoes and a high-necked sailor's jersey.

He repeated with a wide, amiable smile: 'Course you don't understand, miss. Toby here – his name's Toby Dyke and mine's George – he can't ever express himself really coherent like to a young lady. Reckon it was one of the faults in his early upbringing. All that happened this evening – I'll tell you in a word – was that the old gentleman was tryin' to chuck himself over the edge of the cliff, and that young chap with the big ears was stoppin' him. Then Toby and me turned up and finished the business of stoppin' him. Believe me —' He gulped down some whisky, and as the man called Toby Dyke turned on him with a scowl, concluded blandly: 'That's absolutely all there was to it.'

'You damn fool, George,' said Toby Dyke.

Joanna's eyes had widened a little. The slightly blank look in them was at that moment more than ever pronounced. Her stare went between the two men, to be held by the smirking cupids that supported the clock on the mantelpiece.

Toby Dyke started again, hurriedly: 'As I was saying, it was when we were down there on the beach that we heard a voice shouting "Help!" It was right over our heads. It went on shouting, and so—'

'And so,' said Joanna slowly, 'he was trying to throw himself over the edge of the cliffs.'

'Well,' said Toby Dyke apologetically, 'that does seem to have been what was happening. When we heard that shouting we went mountaineering up the face of the cliff, and when we got to the top, there in the rain, right at the edge, were two men, fighting like fiends. It was too wet and too dark for us to see what they were really up to, but we managed to get them apart. It was the young one who'd been doing the shouting, and the moment we'd separated them he started thanking God we'd been in time, because he didn't think he'd have been able to hold out much longer. Your father just lay there. The moment he stopped struggling he simply collapsed. The young man told us where he belonged, and we got him into the car, and the young man came along with us to show us the way, and told us how it had happened. Seems he works under your father, and he'd been worrying about him for some time, and something that happened to-day made him worry particularly; so when your father set off for home on foot, he followed, and then when your father suddenly made for the edge of the cliffs and looked as if he were going to take a dive off them, he grabbed him. He saved your father's life all right.' He stopped, regarding her rather anxiously.

Joanna was looking down, her wide-eyed gaze fixed on a scrap of mud that clung to the grey carpet.

She asked in a stiff, hesitant voice: 'Didn't my father – say anything at all – until what he said when he got here?'

An unamused smile pulled his mouth crooked. 'As a matter of fact, he did. He said one thing. He said: "Why the something hell can't you keep your something noses out of other people's business instead of helping this something something with his devil's work?" It was just then he fainted. I should think on the whole that simplified things for us.'

The short man in blue made another remark: 'Mind you, lady, I kind of sympathised. Suicide *is* a bloke's own business.'

Suddenly Joanna clenched her hands and drummed with them on the arms of her chair. 'I won't stand it,' she cried violently. 'He's got no right to treat me like this. Did you see how he looked at me and then said he didn't owe anyone anything? He meant he didn't owe *me* anything. He meant I'm such a disappointment to him after all he's done for me – but what has he done for me, except go on working in that old Haybox, which he loves for its own sake more than he's ever loved anything in the world? – But he can't ever think about anything but what he's done for me and my ingratitude, and . . .' She dropped both hands limply into her lap. 'No,' she said quietly, 'it can't really be that. No . . . he wouldn't really try to kill himself, would he, just to show me he thinks I'm so ungrateful he doesn't owe it to me even to live?'

Toby Dyke was looking at her in some astonishment. As if to find some remark to make, he said: 'Did you say he works in a Haybox?'

George said thoughtfully: 'Reckon that'll be the name of a night-club or somethin' in Asslington.'

At that there came a great guffaw of laughter from the doorway. Gerald Hyland, edging his overhanging form round the door, exploded: 'Night-club – Edgar boss of a night-club! Goodness me, that's the best thing I've heard for years.'

He came forward into the room. He beamed at everybody. He crossed to the table and stood looking down pensively at the whisky decanter.

'Now if there was another glass . . .'

Then deep chuckles rumbled inside him.

'Night-club! . . . If you'd like to know, the Haybox was the name Joanna gave, when she was a small girl, to the herbarium attached to the Asslington Botanical Gardens. Her father's curator there. And in case you don't know, a herbarium is an institution in which studies in systematic botany are prosecuted. They keep a collection there of as many type-species as possible – I think Joanna found them all very dry and haylike. Joanna, my dear, as I was saying, if there was another glass . . .'

He noticed the expression on her face.

'Cheer up,' he said, 'Edgar's quite all right, tucked up all safe and sound in bed, with two hot-water bottles and a gallon or so of tea. There's nothing to worry about. Matter of fact, I was going to say, if you haven't already rung up Dr. Jones, I don't think there's any great need to.'

She got to her feet. 'I'll fetch a glass.'

He stopped her. 'Joanna, what's the matter?'

She answered: 'You see, Gerald, it wasn't an accident. Mr. Dyke here has been telling me what actually happened. Father tried to throw himself over the edge of the cliffs. Gordon and Mr. Dyke and his friend stopped him.'

'Suicide!'

'Yes, Gerald.'

Intensely startled, Hyland's blue eyes flashed round to Toby Dyke.

Toby Dyke nodded.

'I see,' said Hyland. 'My God! Yes. . . . Well, about that glass . . .'

Joanna went to fetch it.

When she returned to the sitting-room, Hyland was just doing the quick, folding-up movement that was his way of sitting down.

'And of course,' he was saying, 'in the eyes of the law, suicide's a crime.'

22

'That was why I advised Miss Prees to be rather careful about calling in a doctor she didn't know,' said Toby Dyke.

'Just so.' Hyland's voice sounded more than usually grating. He looked up at Joanna and nodded his thanks as she brought him a drink. 'Joanna, I'd realised that something was wrong with Edgar, but that it had come to this . . . Have you any idea . . . ? Can you understand why . . . ?'

She gave a shake of her head.

'Anyway,' said Toby Dyke, coming forward and holding out his hand, 'you'd sooner go into that side of it without strangers present. Good-bye, Miss Prees. Unless there's something more we can do to assist, I think we'd better get going.'

'Going?' Automatically Joanna took the hand held out to her. 'But you'll stay and have dinner, won't you? It'll only be dinner of a sort, but please stay. Mrs. Searle's just been laying places for you.'

Toby Dyke glanced round at George. Probably they would have refused.

But before either could reply, Hyland, shooting on to his feet again, rubbing his hands together enthusiastically, and looking filled with good ideas, exclaimed: 'Look here, don't go home to-night at all. Rotten night, no one ought to be out in it. Come along to my cottage. I can put you up. I can give you some supper too – that'll be better than staying and making extra work for Mrs. Searle, who's been put out enough already – and I've got some pretty good whisky. And I've got some grand records I'd like to play over to you to see what you think of them. Can't remember the names offhand; never can – all opuses, you know, classical stuff. You'll come?'

'It's very good of you,' Toby Dyke was beginning, 'but—'

'Excellent,' said Hyland. 'It's only a few minutes' walk to my cottage, and there's most of a cold chicken in the larder, and a good cheese. And there's one record I've got that—'

'Gerald,' said Joanna, 'perhaps Mr. Dyke and his friend really want to get back to London.'

'On a night like this – nonsense. Come along, Mr. Dyke. We'll go straight away. I'll give you some dry clothes, and get your supper, and then I'll just pop up here again and go into this sad affair with Joanna. I won't be long, Joanna. You don't mind my

23

leaving you for a bit, do you? I'm sure these two gentlemen ought to get out of their wet things, and then I'll just give them my file-index – I spent this afternoon making a file-index of my records – and while I'm gone they can be eating and making up their minds just what they'd like to hear. Come along, come along, one short dash through the rain and we're there. Goodness me, what a piece of luck that you were down below when Edgar started his tricks on the cliffs; I haven't had any good company in the evenings for I don't know how long.'

With a vivacity that had in it a good deal of dogged determination, Gerald Hyland proceeded to remove the two strangers to his cottage.

But they had only reached the hall of the bungalow when he returned to the sitting-room. He had on his oilskins and gum-boots.

'Joanna, my child,' he whispered, tiptoeing up to her and tapping her on the shoulder, 'don't worry too much. I dare say it's an excellent thing this has happened; it'll bring everything out into the open. That always makes things a lot better. Besides, I've had an idea, a marvellous idea. I'm going to put it into execution to-morrow. So don't worry any more – it's really a grand idea.'

She gave him an affectionate but weary smile.

'Is it like most of your grand ideas, Gerald? – because if it is I expect it'd really be best to do nothing about it.'

'It's a grand idea, a grand idea.'

A moment later the front door slammed behind them.

2

The only light in the bedroom came from a small reading-lamp by the bed. Its brown parchment shade had been turned so that the light wasted itself uselessly on a blank space of wall, leaving the face on the pillow the protection of deep shadow. It was so dim just there that it was impossible for Joanna to see, as she came into the room, whether her father's eyes were open or not.

The room was a small one, but the furniture in it was the bulkiest in any room in the bungalow. Of solid, polished mahogany, it had been in the family longer than Joanna herself. Brown velour curtains hung over the windows. On the walls were dusky oil-paintings of cattle and sunsets.

Moving quietly to the end of the bed, Joanna stood looking down at her father.

She could see now that the eyes were closed. The puffy flesh of his face seemed to have fallen in against the bone behind, the small mouth sagged. In the way in which the head lay on the pillow there was the abandonment of total exhaustion. It was a drained, meaningless husk of a man that lay there, either asleep or simply blotted out, finished.

The cold, defensive look in Joanna's eyes gradually melted. Pity appeared, and tenderness. Expression came into the lustrous, rather blank, dark eyes. Her lower lip quivered.

'Why can't you dress yourself decently? Why d'you have to go round all day in those trousers?'

She started.

The eyes in the face on the pillow were no longer closed. Narrow slits had opened in the pouchy flesh of the eye-sockets.

Joanna's mouth became a hard, scarlet line against the pallor of her face.

'And I don't like that lipstick.' Though the voice was weak, each word was formed with pedantic precision. 'Why isn't your own colouring good enough for you?'

'I only came to see how you were,' said Joanna. 'Do you want anything?'

'What I've never had in my life – peace and quiet.'

There was a pause. Then Joanna resumed: 'Would you like me to bring you some supper?'

'Thank you, I feel no desire for food.'

'Isn't there anything I can do?' Her hands were gripping the rail at the end of the bed.

He made no answer, and though it was difficult in the dimness of the room to be certain of it, it seemed that after a moment his eyes closed again.

Joanna waited at the end of the bed for about a minute. Then she turned and went softly towards the door. She had almost reached it when the precise tones once more addressed her.

'I should like to be left alone. I should prefer no one to intrude on me. If you are afraid of what my actions may be you may leave the door ajar. But I should prefer you to close it. You need have no anxiety; I intend to do nothing but rest. And now that I come to think of it, there is something you might do for me.'

Joanna spoke impulsively: 'Father, can't we – isn't there any way you and I could . . . ? Oh —' Her voice was shaking with tears. 'I don't understand what's happened. It used not to be like this. We used to talk to each other.'

He said: 'I notice you change the subject the moment I ask you to do something for me.'

A red stain appeared on her cheeks.

'And I've noticed,' he went on, 'that that might almost be described as a habit of yours. An ungracious one. I disapprove of it.'

'What is it you want?'

'Don't let me trouble you. I can see to it myself.'

'What is it you want?' Her voice rose slightly.

'I told you, I can see to it myself. I merely asked you to do it for me because, in view of what it happens to be, I thought it might reassure your mind if you yourself had seen to it.'

'What is it? I'll do anything you want.'

26

'How I do hate those trousers. Why can't you wear a nice dress – something suitable for the evening? Heaven knows you spend enough on them.'

'*What is it – what d'you want me to do for you?*'

At the note in her voice he stirred restlessly. He said in an irritated but less frozen tone: 'I want a couple of those sleeping-tablets, Joanna. They're in the bathroom, in the cupboard. Just bring them to me, and a tumbler of water. You see, I thought if you saw me fetching them myself you might imagine the worst.'

He laughed.

The sound sent a shudder through Joanna.

She replied: 'All right, I'll get them.'

As she turned swiftly and went to the bathroom, two tears that had been swimming in her eyes brimmed over her lashes and trickled down her face.

She returned in a minute with the sleeping-tablets. He swallowed them, murmured: 'Thank you,' and made a gesture that she should leave him. She went out again, this time closing the door behind her. She took the glass back to the bathroom.

As she was rinsing it out under one of the taps a thought suddenly occurred to her. She put down the glass and went to the cupboard again. Locking it, she slipped the key into her pocket. Then she changed her mind, unlocked the cupboard, took out the box of sleeping-tablets and put that in her pocket.

The dinner that Mrs. Searle served up a few minutes later consisted of chops that had been ready to eat at least an hour earlier, mashed potatoes that had gone dry and heavy through being kept warm in the oven, and tomatoes that somehow had missed being kept warm at all.

Joanna, Peggie Winnpole and Gordon Weedon chewed in dispirited silence. Gordon Weedon had been given a dry pair of flannels and some slippers belonging to Mr. Prees. He had washed the streaks of mud from his face and hands. Peggie also had washed her face and had used powder to mask the tearstains.

After the chops there was rice pudding. Joanna left hers on her plate and went to the sitting-room. She went straight to the table where the whisky decanter still stood, filled one of the glasses and drank it down.

Peggie came in.

'You don't mind if Gordon sleeps here, do you?' she said. 'He can sleep on the divan in here. He was going to walk home, but I didn't think he ought to get into those wet things and risk another soaking. It's raining as hard as ever. You don't mind, do you?'

'Of course not.' Joanna struck a match for her cigarette. 'Peggie, please tell me something. You said you knew something was bound to happen. Was this what you meant?'

Peggie's eyes dropped. 'I don't know what I said.'

'That's what you said – that you knew something was bound to happen.'

'Oh, I was excited and upset,' said Peggie. 'I just said anything. I don't expect I meant anything in particular.'

'But you seemed almost to expect this.'

'I tell you, I was just saying anything. I'd only just woken up and my head was still awful.' The words slipped out hurriedly and anxiously and she turned to go.

But at a sound that reached them at that moment she stood still and looked at Joanna.

A car was stopping at the gate.

Joanna said irritably: 'Who on earth's that at this hour?'

With a nervous smile and in a tone that tried to sound casual, Peggie remarked: 'As a matter of fact, it's Dr. Vanedden.'

Joanna's face showed that that told her nothing.

Peggie said: 'I do hope you won't mind, but I took things rather into my own hands. I thought I ought to. I mean, this must have been a dreadful shock for you; I didn't think it fair to leave all the responsibility on your shoulders. Of course I understood why you didn't ring up a doctor – in a way I dare say you were quite right. But I do think it was an awful risk all the same. You don't mind my saying so, do you? After all, I know your father better – I mean, I've seen a lot more of him lately than you have, and I know how delicate he is. And he did look dreadful to-night. I'm quite sure he oughtn't to have been left without seeing a doctor.'

'But Dr. Vanedden isn't a doctor.' Joanna dropped on to the divan. 'I remember about him now. He's a Doctor of Philosophy or something at one of those awfully obscure American universities. But he isn't a doctor of medicine.'

28

'That's simply because of the bigotry and prejudice of the medical profession. Dr. Vanedden knows much more than any doctor I've ever come across. He's a wonderful man.'

'Oh, God, you're an awful fool sometimes, Peggie. Father'll never see him.'

'It was Mr. Prees who recommended him to me.'

At Joanna's incredulous look Peggie nodded triumphantly.

'And I can never be grateful enough to him for having done so,' she said. 'I went to Mr. Prees some months ago and told him what agony I was having with headaches, and how I thought the trouble was probably psychological, and how anyway I didn't feel properly adjusted to my environment and would benefit from some psychological treatment, and he told me about Dr. Vanedden and gave me an introduction to him.'

'If that's so,' said Joanna, 'I suppose it's all right.'

But just then Mrs. Searle put her head round the door.

'It's that young Mr. Moon,' she said.

Joanna sat up. 'Dan Moon?'

'And he wants to see Mr. Prees. I've told him Mr. Prees is ill in bed, but he says he's going to see him all the same. He seems kind of in a temper.'

'Oh, dear, I thought it was Dr. Vanedden,' muttered Peggie.

Joanna began to laugh.

'Send him in here,' she cried. 'Let's have everyone in here. Let's have a party. Let's celebrate. Let's celebrate the altogether remarkable event which everyone seems to have expected but me. Dan!' – she raised her voice – 'Come in here. It may not look like it but it's a party and you're welcome. We're frightfully merry – come in!'

She suddenly twisted herself on the divan, stretched herself prone upon it and buried her face in her arms.

A young man appeared in the doorway. A tall young man, of slightly cumbrous yet shapely build, he had thick brown hair and a brown face with firmly moulded though still immature features. It was one of those faces that are intelligent and naïve at the same time. At the moment it was lit by a sultry glow, beyond doubt the fire of righteous indignation.

He looked at Joanna lying on her stomach on the divan.

'What the hell?' he said. Then he saw Peggie and nodded at her.

29

Peggie murmured good evening and went out.

Dan Moon took a couple of steps towards the divan.

'Hi!' he said.

He waited.

'Hi, Joanna!'

He said it a third time: 'Hi, I say!' He had a deep, rough voice with a pleasant, warm resonance in it. 'I say, you aren't—'

With a wriggle Joanna turned over and sat bolt upright on the divan. There were bright spots of red on her cheekbones.

'You've a perfect genius for arriving at the wrong time,' she said. 'You always manage to come here when one feels one hates the sight of you.'

'All right, all right,' he said, 'but it isn't you I've come to see. It's your father. Seeing you like that, I thought you must be crying or something. What's the trouble? Stomach?'

'But it's father you can't see.'

'I've got to see him. If I don't I'll calm down and I shan't say all the things I've got ready to say to him. Where is he?'

'You can't see him, I'm telling you. Oh, I don't know what's the matter with you – you always do it, you always arrive when one's just feeling ready to murder somebody, and you go and plant yourself right in front of one, looking like a great mooing cow – and if I'd a hatchet or a hammer I'd—'

'Hi,' he said resentfully, 'not a cow, that's female.'

Taking a couple of long strides, he seated himself on the arm of a chair. His movements were ponderous and deliberate, but had the same kind of vigour that is almost grace that belongs to the movements of a young cart-horse. He took a pipe out of the pocket of his raincoat.

'Anyway,' he said, 'where is your father?'

'It doesn't matter to you where he is, because you aren't going to see him,' said Joanna. 'As a matter of fact, he's in bed ill, and doesn't want to see anybody.'

He said: 'I'll see him all right. I came out here to see him, right through the storm. I knew if I left it I'd calm down and then I'd never say the things somebody ought to say to him before he's much older.' He was fumbling through his other pockets for his tobacco-pouch. 'You can't go on doing that kind of thing without somebody saying something to you sometime.'

30

'Doing what?' she asked.

He suddenly discovered the pouch in one of those pockets that only athletes can reach. While he was contorting himself to extract it, she repeated: 'Doing what?'

'Don't worry,' he said, 'I won't say one word more than's absolutely necessary, and I won't do anything but say what I think.'

She gave a little crow of laughter. 'And I'm not to worry! But what's happened, Dan? What's he done? Or what've you done, because it's much more likely to be your fault than his? You're such a complete fool. If you knew how I hate fools . . . But you needn't think you can see him, because you can't. He's ill, he mustn't be worried by anybody.'

'I'm not going to worry him,' said Dan. 'I'm just going to impart some of my views. They're reasonable views; if they worry him that's his funeral.'

'What views?'

'Oh, it's something quite technical, Joanna, you wouldn't follow.' Dan started contorting himself again in a search for a box of matches.

She asked: 'How d'you know I shouldn't follow?'

'Because I did once try to explain to you some elementary facts about my job.'

Joanna got up, picked up the box of matches on the mantelpiece and tossed it at him. She said in a constrained voice: 'As it was I who got you the job in the first place, it strikes me I must be able to understand a few things about it.'

He stooped to pick up the box of matches that had slipped through his fingers to the floor. 'I know, Joanna. And as part of what I want to tell your father is that I'm chucking the job . . .' He struck a match. As he raised his eyes to her face again he found her gaze boring into him with startled intensity. His eyes quickly avoided hers and his brows puckered. 'I'm sorry – I dare say a good deal of it's my fault. I was damn glad to take the job. But I didn't quite reckon on your father. Honestly, I don't know how I've stuck it this last couple of months. Don't know how anyone has. Look at that row he had with poor old Peggie yesterday. God knows what she'd done, but whatever it was he's got no right to sack someone who's slaved for him the way that woman has.'

31

'Sack her?' cried Joanna. 'Has father sacked Peggie Winnpole?'

'Didn't you know?'

She shook her head drearily. She dropped down again on to the divan. 'No, Dan, I don't know anything.'

'Well,' said Dan Moon with a shrug of his big shoulders, 'it's all got a bit beyond me. There are some reasons why I'll hate to go, but I can't really see that there's any possible future for me here, and though they say it's a mug's game to look ahead in the sort of world we inhabit, I don't really like seeing nothing ahead of me but a blank wall – with some damned unpleasant spikes on it. And now that this last thing's happened—'

'But what *has* happened?'

Dan was silent.

Their eyes met again for an instant and though Joanna's tried to hold his Dan's immediately evaded them, settling instead on the toe of a muddy shoe.

After a moment, in a hesitantly explanatory voice, he produced what sounded like carefully chosen words: 'It's just about some pods, Joanna – and a Russian.'

A vivid smile lit up Joanna's face. The smile developed into laughter. Dan Moon shifted uncomfortably at the rasp of hysteria in the sound.

'Pods,' cried Joanna, 'and a Russian! International complications. No wonder you had to come all the way out here in the middle of a thunderstorm at almost midnight. Is it war or revolution?' She sprang to her feet. 'But you aren't going to see my father, Dan. I don't know what he's done and I don't care. He's ill, he's been ill for ages. If any of you had had any sense or any sympathy you'd have seen it weeks ago. But all you seem to have been able to think about was that he was difficult to get on with. Of course he was – people working up for nervous breakdowns always are. Why couldn't you see what was happening? You're working with him, aren't you? You see him all day, not just for an hour or two in the evenings. Why couldn't you see it and warn me . . .?' Suddenly she stopped, and, drawing a deep breath, seemed to shrink together.

Dan reached out and laid a hand on her shoulder.

'Jo! For God's sake, Jo . . . A nervous breakdown, is that it? Poor old chap. I hadn't an idea . . . I'm damned sorry. Hi, Jo, look up.'

But Joanna slid her shoulder away from under his hand.

She said in a low voice: 'Please go, Dan. Go home. It's been the most ghastly evening I've ever known in my life.'

'But look here, what's actually happened?'

'Oh, go home, go home,' she said. 'I'm dog tired. I can't think about anything. He tried to kill himself. Do please go home.'

He got to his feet. 'But look here—'

'We'll talk it over another time,' she said. 'To-morrow perhaps. And at the same time you can tell me whether it was the pod that didn't agree with the Russian or the Russian who didn't agree with the pod.'

'All right,' he said.

He stood looking at her for a moment, then he crossed to the door.

'Of course,' he said, 'a nervous breakdown explains a lot. Really, if I'd known I'd never —' He gave his head a shake, opened the door and went out.

'Dan,' said Joanna.

He looked back into the room.

'Dan, when you chuck your job here – what will you do instead?'

'Find another eventually. In the meantime – well, I ran into a chap some weeks ago who was getting up an expedition to Peru to map the vegetation. They wanted another botanist to go with them. He asked if I liked the idea. I told him no at the time. But I dare say it wouldn't be too late to fix it up. They weren't going for two or three months. I think I'll write to him.'

'I see,' she said. 'Well, good night.'

'Good night,' said Dan.

A minute or two later, through the soft swishing of the rain, the sound of Dan Moon's car driving away down the road towards Asslington reached Joanna where she sat on the divan.

Presently that sound faded.

In the room in the bungalow it seemed perfectly silent. The thunder had stopped, and though the rain still fell it fell so steadily that the hearing, accustomed to the sound of it, lost it.

Suddenly Joanna flung herself prone on the divan, and with her head buried in her arms, in the position in which Dan had found her when he first came in, broke into violent weeping.

She was still lying like that, but her body had gone limp and her swollen eyelids had drooped over her eyes in a nightmarish half-sleep when, just after the clock on the mantelpiece had given the little *ping* that meant half-past twelve, the door of the sitting-room was softly opened again, and Peggie Winnpole, in an excited whisper, hissed at her: 'Dr. Vanedden!'

Dr. Vanedden was a small man with a big head. The big head was crowned with thick hair of a silky, silver grey. His features were aquiline. His skin was of a smooth parchment colour, covered with a delicately etched pattern of fine wrinkles. He had the arched eyebrows, the prominent, finely modelled nose, the full, subtle lips and the long chin that look distinguished and slightly wicked under a tiewig. His raincoat was exceptionally shabby and old; so was the felt hat he held in his hand; but the double-breasted grey suit he wore had the easy, prosperous look of excellent tailoring.

As he advanced into the room he let his eyes rest for an instant on Joanna's tear-marked face, then he directed them at the clock. He gave it a whimsical look of disapproval when he saw the lateness proclaimed there. He had that frank air of apology possible only to those who are perfectly sure of themselves.

He said: 'I'm dreadfully sorry. I'd have been here an hour ago if I hadn't had trouble with my car. I had to take it to a garage. They were so slow I almost abandoned hope of getting here at all. However, here I am.'

His voice was a tenor one; he had a light, graceful way with his words.

Joanna took the hand he held out, but her gaze went confusedly from him to Peggie. Beyond Peggie, with his hand up to his mouth to stifle a yawn, was Gordon Weedon.

Joanna fixed her attention on him.

'Oh, Gordon, you wanted to sleep in here, didn't you? I've been keeping you up. You ought to have come in and reminded me. I could have gone to bed, only . . .' She rubbed a hand across her forehead. 'I was staying up for something. There was something. . . . Of course, Gerald said he'd come back. He must have forgotten.'

'How like him,' said Peggie. 'However, here's Dr. Vanedden, and he'll be much more help than Mr. Hyland.'

34

Joanna looked again into the face of the small, silver-haired man. 'But I expect my father's asleep.'

'If that's so,' he answered, 'we can be thankful for it. Of course we won't disturb him. I can come again in the morning, that is, if you still want me to.'

Peggie at once protested: 'Oh, but you don't want to have made the trip out here on this dreadful night for nothing.'

His eyes were still on Joanna. Cool, grey eyes, penetrating and full of gravity, they studied her with an openness and at the same time a detachment that eyes are usually too diffident, too uncertain of themselves to display.

Joanna got up. She said: 'I'll go and see if he's asleep. He took some sleeping-tablets, so I expect he is.'

He checked her movement towards the door.

'Miss Prees, I'm afraid I've made a mistake in coming here. I don't think you want me here at all. It was Miss Winnpole who telephoned, and I think it was only Miss Winnpole who wanted me.'

Joanna said nothing. They looked at one another. Then Joanna looked down.

She murmured: 'I'm very grateful to you for coming.'

'I'd far sooner you were honest with me,' he said. 'I shan't be at all offended if you simply ask me to go home.'

'Not at all, Dr. Vanedden. I'm very glad. . . .'

He laughed softly.

She flashed a quick glance at him.

'Miss Prees,' he said, 'do I really look the kind of person who can't tell when a person thinks I'm both a quack and a nuisance? You know, I can see how hard you're hoping that your father's sound asleep, so that you needn't let me in to see him. But now tell me, isn't it right that Miss Winnpole asked me to come here without your concurrence?'

Peggie Winnpole, who had been hovering at his elbow with a mixture of proprietorship and humble propitiation in her manner, began: 'Oh, but Dr. Vanedden—'

'Isn't it so, Miss Prees? You do think I'm a quack, don't you? Now, be frank.'

His smile seemed to be seeking something out in her, probing, prompting.

35

After a moment, unwillingly, a smile appeared on Joanna's face.

He said: 'Good, that's settled.' As he laughed again, his eyes had a vivid twinkle in them. 'Now I can go home to Asslington and get to bed. Still, you know, Miss Prees, your father and I are quite well acquainted, and if I were just to look in on him – only if he's awake, of course – and ask him how he is, I don't think he'd mind in the least. There needn't be anything at all professional about it.'

'Please do,' she said, with the haste of embarrassment. 'I didn't mean . . . I mean, even if . . .'

'Let's just leave it at that,' he suggested. 'You'd sooner I didn't see him.'

'Oh, *no!*' She was flushed and her hands were fidgeting. 'Please – of course I want you to see him. It's true Peggie asked you to come here without telling me beforehand – and I didn't know you were a friend of my father's. Oh, forgive me, I'm in such a stupid muddle, I don't know what I'm saying. It's been such a queer kind of shock.' She stopped. Her look changed. 'I suppose,' she said, 'you do know *why* Miss Winnpole asked you to come here?'

'Oh, yes.'

Peggie put in: 'We can trust Dr. Vanedden *absolutely*, Joanna.'

'Thank you,' he said, and at the earnestness in his tone Peggie coloured with pleasure.

'Well, let's go and see if my father's awake,' said Joanna.

He was awake.

In spite of his exhaustion, in spite of the sleeping-tablets, Edgar Prees was lying with his eyes wide open. There was a feverish light in them. He seemed to be more restless, less limp. When the door opened and Joanna, followed by Dr. Vanedden, came into the room, his whole body gave a jerk and he almost sat up in bed. But there was no special surprise on his face at the sight of Dr. Vanedden. Perhaps he had heard his voice in the hall. He said nothing. Dr. Vanedden gave a slight nod to Joanna and she went out, leaving them together.

As she rejoined Peggie and Gordon in the sitting-room, Peggie greeted her eagerly: 'Don't you think he's got a wonderful personality, Joanna?'

Joanna was looking round fretfully.

'Don't you think so?' said Peggie.

'Where are those cigarettes?' asked Joanna.

'*Don't* you?'

'All I know is,' said Joanna, 'he embarrassed me until I had to ask him to go in and see father. Where the hell are those cigarettes?'

Gordon found he was sitting on them.

'Thanks,' said Joanna. 'And his smile's too beautiful.'

Peggie said: 'The first time *I* saw him I recognised at once the extraordinary power of his individuality. And there's a wonderful integrity in his face; one feels certain immediately of his complete disinterestedness. But perhaps one can only have those vivid perceptions if one's an intuitive type. He says I'm very intuitive indeed. Actually, though I haven't told anyone but Mr. Prees and Gordon, I've been going to him every week for treatment. It's made a great difference to my life already. Really, it's very, very kind of him to treat me, because of course his house in Asslington is only a week-end place; when he's down here he's on holiday. His practice is in Harley Street.'

'If I were Gordon,' said Joanna, 'I shouldn't feel too flattered at your needing all that difference made to your life. Where are those matches?'

Gordon was sitting on them too.

Peggie exclaimed: 'Oh, heavens, I don't understand you. Aren't you glad there's someone with Dr. Vanedden's experience and insight ready to help your father through this frightful spiritual crisis?'

'I don't know anything about his experiences. I expect there've been plenty of them, but somehow I don't feel at all certain they're the right kind to help my father.' Puffing impatiently at the cigarette, Joanna retreated to the window.

She pulled one curtain a little aside and put her face close to the glass so that in the space that was shadowed by her head she could see a little way out into the darkness.

Though the thunder had rolled away, the rain was still driving into the sodden ground. The rain and the darkness were like one thing as they pressed down together upon the earth. All the lights in the other bungalows had been put out. Only one faint light glowed, some distance off. Joanna knew it was in the window of Gerald Hyland's cottage.

Leaning forward a little, she rested her forehead against the glass. Minutes went by.

Presently she heard Gordon Weedon saying: 'I say, Doctor, if you're driving back to Asslington now, I wonder if you'd mind taking me along with you. I was staying because of the rain, but it'd be better if I could get back.'

Joanna turned round. Dr. Vanedden was in the room again.

He replied to Gordon: 'Of course – glad of the company. Well, Miss Prees, there's nothing physically the matter with your father. If a body were all that a human being consisted of you'd have no cause for anxiety at all. But the mind, the mind . . .' He gave a slow shake of his head.

Joanna said quickly: 'You don't mean—?'

He was staring down at the carpet. He said thoughtfully: 'Tell me, d'you know of anything that's been worrying your father lately? Anything special?'

'No,' said Joanna. 'I've realised he was – different. I knew there must be something. But I didn't know what.'

'You're sure you know nothing – nothing I ought to know if I'm to help him? You can, as Miss Winnpole assured you, trust me absolutely. I think perhaps you've begun to feel that by now?' He looked at her questioningly.

'I don't know, Dr. Vanedden, I don't know anything,' she answered.

'Nothing you'd tell me if' – he looked round at Peggie and Gordon – 'if we were alone?'

'I tell you, I wish I did.'

He gave a slight sigh. He passed a hand through his thick, grey hair. It was a little hand, white, with short, square-tipped fingers. Surprisingly, it was rather dirty.

'Well, young man,' he said to Gordon, 'if you want to get back to Asslington, come along. Good night, Miss Prees. I expect I shall see you again shortly. If I can do anything . . .' The smile appeared again. It was less impersonal now; it was gentle, intimate, compelling response. 'If I can do *anything* . . .'

Joanna replied with a twitch of the lips that did duty for a smile, and shook the small, dirty hand held out to her.

Dr. Vanedden and Gordon Weedon left together.

That night, although as soon as the doctor's car had driven away, Joanna went to her room, undressed, got into her pyjamas and lay down in bed, there was no sleep for her for a long time. Outside the rain went on; all through the hours of darkness the hissing sound of it drove through her muddled, wakeful thoughts. Because it was falling at a slight angle, she had to keep the window closed. The room grew hot and airless. Even when she pushed the covers back she felt too hot. She tossed and fidgeted.

Once she switched on the light, smoked a cigarette and tried to read for a while. But she put the book down again after a few minutes.

Once she got up and went to the kitchen for a drink of water.

When at last sleep of a sort came there was already grey light in her room. The rain was stopping and thick clouds of mist were rolling in from the sea.

Joanna woke with someone's hand shaking her shoulder. She started up, wide awake. It was her father leaning over her.

'I want you to drive me in this morning. How soon can you be ready?'

'But you aren't going in this morning!'

'I must. I want to get there early. Can you be ready in a quarter of an hour?'

'Father, you can't go – really you can't. You oughtn't to be up. You're looking dreadful.'

'I'm asking you a simple question, Joanna. Can you be ready to drive me into Asslington in a quarter of an hour?'

'Yes, but—'

'If you don't want to I can drive myself.'

'Father, please go back to bed,' said Joanna. 'Look at yourself in the glass, look how your hands are shaking.' She stood up beside her bed, reaching for her dressing-gown.

'Precisely,' he replied, 'I'm too shaky to drive. But if you won't oblige me I must drive myself. Now can you, or can you not be ready in fifteen minutes?'

'I can,' she said, and fifteen minutes later, dressed in her slacks again and her silk shirt, with a loose jacket over them, she brought the car round to the front door.

The unmade road was still sticky with chalky mud. Yet the morning air had sweetness in it, and there were thin patches in the mist through which a faint blue was beginning to shine. But thick mist still brimmed over the rim of the cliffs; the sea was hidden beneath it.

Mr. Prees did not sit beside his daughter. He got into the back of the car and huddled a rug round his stout, shaking body. He had found some spare pince-nez; behind them his small eyes stared out with a sightless glow. His face was almost the colour of the chalk track. He spoke once or twice, but not to Joanna.

There were no other cars on the road yet. About half a mile from the bungalow the track joined the main road from Asslington to Lythe. Here they passed a farm-cart and presently a cyclist. At the outskirts of Asslington they found milk-carts abroad, a small number of people and a little other traffic. A church clock told them it was ten minutes to seven.

The Botanical Gardens are at the centre of Asslington. The town, with its hotels, boarding-houses, promenades, cinemas and shops, gathers around this park of pleasant lawns, rare trees and shrubs, glowing flower-beds and glasshouses.

Joanna set her father down outside the herbarium. It was built along one side of the Gardens, and could be entered either from the Gardens or from the street. Of elegant Victorian Gothic, its narrow, pointed windows were imposing with stained glass, its portal might have been copied from some nineteenth-century cathedral or the municipal buildings of a Midland town.

Edgar Prees was not a man who ever had to fumble for his keys. A key to the herbarium and a key to his private office hung on a chain that was looped across his chest. Though he stumbled a little as he stepped on to the pavement, and though, from the strange way he was staring ahead, he might scarcely have been able to see, he already had the right key in his hand as he reached the doorway.

As he pushed the door open Joanna called after him: 'Shall I come in with you?'

He did not answer.

She repeated her question. Again he did not answer.

'Well, when shall I call for you?' she asked.

'What's that?' he said. 'Call for me?'

'Are you going to be long? Shall I wait for you? Or shall I call for you presently? You aren't thinking of doing a day's work, are you?'

'No, no, go away. Call for me if you like. I don't know.'

He took one long, extraordinary look at her, then without saying anything, went inside and let the door swing shut behind him.

After a few minutes Joanna started the car and drove on. Her features were set in depression. Driving to a car park, she left the car there and, with her hands thrust into the pockets of her loose jacket, went walking along the promenade.

It was still early enough for the streetcleaners to be out. One went ahead of her, collecting pieces of newspaper and orange-peel on a spike. Now and then some determined-looking, early morning bather strode across promenade and shingle and plunged into the mist-wrapped sea.

Joanna walked to a café, only to find that it was not yet open.

Turning back and walking this time not on the promenade but on the beach a couple of feet above the line where the tiny ripples that edged the dead calm sea twisted silently over, she made for a coffee-stall at the head of the pier. She drank a cup of coffee there and ate some biscuits. Then she went and sat on a bench. The thinning mist was shot through with a glitter of sunshine. The mingling of sun and mist caressed her skin with gentle freshness.

She smoked two cigarettes. Then she got to her feet and, strolling at first but suddenly beginning to hurry, returned to the herbarium. But the caretaker had evidently not arrived yet, for the nail-studded, Gothic door was still closed. She pushed at it, controlling a momentary impulse to start a panic-stricken battering on it with her fists. But the door did not yield.

It was nine o'clock, when the shops opened, that Joanna appeared in the doorway of a hairdresser's and asked to have her hair shampooed and set. Ushered into a cubicle, draped in a white cassock, sprayed, lathered, rinsed, combed, given a cowl of net and pads of cotton-wool over her ears, and placed under a dryer, she got through another hour. By the time she came out of the shop the mist had cleared, the street was brilliant with clear sunshine, and busy with shoppers and cars.

The heat and the buzzing of the dryer had made her drowsy. She stood blinking in the bright light, still dazed with the warm, scented stupor of the cubicle.

Again she approached the herbarium. She did not hurry. It was half-past ten when she passed the gates of the Botanical Gardens. The gates in summer opened at nine o'clock; by half-past ten the paths were usually dotted with perambulators and the lawns with romping children, while old ladies and gentlemen sat on the benches, reading the *Daily Telegraph* and digesting their boarding-house breakfasts.

But to-day at half-past ten the gates were still closed. They were not only closed, but there was a policeman to keep back the chattering, curious crowd.

Outside the door of the herbarium there was another policeman.

Joanna saw the policeman and the knot of people on the pavement. For a moment she stood still with a look of complete paralysis. Then desperately, with a ruthless jerking of her elbows left and right, she forced her way through. She stood in front of the policeman.

'Please,' she said, 'let me in at once.'

A big, slow-spoken man, he shook his head at her.

'Sorry, miss, you can't go in there. Place isn't opening to-day.'

'But I've got to get in. I – I want to see someone.'

'Sorry, my dear, it's closed. They're not letting anyone in.'

'But I want to see someone. It's important. Please, please let me through.'

There came a change in the way he was looking at her.

'Who is it you want to see?'

She said in a low voice: 'Mr. Prees. I'm his daughter.'

Without a word he unlocked the door.

As he let her through a sudden crescendo in the sibilant undertone of chatter on the pavement followed her from the sunshine of the street into the vaulted entrance-hall and camphor-laden air of the herbarium.

The first person she saw was Dan Moon.

He was coming down the wide flight of stairs before her. He looked white and shocked. For an instant, when he saw her, a gleam of fright appeared in his eyes and he stood still, as if he could not bring himself to be the one who had to tell her what had happened. Then, as a policeman came through a door and approached her, Dan ran down the stairs and thrusting past the man in uniform, put an arm round her shoulders.

He took a hard grip on her arm.

'Look here, Jo, hold on to yourself tight while I tell you—'

'He's dead,' she said.

'Yes.'

She twisted her head to look up at him. 'That's why he came here. I understand now.'

'Sh!' said Dan sharply.

'But that *is* why he came!' she cried. 'He made me drive him here so that he could go up to his room and kill himself.'

The policeman was standing looking at them.

'No,' said Dan.

'No?' said Joanna. Dan's fingers were digging into her arm. 'But that *is* why he came. I feel now as if I'd known it all along, and if I hadn't left him—'

'All the same,' he told her harshly, 'he didn't kill himself, he was murdered.'

3

Inspector Tingey liked simplicity. He liked simple virtues and was sympathetic to a few simple vices. He liked to be thought a simple man who believed what people told him.

His love of simplicity had been carried into his way of living; he seldom ate anything but steak and chips, never drank anything but tea and beer, and if he could not remember the name of a man, he always called him M'Clusky.

It was in the Inspector's calm, kindly tones that the details of her father's death were told to Joanna. Edgar Prees had been shot through the head. Seated at his desk in his private room in the herbarium, he had been shot at close range with his own revolver. This revolver, as most people seemed to know, he had always kept in a drawer of his desk.

There had been an attempt to produce an appearance of suicide. But the attempt had been a careless one. Though the revolver had been left lying on the floor as if it had fallen there from the dead hand, and though the fingerprints of Edgar Prees and of no one else had been found on the revolver, the truth was that no human hand could have held the revolver in the position which the fingerprints suggested. Inspector Tingey inferred that the murderer, who had either worn gloves or else had wiped his own fingerprints away, had himself pressed the finger-tips of the dead man down on the metal surface – but in the wrong places. According to the medical evidence death had occurred not later than eight o'clock.

Joanna had one short, sickening glimpse of her father. After that the Inspector had a great many questions to ask her.

Gerald Hyland, who stayed at her side, reminded her: 'You don't have to answer these questions, you know, if you don't want to. If you don't feel up to it I'll damn well see they let you go home straight away.'

But she only nodded impatiently. Her eyes dwelt steadily on the face of Inspector Tingey.

The Inspector, with all his simplicity and all his kindliness showing in the smile that hovered beneath his drooping moustache, said to her: 'You know, I've got a daughter myself, Miss Prees – just about your age too. Sally her name is. She lives in New Zealand; I haven't seen her for three years. She's married and she's got a little girl of her own – Irene Dawn they called her. Pretty name, isn't it? Irene means Peace, you know – kind of a nice thought, don't you think?'

They were sitting in Gordon Weedon's room. It was a high, narrow room with two narrow Gothic windows. There was stained glass in the top of each window; the sunshine, falling through panes of ruby, cobalt and amber, made pools of coloured light on the table at which the Inspector had seated himself, and touched the tips of his ears with a rainbow-tinted glow.

'And now, Miss Prees, just tell me in your own words everything that happened this morning.'

As Joanna stayed silent he repeated his question.

She had crossed her arms and looked as if she were huddling herself together against cold, though the air in the room, laden with the pungent smell of Xylol which came from some wax in the dishes of an electric embedding-oven standing on the bench just behind her, was over-heated and fusty.

Her answer came jerkily: 'My father woke me up this morning – I don't know what the time was – he asked me to drive him in here. I didn't want to. He was looking much too ill. He said if I wouldn't drive him he'd drive himself. So I did. I suppose—' She snatched a swift glance at Gerald Hyland. 'I suppose they've told you about last night?'

'Yes, Miss Prees, but I should be glad to hear your version of it.'

So she gave it, a short, abrupt narrative.

'Thank you,' he said, 'we'll come back to that later. Now can you tell me, what time was it when you got here this morning?'

'A few minutes to seven, I think.'

'You aren't sure?'

'Well, it was ten minutes to seven when we passed the church.

45

It'd have taken me five or six minutes, I think, to do the rest of the distance.'

'And you say you didn't come in with your father?'

'No,' said Joanna.

'Although,' said Inspector Tingey, 'you thought he was ill, perhaps even not quite responsible for his actions?'

'No, I didn't come in.'

'Remember,' came the grating voice of Gerald Hyland, who was standing by one of the windows, a long, thin sliver of a man, fidgety and pale, 'you don't have to answer that kind of question if you don't want to.'

The Inspector said earnestly to Joanna: 'I don't think Mr. Hyland's giving you particularly good counsel this morning. I'm sure you'll be best advised simply to tell me everything you can.'

'I think so too,' she said.

'Good. Now why didn't you follow your father, Miss Prees?'

'He didn't want me to.'

'But if you thought he was ill . . .?'

'Oh, I know I ought to have gone with him. But he and I' – she pinched up a fold of her jacket between two fingers – 'we haven't been getting on well. In fact, I think he hated the sight of me. I was afraid, I suppose, to insist on going with him when he didn't want me. We've done nothing but quarrel recently, and—'

'Joanna!' Hyland's blue eyes were blazing at her out of his bony face.

'Oh, Gerald, do leave me alone!' she exclaimed. 'Everyone knows how father and I have been quarrelling recently.'

'But you shouldn't let words be put into your mouth.'

'I haven't let any words be put into my mouth.'

'For heaven's sake,' he said, 'do realise the seriousness of – all our positions.'

'But there's no point in pretending a thing when everyone knows it isn't so – is there?' she asked Inspector Tingey.

'Of course not, of course not.' He stroked his drooping moustache. He looked such a mild man, such a simple man, with his serious expression and his rainbow-tinted ears. 'Talking of quarrelling, Miss Prees, isn't it true that Mr. Moon had a quarrel with your father yesterday evening?'

'No, he didn't.'

Tingey was looking at some notes. 'Miss Winnpole says that late yesterday evening Mr. Moon arrived at the bungalow and wanted to see your father. She said he appeared to be in a "furious temper." She heard his voice raised, saying he couldn't stand working under your father any more, and that he was going to tell him what he thought of him. Is that correct, Miss Prees?'

She stared down at one sandalled foot. 'I'm afraid an awful lot of people have had quarrels with my father recently. I don't think he's been normal for some time. He's been finding fault with everyone – even people he'd a very high opinion of. For instance, he sacked Miss Winnpole whom he knew would do anything on earth for him. And when Mr. Weedon saved his life on the cliffs yesterday he called it devil's work.'

'Yes, but *did* Mr. Moon arrive at your home last night, in a furious temper, wanting to see your father?'

Unwillingly she admitted it.

The Inspector proceeded: 'What was he in a temper about?'

'I don't know.'

'He didn't give you any explanation?'

Her gaze shifted to a row of dried plants laid out on sheets of paper on a table under one of the windows. They were large-leaved plants, a peculiar species of *Hamamelis* from the Amazon valley.

'Not much,' she said slowly. 'He said it was technical – something about a Russian. It won't have been anything important; he's very quick-tempered.'

'A Russian?' Interested kindled on Tingey's face. 'A Russian – fancy. I suppose' – he looked at her searchingly – 'that young man isn't a Communist or anything like that?'

She shrugged her shoulders. 'All I know is, whenever scientific people start quarrelling, the Russians come into it sooner or later.'

'But you've known Mr. Moon for some time, I believe? Wasn't it you who obtained him this post here under your father?'

She nodded. 'We were at Oxford together.'

'Thank you.' He picked up a pencil. 'And now, after you'd left your father, where did you go next?'

She told him.

47

She told him how she had taken a car to a car park and gone walking along the promenade, how she had drunk coffee at the coffee-stall and sat on a bench, how she had tried to get into the herbarium, had failed, and had gone back to sit on the bench until, at nine o'clock, she had gone to the hairdresser's.

He made notes with a slow-moving pencil. While he was doing it Joanna fidgeted, twisting sideways in her chair. She sniffed at the smell of Xylol coming from the wax in the dishes of the embedding-oven on the bench, and poked with one finger at the wax in one dish. The wax was softish and took and held the imprint of her finger.

When Tingey laid down his pencil she faced him again.

'Please,' she said, 'would you mind telling me, who found my father? Please tell me a little more about it all. I keep trying to see it – in my mind's eye. I can't.'

Tingey glanced at the tall man by the window. He said: 'Mr. Hyland found him.'

'Yes,' said Gerald Hyland quickly, 'yes, Joanna, I found him. I came here. . . . You see, I was looking for him. I rang up the bungalow this morning . . .' He broke into a fit of coughing. 'As I was saying, I rang up the bungalow – it must have been about eight-thirty – to ask how he was. By the way, I'm frightfully sorry I never came round last night, Joanna. I got playing some Wagner to my visitors and never realised how late it was, and then when I did realise, I thought you'd probably have gone to bed. Anyway, I rang up this morning, and Mrs. Searle told me that you and Edgar had gone already. I felt a bit anxious, so I came along here. The place was open, but Edgar's door was locked. I didn't like that much somehow, so I went and got the caretaker and persuaded him to open the door for me with his spare key. And there he was – Edgar, I mean.' Hyland's face had coloured oddly while he was speaking, and there was agitation in his manner.

As he finished the door opened and a constable came in.

'A telephone call from London for Mr. Hyland,' he said. 'Shall we have it put through to here?'

'No,' said Tingey, 'put it through to one of the other rooms. I want to talk to Mr. Moon.'

As Hyland hurried out Joanna rose to follow him. But Tingey

motioned her to stay. He had still a few questions to ask her, such as whether she knew of anyone with any enmity towards her father, or whether she had any ideas concerning his attempt at suicide.

When she had shaken her head at each question, he told her that that was all.

She lingered at the door. 'Inspector . . .'

'Yes, Miss Prees.'

'Are you certain – isn't there any doubt at all – that it's murder?'

'There's uncertainty in all earthly matters, Miss Prees.'

'But you are sure?'

'Well' – he sounded apologetic – 'those fingerprints didn't land on the revolver in a natural way, did they? And the fingerprints aren't all.'

'What else is there?'

Tingey picked up his notebook. Ruffling the pages with a broad thumb he seemed about to speak when, fluttering from between the pages of the notebook, something glided to the floor.

Picking it up, he gave an exclamation.

'So that's where I put it!' A smile shone all over his face. 'My, I'm glad I found it – I've hunted all over the place for the thing. Look, Miss Prees. There, isn't she sweet?' He held it out to Joanna.

It was a photograph of a child of about two years old. A child of solid structure with an expression on its face of uncommonly grim determination, it was amazingly like a more censorious, less liberal-minded Inspector Tingey.

The Inspector beamed with pride.

'That's Irene Dawn, Miss Prees.'

A mild man, a simple man . . .

Joanna went quickly from the room.

She found Dan, Gordon and Peggie gathered at one end of the long, vaulted room where all the box-files containing dried specimens of plants were kept. Tall cases, filled with these files, lined the four walls. Down the centre of the room were more cases, filled with more files. Everywhere there was the same musty smell of camphor.

The three people at the end of the room were smoking. Though they were standing together there was an air of separatedness about them all; each face revealed how thoughts were drawn inward into an unshared, uneasy brooding. Joanna joined them without speaking. She accepted a cigarette from Gordon, and turning to the window, leant an elbow on the sill, and looking out at the lacy foliage of the strange maidenhair tree outside, made a fourth in this group of silent, isolated people.

After a minute or two Dan Moon was summoned to speak to Inspector Tingey.

A moment after he had gone Gerald Hyland came into the room. Still nervous and excited, he now looked angry as well.

He said: 'I've just been speaking over the telephone to that man Dyke. I sent him a wire this morning, and he says he and his friend are coming straight down. I told him it wasn't necessary. I dropped the broadest hints I could that none of us here is going to feel like entertaining strangers at the moment. He wouldn't take any notice – actually said a murder ought to be enough entertainment for anybody without our worrying to supply anything extra. I almost went the length of telling him we damn well didn't want him poking that big nose of his into our affairs. It didn't do any good. The man must have the thickest skin imaginable.'

'But why did you wire him, Gerald?' asked Joanna.

'Had to, he's my alibi.'

'But —' Joanna looked round at them all. 'Have they been asking you all for your alibis?'

'Of course,' said Gordon. He gave a little giggle. 'Peg's the only one with a good one; your Mrs. Searle knows that she didn't go out till we rang up for her. But I couldn't produce one to satisfy them. I was out for an early morning walk. Sinister, don't you think?'

'Don't, Gordon, for God's sake!' Peggie barked the words at him. Then she put a hand to her forehead. 'This head – it'll drive me mad. I woke up with it, and it seems to be getting worse every minute.'

'I suppose I've got an alibi,' said Joanna thoughtfully.

'My alibi,' said Hyland, 'is absolutely watertight. Edgar died sometime between seven and eight. Well, until about a quarter to nine I was looking after my visitors. I cooked liver and bacon for their breakfasts. I cooked it very well, too – it's one of the things I'm good at. I do feel they might show their appreciation by exhibiting a little perception. I almost told them so in so many words.'

'Oh, what does it matter if they do come?' Joanna turned back to the window. 'We'll have enough people interfering with us anyway during the next few days . . . weeks . . . months. . . .'

'Oh, God,' moaned Peggie, 'I think I'm going to go mad with this head – and everything.'

Gordon looked at her frowningly, without sympathy.

Someone standing just behind Gerald Hyland suddenly cleared his throat loudly.

They all started.

Hyland stepping aside, revealed a small, leather-faced man in an apron. It was the caretaker, Barnes.

'Oh, hullo, Barnes,' said Hyland.

'Mornin',' said Barnes.

He stood there, leaning on a long-handled mop.

'Well,' said Hyland after a moment, 'what is it, Barnes?'

'That's just it,' said Barnes, 'that's just what's worryin' me.'

'What d'you mean?'

'That's just it,' said Barnes again. 'That's what I wish I could remember. I've got somethin' on my mind, Mr. Hyland.'

'We all have, Barnes.'

'Ay, but I reckon you know what you got on your mind. Mine's slipped.' He nodded dourly, gripped his mop and wandered off.

'What did he mean?' asked Gordon Weedon.

'Oh, Barnes is always like that,' said Hyland. 'A somewhat incoherent thinker. Oh, hullo, Barnes' – for the small man with the weather-beaten face was back at his elbow – 'what is it now?'

'I wish I knew, Mr. Hyland,' said Barnes gravely. 'It's heavy on my conscience. But I know I seen somethin' wrong. Somethin' queer. This mornin'. You know you asked me to open the door of Mr. Prees' room, and I done it and we found him there, and then I went to telephone the police, and then I came back and there's you and Mr. Weedon in the room, and then after a bit there's the Inspector. Well, I been goin' over and over all that in my mind, tryin' to remember somethin'. But it's slipped. All I

51

know is, there's somethin' wrong, somethin' queer.' He gave a shake of his head and pushing his mop ahead of him over the polished floorboards, again departed.

Joanna said: 'Gordon, were you here already when – Gerald found him?'

He gave his uneasy little giggle again. 'No, I arrived while Barnes was telephoning. That's what I meant when I said it was really horribly sinister. You see, no one saw me arrive, so I can't prove I wasn't here much earlier.' The same nervous titter blurred the end of the last word.

Peggie shuddered, and with a slight, moaning sound, leant against one of the glass cases.

'And where was Dan?' asked Joanna.

A door at the far end of the room opened. It was Dan himself who appeared. He came strolling down the length of the room towards them. His thoughtful but immature face was set in an expression of glowering concentration.

'Dan, where were you between seven and eight this morning?'

He looked bewildered, as if the question were miles away from his thoughts.

'In bed, asleep,' he answered. 'What d'you take me for?'

Joanna's tense shoulders relaxed. She turned back to the window. Where the full sunshine fell on the maidenhair tree its light green leaves were almost golden.

'But I wish to God,' said Dan violently, 'I was in Peru!'

From the top of the cliffs the summer sea looked as if it had been stroked into motionless ridges, each reflecting its own separate beam of the brilliant sunshine. The sea's expanse was dappled in patches of light turquoise and, where the water was deeper and the seaweed grew long and waving in the depths, of almost sullen blue. Over all was the sheen of the afternoon sun. A white flash now and then showed where a gull swooped down to the water from its perch on the side of the cliffs.

Soft footsteps sounded on the turf. A voice said in artificial astonishment: 'Look who's here, George!'

Joanna, lying on the springy grass that was sweet with the honey smell of small heath-flowers, rolled on to her side and looked up.

52

Removing a grass-blade from her mouth, she said: 'Hullo,' and then bit into the grass-blade again.

Toby Dyke dropped down on the turf beside her.

Today he was dry and free from mudstains. His black hair was sleekly brushed. He was wearing a rather vivid blue sports coat and freshly creased flannel trousers. If one liked a swarthy skin, a beaked nose and dramatically sunken eyes, one might almost say that he looked handsome.

His friend George appeared to be in the same clothes as the evening before, merely dried and brushed. He squatted down beside Toby, nodded to Joanna, and imitated her in her grass-chewing.

Toby Dyke said: 'So you came to take a look at the spot.'

'What spot?'

'This one.'

She took a quick look round her.

'D'you mean that this was where it happened last night?'

'That's right.'

'I didn't know.' She looked round her again, more thoughtfully. 'I didn't know, I just came. I couldn't stand sitting there and watching while Gerald ate that enormous lunch. He always eats and eats when he's upset. What are you doing here?'

'Primarily, taking a look round. Secondarily – taking a look round.'

'Oh!'

'Just one of those things it seemed sensible to do, you know. I don't really think there's anything to see here.'

'D'you mean you think that what happened last night had anything to do with what happened this morning?' She rolled the grass-blade from one side of her mouth to the other.

'Frankly,' he said, 'I don't see how it can have. A man tries to commit suicide in the evening; in the morning he's found murdered. Both those events involve death. But apart from that they're about as difficult to connect with one another as two events can be. I mean, why murder a man who's so anxious to get rid of his life anyhow? Unless . . .'

'I know what you're thinking,' she said, 'or, anyway, what I'm thinking. I've kept thinking about it.'

He looked at her curiously.

'You've been wondering,' she said, 'whether or not – no, I don't think I'll say it. It's horrible. But how can one help having horrible thoughts – nothing but horrible thoughts – at a time like this? I've had horrible thoughts racing through my brain all day. Suspicions, quite crazy ones, ideas that couldn't have any possible foundation – they come bang into my mind and shut out every scrap of sense I've got. And then literally I start feeling sick. So I came out here by myself.' She plucked a fresh grass-blade and substituted it for the mangled scrap of green that clung to her lip. 'Anyway, people shouldn't behave so queerly if they don't want one to have queer thoughts.'

He asked: 'Who's been behaving queerly?'

'Oh, everyone, everyone. But all the same, Gordon couldn't have been trying to push my father over the cliffs last night – that was what you were wondering, wasn't it? – trying to push him over and only pretending to save him when you arrived. He couldn't have been doing that.'

'Just so,' said Toby Dyke, 'he couldn't have. Because your father himself was in a black fury with him for saving him.'

'Of course,' she said, 'father was so sick and ill, he might not have been able to tell the difference between pushing and pulling, and suppose that Gordon didn't believe that father really meant to . . .'

'Just so,' said Toby Dyke.

'There, you see!' Joanna suddenly sat upright on the warm, sweet-smelling grass. 'That's what I mean. I keep trying to make sense of horrible, ridiculous thoughts like that – when I know it couldn't have happened like that.'

One of Toby's dark eyebrows arched itself over a quizzical eye.

'But it couldn't have,' she asserted. 'He's got no reason to push my father over the cliffs, or to shoot him through the head. You've got to have a reason before you start killing people.'

'Somebody had a reason.'

Dark eyes with an odd, rather blank innocence in them, stared into his.

He said: 'A good many human actions are reasonless, but people don't kill unless they believe they've a reason for killing. Even if it doesn't look that way to other people, the killer believes for at least one moment that there's stark, unavoidable necessity to kill.'

She shifted her gaze from his face to the sea's dappled greens and blues. Her own face had a strained unhappiness in it, with eyelids thickened by recent tears and bleak bewilderment in the eyes.

It was in answer to something about that bewilderment that: 'Look here,' said Toby Dyke, 'I want to make an explanation. I want to explain just what George and I are doing here. You see, it was quite by chance that we got landed in this business last night. O.K. – we did what we could and went home. This morning we got a wire; it was your tall friend Hyland, wanting us to check his alibi. O.K. again – we say delighted, assuming that the simplest way to do it will be to run down here again and tell old Tingey ourselves that Mr. Hyland definitely didn't leave his home until at least a quarter to nine. We knew we'd have to do it sooner or later anyway, because Tingey was bound to want our version of what happened last night, so's to check whatever Weedon told him. Well, at that point Hyland starts laying it on with a trowel in the most heavily tactful fashion that if we come down we'll be nothing but damnably in the way. He hardly even gives us a chance to say all right then, we won't come; he simply starts rubbing our noses in the fact that he doesn't want us. And that's the cue for this somewhat suspicious brain of mine to give me a reminder that if he doesn't want us here this morning, he was mighty anxious to hang on to us last night. When we realised that he intended to spend the evening playing most of *The Flying Dutchman* to us we made several attempts to get away and go home, but he wouldn't have it at any price. Now that may have been simply because he wanted to show off his new gramophone; there are plenty of people like that. Yet it's turned out rather useful to him that we were there to corroborate the fact that he didn't leave home before a quarter to nine. D'you see what I'm getting at?'

She said in a tone of surprise: 'But you aren't seriously telling me that you suspect Gerald Hyland of having murdered my father?'

'No, as you say, not seriously – not particularly seriously.'

'But then—'

'There's one thing I *am* serious about, and that's a dislike of being made use of for dubious purposes – anyway without my permission.'

55

'But there's never anything dubious about Gerald's purposes. He's the most candid soul alive. And he's my father's oldest friend – his only friend. As a matter of fact, he's my godfather. And that's why we came to live out here, you know – because Gerald lived here.'

'Listen,' said Toby Dyke, 'we've just come from his cottage. When we'd seen Tingey and then booked ourselves rooms in The Ship in Asslington, we thought we'd just let Hyland know we'd done the job of clearing him. And he practically slammed the door in our faces. He was looking very white and excitable too, and his breath was well loaded with whisky. Now, making all allowances for grief at the loss of a friend, isn't there a good deal of the smell of a fish about his actions?'

Before she could reply, George said casually: 'Mind you, some things smell fishy to some people, and smell just like a sweet summer morning to others. Often, if you know enough about a thing, you never even think of thinking it peculiar. F'rinstance, once I was in Manchester. It was a wet Saturday afternoon. Don't know if you've ever spent a wet Saturday afternoon in Manchester. Anyway, there I was, waiting for a bus in the rain outside a big building. Don't know if you've ever waited for a bus in the rain on a Saturday afternoon in Manchester. . . . Anyway, there I was. Bit by bit I sort of realised what a lot of people was goin' past me into this buildin' – and doin' it in a queer, grim-faced, determined sort of way. I didn't take much notice at first. But then I began to wonder a bit; I reckon it was the stubborn way they were ploddin' through the rain that made me feel curious. Struck me suddenly I might look inside and see what it was all about. Well, what d'you think it was? Was it a meeting to vote for universal peace? Was it an indecent picture-show? No, it was a lecture on a comparison between the Rules of Gautama Buddha and Saint Benedict.' George spat some grass out of his mouth. 'Now me, I thought that queer. What with the rain, and its bein' Saturday afternoon, I reckoned there must be somethin' behind it. So I went in and sat right through the lecture to see what it'd turn out to be. Well, there wasn't nothin'. It was all above board, nothin' queer – honest there wasn't. It's just what does happen in Manchester, particularly on wet Saturday afternoons. If only I'd realised that I'd never have thought of anythin' bein' fishy.'

There was a silence.

Then Toby Dyke cleared his throat, and said: 'Yes, well, about this odd attitude of Mr. Hyland's, I was going to say—'

Joanna stood up. 'I think there's something in your friend's story. If you knew Gerald you wouldn't be exercising your suspicious mind on him.'

'Just a bit worried about him yourself all the same, aren't you? *Everyone's* acting queerly – you said so yourself.'

She brushed some fragments of grass from her clothes. 'Isn't it always rather a mistake to jump on every phrase a person uses? And, by the way, it struck me just now when you spoke of Inspector Tingey, it sounded rather as if you knew him. Do you?'

George replied: 'You never met a man in your life knows as many policemen as Tobe does. And he always believes they start perkin' up and feelin' pleased the moment he turns up. Which is his mistake.'

'If you know Inspector Tingey,' said Joanna, 'perhaps you can tell me something. Why's he so absolutely certain it's murder? Suicide's so much more reasonable. My father *wanted* to commit suicide.'

'Don't you know about the fingerprints on the revolver?' asked Toby.

'Oh, yes. But wasn't there something else?'

'There was the key.'

'What key?'

'The key to the main door of the herbarium. I believe he always wore it on a chain. It's missing.'

'Oh,' she said, 'I see.' She went a few steps nearer to the edge of the cliff. Standing with her back to the two men, her hands in her pockets, she asked next: 'Did Inspector Tingey tell you anything else?'

'Yes,' said Toby, 'he told me about a quarrel a young man called Dan Moon had with your father.'

'He didn't have a quarrel with him. He only wanted to have one, and when I told him father was ill, he said it didn't matter and went away.'

'What was it he wanted to have the quarrel about?'

'I don't know.'

'I rather wish I knew what it was,' said Toby Dyke. He dug

57

with his long fingers into the turf at his side. 'Tingey's taking it seriously – all the more so since Moon gave him an explanation of sorts and left poor Tingey more puzzled than when he was altogether in the dark. I was just thinking . . . don't you think it might be a good idea to get at the truth of all that before the mystery of it starts looming too large in the business? If we went along into Asslington and asked him—'

'Good heavens,' she exclaimed, 'what on earth has it got to do with you?'

He hesitated, and she went on vehemently: 'It's all crazed and ridiculous. It's unreal!'

'On the contrary – unfortunately.'

'And I'm not going chasing round after Dan Moon asking him for explanations of his conduct.'

'It was only an idea,' said Toby.

'I'm going home, I think,' she said. 'I think I'd better go home and see if – anything's happening. I didn't mean to stay out here so long anyway; I only came because I wanted to get away from people. And' – with chill emphasis – 'I didn't manage it. But since you're taking so much interest in our affairs I'll tell you something; Gerald Hyland's the only friend my father ever had. They used to fight with each other, and jeer at each other, but they'd have done anything on earth for one another – at least, I know Gerald would have for father. I dare say he does strike people who don't know him as a quite fantastic character; he's always lived alone, writing those dreadful books about Passion in the Desert, and Love among the Pyramids, and he's always having one absurd craze after another; at the moment it happens to be his new gramophone, but not long ago it was the importance of everyone having their teeth out, and before that it was photographing birds. But underneath all that he's shrewd and reliable and very, very kind. If you're here simply because you think there's something odd about Gerald Hyland's actions there's no reason why you should stay. In fact, there isn't any reason why you should stay.' The words had been coming faster and faster. As she finished she gave an abrupt nod to Toby and started walking away quickly in the direction of the bungalow.

Toby Dyke looked after her with sardonic sympathy in his eyes.

58

At first she walked quickly. But once she was well away from the two men her pace slowed down, and by the time she reached home her feet were dragging. She was so sunk in her own thoughts that she circled the black Cadillac that stood at the gate without paying any attention to it. But when she was half way up the path she paused and glanced back, suddenly concentrating on the car's unexpected presence.

Then she moved swiftly. A few rapid steps took her up the path and into the hall of the bungalow.

In the sitting-room, seated beside Peggie Winnpole, holding a cup of tea in his small, rather dirty hands, was Dr. Vanedden.

Dr. Vanedden rose. He made a small, stiff bow.

'My deepest sympathy.'

It was reserved, it was dignified, it was quite nicely judged.

Joanna said: 'Thank you,' and dropped into a chair. 'Any tea going?' she asked Peggie.

Peggie bent over the silver tray, pouring milk and tea into one of the Davenport cups. Her eyes were bright, her cheeks were pink; she looked as animated as Joanna had ever seen her.

Taking the cup that Peggie handed her, Joanna asked: 'Has anything been happening?'

Dr. Vanedden answered: 'I'm afraid I've been happening. I came out here knowing nothing. Nothing. I came simply to see your father. I thought I might talk with him for a while, and perhaps – well, I admit I had a certain scheme in my mind. I wanted to persuade him to let me give him psychological treatment.' He gave a shake of his big, silver-crowned head. 'It would have made all the difference, Miss Prees. You may think it was taking a great responsibility on myself, trying to persuade him instead of letting him come to me. But my methods are absolutely scientific – their soundness is beyond question. If I had been given time I could have saved him.'

'I don't see,' said Joanna, meeting the impersonal gaze of his grey eyes and frowning slightly to prevent her own gaze from growing nervous as his explored her face, 'how being psycho-analysed could have saved my father from being murdered.'

'Not psycho-analysed,' he said gently. 'Psycho-analysis, properly speaking, is that particular method of psychotherapy employed by the great Freud. My method differs from his a little. A little but fundamentally. It is, I think, more truly scientific. Your father, as a scientist himself, appreciated it.'

'Still I don't see how any kind of psychological treatment could have saved him from being murdered,' said Joanna.

Peggie broke in eagerly: 'But Dr. Vanedden doesn't believe he was murdered. He's absolutely certain it was suicide after all.'

As Joanna looked from one face to the other Dr. Vanedden gave a slight, earnest nod.

Joanna put down her teacup. She stood up. But instead of going abruptly from the room, she lingered irresolutely, and Peggie, filled with the unusual vitality she seemed to derive from Dr. Vanedden, said: 'He thinks it's absolutely natural that Mr. Prees, in the state of mind he was in, should have committed suicide in such a way as to make it seem like murder. Please explain it to her, Dr. Vanedden. Apart from everything else, it's *so* interesting.' Peggie's face glowed with a white and rosy prettiness.

Joanna said shortly: 'He was murdered. There were the fingerprints, and the key.'

'The key?' said Dr. Vanedden.

'His key to the main door of the herbarium. It's gone. He always carried it on a chain, and it was there this morning, because I saw it when he got out of the car and let himself in. But it's gone now.'

'Ah,' said Dr. Vanedden. 'Interesting. Let me think, let me think.' He placed the tips of his short, delicate fingers together. But while he was thinking his gaze did not stray from Joanna's face, even when she, with a movement of discomfort, turned away.

Peggie sat in a deep-breathing, worshipping silence while he thought.

'I wonder . . .' said Dr. Vanedden.

'I don't *want* to think he was murdered,' said Joanna sombrely. 'Suicide would be easier to face; it doesn't leave the same trail of suspicion and fear. And it'd be less incomprehensible. But it's merely stupid to try and overlook evidence.'

'You see, Miss Prees,' said Dr. Vanedden, 'Miss Winnpole has been telling me a great deal about your father. She's been working with him, living in the same house with him, and she has besides an unusually sensitive and perceptive nature. A deeply loyal and affectionate one too. What she's told me has given me an insight into the situation which it might have taken me many weeks of careful work to achieve by myself. As it is, I understand perfectly, I believe, the condition that had developed in your father's mind during the last few months. I could explain it to you all in technical language, but perhaps you wouldn't follow that. I can explain it quite simply, I think, by saying that the self-hatred which had been increasing in him, due to certain conflicts in his conscience – all of which go back, of course, to his relationship with his own father, but I needn't go into that – had turned outwards lately, changing into a malevolence against everyone he knew. You can recognise that, I imagine, in his changed attitude to yourself. But the self-hatred remained, turning to a desire for self-annihilation. Self-annihilation, world-annihilation – what's the consummation of those two desires? What indeed but suicide, designed to look like murder?'

'But the key, the fingerprints?'

'Ah, the key. I wonder where they've looked for the key. I imagine they've searched the room very carefully. But I wonder, for instance, if they've looked . . .' He considered. 'I wonder if they've looked for it outside the window.'

'Of course, the window!' said Peggie. 'He could have thrown it there, couldn't he?'

'Yes, I feel sure that's where they'll find it – outside the window. It stands to reason. He would have thrown it out there in order to produce the precise effect its absence seems to have produced on the police and others.'

'But the fingerprints,' said Joanna stubbornly. 'Did he shoot himself through the head and then polish the revolver and press his fingers on to it again in the wrong positions?'

He smiled. 'I don't know. I don't pretend to know everything. There are ways in which such things can be contrived, but the police will know more of them than I do. What I know is the state of mind of the dead man, and the actions likely to result from the state of mind.'

Joanna said: 'I don't believe it.'

'But my dear Miss Prees, it's true.'

'I don't think so.'

61

'I'm sorry,' he said. Then with simple, compelling gravity: 'It's true, it's true, Miss Prees. I know you think I'm just making it up as I go along, but theories like these are based on long years of observation and careful reasoning. And consider – consider the probabilities. Your father tries to commit suicide in the evening; in the morning he's found murdered. What an absurd situation. Isn't it much more probable that his death was suicide – the suicide that failed the evening before? Dismiss the preconceptions the police have planted in your mind; answer me, isn't it much more *probable?*'

'Oh, yes, of course it's more probable,' she said wearily, 'but it isn't what happened.'

Shrugging his shoulders rather sadly, he rose. He seemed, holding out one of his little paws, to be cogitating something more to say to her. When she let him take her hand he kept it in his, looking thoughtfully down at the slender fingers.

But whatever he might have said at that moment was checked by the entry of Gerald Hyland.

Seeing Dr. Vanedden, Hyland stood still, surprised and put out at finding a stranger.

Joanna introduced them, adding a curt explanation of Dr. Vanedden's presence.

Grunting, Hyland folded himself up into a chair. He had changed since the morning from his usual flannels into a dark suit of antique cut and mothball fragrance, a change intended, presumably, as a gesture of respect to the dead.

Dr. Vanedden kept one little, soiled hand extended. He made delicate weavings with it as he spoke. He said: 'Mr. Hyland, I wonder what you'll have to say to my theory. I've just been explaining it to Miss Prees, but finding it, I confess, very difficult to convince her. It's my view that Edgar Prees was not murdered. It's so clear if you understand the psychological situation. He committed suicide.'

Arresting his search through his pockets for his pipe, Hyland said, 'Eh?'

'But of course.' And Dr. Vanedden went over it all again.

Looking more pleased with the theory each time she heard it, Peggie gave a satisfied sigh and murmured, 'It's so *scientific*.'

Slowly, deliberately, Hyland resumed his search for his pipe.

He found it, filled it, stuck it between his teeth; he picked up a matchbox. But with the box in one hand and an unlit match in the other, he paused. The contraction of his cheek-muscles showed how viciously he was biting on the stem of his pipe.

'So you see,' said Dr. Vanedden, 'it's almost a foregone conclusion. Murder in those circumstances would be too bizarre. And life is very seldom bizarre, Mr. Hyland, it proceeds with astonishing regularity to rule, a rule that used to be entitled Divine Providence. We have other names for it: one name is Probability. And there are laws of Probability – exact, mathematical laws. I rather think,' – his vivid, authoritative glance fastened on Gerald Hyland's face – 'yes, I can see it; you agree with me.'

With a slow movement Hyland took his pipe from his mouth. His lips curled back from his teeth. 'You damned, hypocritical, little charlatan!'

Dr. Vanedden took a startled step backwards.

'What's your game?' shouted Gerald Hyland. 'What are you doing here? What d'you mean by trying to ram your cracked theories down our throats? Why d'you want to upset Miss Prees with all this – all this damned mumbo-jumbo? What d'you mean by it? Well, why don't you answer? What d'you mean by it, I'm asking – *what d'you mean by it?*'

Peggie had flushed crimson. 'How outrageous, how disgusting!'

'That's right, outrageous *and* disgusting!' cried Hyland violently. 'Coming here at a time like this, trying to wheedle into the confidence of a young girl – who's luckily got a lot too much sense to listen to you – but a young girl who's got the right at the present moment to be spared this interference and unnecessary vexation. Get out, you bogus little weasel – get out!'

'It's what I've always suspected,' breathed Peggie thickly. 'Half mad! Living alone, writing those loathsome, sensual novels – it was only to be expected. I'm trying to control myself, Mr. Hyland, because I don't believe you can help it, but if you'll take my advice you'll start having psychological treatment yourself without delay.'

Dr. Vanedden checked her with a hand laid lightly on her arm. After his swift step backwards out of reach he had quickly

63

recovered his dignity. He was regarding Gerald Hyland with thoughtful interest, to which his arched eyebrows gave a twist of humour.

He remarked, 'In my profession, you know, we're never surprised and never shocked.'

'You'll be both surprised and shocked if you come here again with that theory of yours,' said Hyland. 'Suicide! What's to be gained I'd like to know by bringing that kind of confusion into things? Or is it just that you've got to find something to talk about when you come here? You're going to send in a bill for all these visits – is that it?'

Dr. Vanedden again checked Peggie before she could break into words.

'My patients say far worse things than that to me, I assure you,' he told her. 'I welcome them, they often teach me a great deal about the patient's condition. Well, Mr. Hyland, I see you and I aren't going to agree for the moment, but I hope that may change. Myself, I should be glad of our better acquaintance. Now, however, as you wish it, I'll leave. Indeed, I was just about to do so when you came. Good-bye, Miss Prees. I hope I've at least managed to make you feel that you can turn to me if there's any way – *any* way – I can help. I understood and respected your father. Good-bye.' He went out. Peggie followed.

Hyland shouted after him. 'Send the bill to me, I'll enjoy paying it!'

As soon as the door had closed Joanna, who had watched the scene expressionlessly, turned on Hyland, saying: 'What on earth's come over you?'

He responded raspingly: 'What d'you mean?'

'Of course you know what I mean. Behaving like that – it's the most childish thing I've ever seen.'

'I don't understand,' he replied. 'I was angry with the little rat. I told him so. I believe in being frank.'

'You don't believe in anything of the sort. You just went and made a hideously uncomfortable and totally unnecessary scene. It's not at all like you.'

'He makes me feel sick. He's a fraud, a charlatan. I don't want him about the place.'

'Nor do I particularly,' said Joanna. 'He does make one feel sick somehow – sort of tight inside – when he looks at one. But I don't like scenes like that. Peggie was quite right, it was outrageous and disgusting.'

'Well, I'm sorry. I never dreamt that's how you'd feel about it. I was doing it for you. I didn't think you'd want to be bothered with him.' He had taken offence.

'But it was so unlike you,' she said. 'I don't know what's happened to people. No one seems normal. I'm beginning to feel . . .'

'What?' he asked suspiciously.

'Oh, I don't know. But I'd like to talk to somebody normal. Somebody whose nerves don't seem to have gone to pieces. I've got to hang on to a bit of detachment. I mustn't get swept *into* this thing. Father's dead – that's all of it that really matters to me. Tension, fear, suspicion – they don't really matter if you don't let them get you. Why've you let them get you, Gerald?'

He stood up.

'Sorry, Joanna, I *am* all upset. Don't let it worry you.'

'Gerald, what do you believe was the reason it – the murder – happened?'

He shrugged his shoulders. 'I think I'll go home and play my gramophone. There's nothing so soothing and stabilising as good music. By the way, you remember last night I told you I'd had a grand idea, something to help poor old Edgar and pull him out of his troubles? Well, that was my gramophone – I was going to give it to him.' He sighed. 'I'll be getting along home. I think I'll put on the Double Concerto. It's a new recording, a very beautiful one; I only bought it yesterday.'

'Poor Gerald,' she said, smiling, 'I don't believe you can tell one note from another. Who's it played by?'

'Couple of blokes.' Despondently he wandered out.

In the doorway he passed Peggie Winnpole. They eyed one another but neither said anything.

After he had gone Peggie, coming swiftly into the room and closing the door, said: 'I don't want to add to your worries at the moment, Joanna, but there really is something very strange about Mr. Hyland's mental condition. Don't you think so? His behaviour just now was perfectly extraordinary.'

Joanna gave a laugh. It had an unpleasant sound. She advanced a few steps towards Peggie.

'But you know, Peggie, your behaviour is perfectly extraordinary too. In fact, it's been extraordinary ever since yesterday evening. D'you remember when I came into your room and told you that father hadn't come in? You told me you knew something was bound to happen. You told me you knew a lot more about my father than I did. D'you remember? And do you remember what your first words to Gordon were when they brought father in from the cliffs? You said: "Oh, my God, Gordon, what have you done?" And Gordon didn't like your saying that, he told you to shut up. I don't know if you thought I hadn't heard it, or thought I'd forgotten it. Actually I believe I'm going to remember for the rest of my life every single thing that's happened during the last two days. And I want these things explained to me – or explained to the police. I want to know, I *must* know' – her voice rose jerkily – 'what all these things are that you know and that I don't. I want to know, for instance, why my father gave you the sack, and – Peggie! Peggie, what's the matter?'

For Peggie's face, from which, while Joanna had been speaking, every scrap of colour had drained, had suddenly gone vacant and lifeless as if she were going to faint.

But recovering herself, she turned on her heel and with an odd, stiff walk, went out of the room.

Joanna did not attempt to stop her. Her gaze remained for a moment on the door which Peggie had pulled shut behind her, then her hand went out, groping for cigarettes on the table.

Her hand had not yet struck against them when she muttered aloud: 'Yes . . . yes, I think so. That might be a good idea after all.'

The words were a prelude to swift action.

4

The Ship Inn is not one of the fashionable hotels of Asslington. It does not face the sea, it does not advertise, it has no band; there is not even water laid on in the bedrooms.

It was about seven o'clock that evening when a young woman in a close-fitting black dress of considerable sophistication, a small black hat with an eye-veil, with big pearls clamped to her ears, and high, slender heels on her shoes, walked suddenly into the lounge.

Roving eyes, mostly the eyes of commercial travellers, but also of a press-photographer and of one or two reporters, turned appreciatively in her direction.

But before anyone had had time to realise that this was the same girl whose photograph, in loose jacket and slacks, was in several of the evening newspapers, she was gone again.

Hurrying nervously, she went to the nearest telephone-box. She rang up the Ship Inn. She asked if she could speak to Mr. Dyke. She refused to say who wanted him.

Waiting in the telephone-box while he was being fetched from the corner of the lounge where, a moment ago, she had caught a glimpse of his black hair and sallow face, her lips moved over the mouthpiece of the telephone, rehearsing a few sentences in which she could tell him, hurriedly, explicitly, why she wanted him. But when his voice said suddenly in her ear: 'Dyke speaking,' she only managed some muddled incoherency.

He cut her short. 'Where are you speaking from?'

'Just outside the hotel.'

'Right,' he said, 'wait there. I'll come straight out. No, don't do that – someone might think of coming along with me. There are some reporters staying in this place, and I'm suspected of having a certain amount of inside information. You'd better go somewhere else and wait for me. D'you know a good place? I don't know this town. Where can we eat in something like privacy?'

She had that part of it thought out in advance. She told him the name of a small Italian restaurant near the station, and gave him directions for getting there.

Toby Dyke said: 'Right, you go there, and I'll be along as quickly as I can.'

'Thank you,' she said. 'I – I'm afraid I haven't really explained yet why I—'

'That can keep.'

She heard the click as he replaced the receiver.

The restaurant she had named was a cheap, steamy place, smelling as richly of garlic as the woods in springtime. The olive-skinned waitresses, an amazing number of them, all with sleek, black curls and chubby, rounded hips, looked so like one another that it seemed probable they were all the proprietor's daughters. Joanna had been here once or twice before with Dan Moon. The tables were separated from each other by high-backed benches, which formed small cubicles down each side of the room; this, from Joanna's point of view at the moment, was an advantage.

She went to the farthest table and sat down with her back to the door. After about ten minutes Toby Dyke joined her.

At the slightly startled look that came to his face the moment he saw her, she said with an apologetic laugh: 'I'm sorry about the make-up. I'm usually so judicious about it. But they don't in the least mind if you bring disreputable women in here, and it did seem a good idea, rather. You know, I walked into your hotel just now and faced all those journalists, and they didn't spot me.'

He grinned. 'Don't apologise; it's a pleasure.' He slid along the bench opposite her. Then looking over the tops of the benches towards the door, he made a sound of disgust.

'Hullo, I thought I'd shaken you off,' he said, as George, coming up to the table and sliding his plump person along the bench next to Toby, gave his head a slight, contemptuous shake and said to Joanna: 'Evenin'.'

Toby sighed.

'I'm sorry about George,' he said to Joanna.

They ordered the inevitable *escalope de veau* and spaghetti.

As the black-haired, round-bottomed little waitress moved off to start screaming in shrill Italian down a hatchway, Joanna, in the stiff, uneven tone that got into her voice whenever she was nervous, said: 'They take ages here to bring one anything. I think, if you don't mind, I'll start talking now, and talking about what I'm here for. I don't think I could keep up a conversation for long on whether Asslington's as charming a resort as Bournemouth, or whether I've seen any good plays lately.'

'O.K.,' said Toby, 'but let's order something to drink first.'

The round-faced, bald-headed proprietor, putting on a bowler-hat and carrying a large jug, went to fetch the beer they ordered from the nearest licensed premises.

The opening and closing of the door as he went out made Joanna look round the high shield of the bench, but seeing no one come in, she settled back again into her corner.

'I'll explain first,' she said, 'why I rang you up just now. It's simply that I started feeling I wanted to – almost had to, really – find someone normal to talk to. You remember I told you this afternoon, everyone's acting so queerly. It's making me almost start wondering whether I'm not acting very queerly myself. That sounds stupid. I'm feeling horribly stupid and helpless. I can't think about anything clearly. But if one can't think clearly, if one can't keep one's head . . . I mean to say . . .' The explanation, which had started rapidly, lost its way a little. Her eyelids, blue with eye-shadow, drooped over her eyes. 'I mean, you sounded this afternoon as if you were interested in – all this. I don't know what your interest in it is; it seemed to be rather cold-blooded. But it seemed sane. And someone cold-blooded but sane to talk to at the moment would be an enormous help.'

She suddenly looked up at him. When she met his eyes, intent, observant and encouraging, a little of the bright nervousness disappeared from her own. She relaxed more easily against the high, hard back of the bench.

But it was George who replied: 'I'll tell you what his interest in this kind o'thing is, miss. It's just a generalised interest in crime. He edits books about it, real and fictional; he writes 'em; he writes articles. Crime – nothin' but crime. You mightn't believe it, but I led a life of crime myself once; it's Tobe here that put me off it. Got me just bored with the subject, fed up with the *idea* of it, if you follow me. He's writin' a little book now for a children's Nature Study series: "Wild Criminals I Have Known." So you want to be careful what you tell him, or you'll find yourself and your friends bein' dished up for the tiny tots in simple language with nice little pen and ink pictures in the margins – see what I mean?'

'Shut up, George.' Toby picked up the jug of beer which the bowler-hatted proprietor had just put down on the table. He filled three glasses. 'I don't think we've got to go on finding reasons for having dinner together and talking over reasonably the thing we've all got involved in. Perhaps it'd be difficult to find a reason why George should be in it too, but his dinner's ordered; we may as well let him stay and eat it. Now suppose you begin by telling me everything that happened since you first started worrying yesterday evening because your father hadn't come home. I think if you do that I may begin fitting things into some sort of shape.'

It took her a long time to tell it.

The *escalope* and spaghetti had arrived, had been eaten, the proprietor had been sent off once more in his bowler-hat for a second jug of beer, before Joanna had finished describing that last odd scene with Peggie Winnpole, when Peggie, on being asked why she had lost her job, had almost fainted.

As at last Joanna came to a stop the three of them sat silent.

Toby was crumbling some bread on the table before him, George was looking down into his glass, tipping it this way and that, watching the liquid spin and find its level again.

After a moment Joanna said tentatively: 'Tell me, I've been thinking and talking about Gerald and Peggie and Gordon – that's stupid of me, isn't it? Isn't it more likely to be mixed up with a quite different lot of people?'

'A pity,' said Toby Dyke, 'but it doesn't seem to be so.'

'Why not?'

'You see, it's a matter of keys.'

'What keys?'

'The keys of that entrance to the herbarium by which you saw your father go in. The other entrance could only have been reached through the Gardens, and anyone trying to get in that way before the Gardens opened would almost certainly have been seen. It's true someone might have hidden in the Gardens all night, but there were no signs that any of the windows had been forced. Again, someone might have spent the whole night inside the building. But could that person have known your father was to arrive so long before other people? Then it's possible too your father himself let the murderer in. But the probability is, don't you think, that whoever it was came in at the main entrance, using a key. From eight o'clock, when Barnes arrived, the door was unlocked, and someone might have got in then – only as it happens Barnes was cleaning the passage outside your father's room and then the entrance-hall, so if anyone had come in Barnes would have seen him. So even if the argument has holes in it, you've got to turn your attention very carefully on people who've got keys to that front entrance. And those are Barnes, Peggie Winnpole, Weedon, Moon and two or three other members of the staff who are having their holidays just now – naturally Tingey's making inquiries about them also.'

'But keys can be borrowed,' she said.

He nodded. 'True.'

'And that kind of key can be duplicated in five minutes at any Woolworth's.'

'Yes, I said the argument had holes in it. Still, it does make certain questions rather important, doesn't it?'

She said nothing. The door of the restaurant opening and closing at that moment, she again looked hastily round. As she turned back to the table, she put her elbows upon it and hid her face in her hands. 'Heavens, I'm tired,' she said in a muffled voice. 'I know this kind of tiredness too – it means one doesn't sleep. Well, I thought when I'd got to the end of my story you'd ask me questions. Don't you want to?'

'There are several questions I want to ask,' he replied, 'but you aren't the one who can answer them. Tell me one thing, had your father and Hyland any financial dealings with one another?'

'I don't think so. Why?'

He did not tell her why. He asked after a moment: 'What's Hyland's income?'

'More than he needs, anyway; he's always giving it away.'

'Is it all from his novels?'

71

'What's the point of this?' she asked impatiently. 'Gerald Hyland's the one person you definitely needn't suspect. Apart from anything, he hasn't a key, and has got an alibi.'

'Yet you said yourself he's acted queerly ever since the morning.'

'Yes, I know.' She moved uneasily. 'Oh, well . . . Yes, so far as I know, Gerald does live on his writing. Sex and religion in the desert seem to bring in a very reasonable income. And my father had his salary as curator at the Haybox – that's been seven hundred for the last few years; and he's also got a good many investments, and if what you're working round to asking is who inherits whatever he leaves, I do.'

'I see.'

She propped her head against her hands once more. She said drearily: 'I don't really know now why I came. After all, I don't believe it's any good talking about it.'

Toby Dyke was drumming with his fingers on the table before him.

'The motive,' he said, 'that's what no one's dropped a single hint about yet. No one seems to have had anything serious against your father, except possibly Dan Moon. Hyland appears to have been an old and reliable friend, Peggie Winnpole says she'd have done anything on earth for him – seems she told Tingey a lot about her unhappy childhood, and having no parents but only a lot of religious aunts and uncles, and how your father meant much more to her than anyone else. Weedon's attitude seems to have been merely negative—'

'Oh, Gordon and my father had no use for each other at all,' she said listlessly.

'Hadn't they? Well, that's something. Why not?'

'Oh, I don't know; they just didn't like each other. Perhaps Gordon was a bit jealous because Peggie was so fond of my father, though I don't think Peggie and Gordon have ever been much in love. They're the kind of engaged couple who'll go on being engaged until they've saved up enough money to buy every last salt-spoon and embroidered guest-towel. No, I think I'm probably wrong, I don't think Gordon can have been jealous; I don't think he's got it in him. God, I wish I weren't so tired. Gordon and my father – they just didn't like one another.'

'And anyway it was Weedon who saved his life last night, so

the dislike can't have gone very deep. And that means we're left with Dan Moon and his unexplained craving for – Miss Prees, are you expecting someone?' For Joanna, at a sound, had again glanced round at the door.

'No,' she said. 'Why?'

'Only that if you don't want to attract the attention of the murder-thrilled public, the thing to do is *not* to look round when people come in.'

She subsided into her corner.

He went on: 'Well, as I was saying, we're left with Dan Moon and his unexplained craving to have a row with your father. But something else I'd like to know about is why Peggie Winnpole was given the sack. Also, what was the real reason that made Weedon follow your father home yesterday evening?'

'And what I'd like to know,' said Joanna, raising her head, 'is whether, if you looked, you'd find that missing key of my father's in the flower-bed outside the window, as Dr. Vanedden suggested.'

George stood up.

'Reckon I'm goin' to stroll up and down outside for a bit, and have a quiet think about whether or not that key's in the flower-bed.'

'Sit down!' Toby pulled him violently into his place. 'I know what your quiet thinks always let me in for.'

'But, Tobe—'

'Shut up! *I'm* doing the thinking at the moment. Vanedden – there's something familiar about that name, something I've heard, or—' He broke off. 'Miss Prees, if you don't want some strolling reader of the evening papers to realise that you're in his midst, *don't* look round every time the door opens.'

She reddened under the rouge on her cheeks.

As she relaxed against the back of the bench and started tearing small scraps of bread from the crust on her plate and working them into hard little pellets, the door of the restaurant opened yet once more. This time she succeeded in checking her involuntary movement to look round.

Toby Dyke chuckled, and with a sardonic gleam in his eyes, said to her: 'That's better – only this time it *is* your friend, Dan Moon.'

Dan Moon looked thoughtful and self-engrossed as, with his lumbering, vigorous strides, he made his way down the room between the rows of tables. He had not seen Joanna. Though Toby had recognised him, Toby's appearance seemed to convey nothing to Dan Moon. He sat down at the next table, immediately behind Joanna. They could just see the top of his head above the back of the bench.

All at once the mask of unconcernedness slipped from Joanna's face.

'Well, suppose I *was* expecting him,' she whispered across the table to Toby. 'He does usually come in here in the evenings. But you needn't look so sophisticated about it. I knew you'd want to go into the matter of that Russian. How was it you recognised him, anyway? Have you met him already?'

'Someone pointed him out to me,' Toby replied.

'You do look into things, don't you?' She leant back; lifting one hand, she made a sudden grab at a tuft of the thick brown hair that showed above the top of the bench. 'Hullo, Dan.'

If the people who frequented the restaurant had been of the kind who are easily upset by obscenity, the remarks that this action of Joanna's called forth from the lips of the startled Dan Moon might have landed him in trouble. But he managed to stop himself in the middle of the second sentence. Getting up and looking more abstracted than ever, he came round to their table and sat down on the bench beside Joanna.

He did not greet her. Giving a hard stare at her complexion, then as hard a stare at Toby, he thrust out a hand on a long, powerful arm, grabbed the menu and buried himself in its text with as much concentration as if it had been a page of Engler and Prantl's *Die Natürlichen Pflanzenfamilien*.

Joanna introduced the three men to each other. Dan glanced up, nodded, and returned to his absorbed reading of lists of soups and entrées. The little waitress came up; she had a familiar way with him, leaning a plump elbow on the bench behind him, and resting a fist on one chubby, protruded hip.

Dan called her Maria and ordered minestrone.

As she trotted away to scream shrilly down the hatchway to the kitchen depths below, Dan got up once more to buy cigarettes at the cash desk.

Though he had not yet addressed anyone at the table, he passed the cigarettes round. He looked with a trace of surprise at the competent ease with which Toby discovered matches in a pocket, and the speed with which one was lit as Joanna placed her cigarette between her scarlet-coated lips. He puffed at his own with quick, impatient puffs, mangling the tip of it, then asked abruptly: 'Well, going to stay and watch me eat?'

'D'you mind?' said Joanna.

He answered: 'No,' but seemed puzzled and uncomfortable. Dodging her regard, he took another questioning look at Toby.

Joanna, speaking round the cigarette that dangled from her lips, said: 'Dan, there's something everyone wants you to talk about. I think you'd better oblige. It's—'

'I know, I know, those damn pods.' He flicked ash on to the floor. 'Everyone's been making me talk about them. Right-oh, it's nothing to me. I'll talk about them all day and all night if you like. Got the story off by heart by now. Wherever I go policemen keep stopping me and wanting to know the story of the pods. Shouldn't be surprised if there's one waiting outside now. Either they can't understand simple language, or they think if they go on long enough they'll get me to tell them something different, or else someone's told them that pods are a sexual symbol, and they just want to go ha-ha; it's usually only dirty stories one has to tell so often.'

'The trouble appears to be,' said Toby Dyke, 'that Inspector Tingey can't believe that anyone would go all the way out to that bungalow in the sort of storm that was on last night simply to shoot their mouth off about some pods. I told him that controversies have raged for years and gone into several volumes of small print about things less remarkable than pods, but he still insisted that the people involved in them stayed at home in their studies and didn't go out in the wet on a night like last night. In which there is some truth.'

'But if I'd waited I'd never have managed to say anything about it at all,' said Dan peevishly. 'I explained that to him. You see, I'm not at all a quarrelsome person, in fact I'm definitely bad at quarrelling; I have to seize the moments when I think I'm up to the job. And last night, when I'd just got back from London, after going to the Museum and finding out that that damn Russian was perfectly right, I knew I was in the mood, I knew I could do it. I knew I could say just everything I felt. Dare say the weather even helped – it kept my bad temper up all the way out to the bungalow. But as I told that blasted police-inspector again and again, if I'd had the faintest idea of the state the old man was in, I mean if I'd spotted he was working up to a nervous break-down, I'd never have brought the subject up at all. For one thing, that explained everything, and meant besides that it wasn't really his fault. But until Joanna told me I simply never realised it. Stupid of me, but there it is.'

'Suppose,' said Joanna, 'we keep to the subject of pods.'

'That's right,' said Toby. 'First of all, what pods?'

'*Citrullus colocynthus.*'

'Ah! And why pods?'

But black-haired Maria arriving just then with Dan's plate of minestrone, his attention was switched to the soup.

After a mouthful or two, however, he put his spoon down.

'Of course, technically speaking, they aren't pods at all,' he said. 'They're fruits really – sort of gourds. Hi, Maria – bring me a roll, please.'

'I hope Inspector Tingey comprehends that precise point,' said Toby.

'Fact is,' said Dan, 'the whole business makes me look an awful fool. That was why I was so mad about it, naturally. I thought the old man must have been doing it deliberately. Couldn't think why he should have, but all the same couldn't think of any other explanation. You see, I'd been making a survey of some desert plants. They're sent over, dried, by an old boy in Cairo who goes out into the desert to collect them. Well, I'd been working on them for some time, and published one or two things about them, and never realised, until one of those damn Russians at the All Peoples' Commissariat for Plant Industry wrote and inquired why my description of the plants didn't tally with Muschler's, that old Prees had been handing me over material which had the pods of about four forms mixed in with it. They were always so mutilated that I couldn't tell much about them anyway. I made several rows about that, but it never made any difference. They were always chewed to bits – looked as if he'd let the mice get at them before handing them on to me. But I've been up to the British Museum to-day to

76

look at the specimens there, and that bloody Russian's perfectly right.' He clamped his jaws together, scowling down at his plate. 'Perfectly right,' he muttered between set teeth, 'and that stuff of mine, passed by Prees, is all published, it can't be called back. And I've made a complete bloody fool of myself.'

Toby Dyke was drawing patterns on the tablecloth with the prong of a fork.

In the pause that followed Joanna drawled: 'That story had the ring of Absolute Truth, don't you think, Mr. Dyke?'

Dan looked at her suspiciously.

'Yes, Dan,' she reassured him, 'it's a nice story, it'll do.'

'Hell,' he said, 'it's true.'

'Yes,' she said, 'that's what I'm saying.'

'But you don't believe it.'

'Oh, I do.'

'You don't.'

'I do, I do, I do!'

Dan turned to Toby Dyke. 'She doesn't believe it.'

'Don't you, Miss Prees?' asked Toby Dyke, his grave scrutiny searching her face.

Dan looked slightly bewildered at the way she dropped the mockery to reply to Toby. 'I don't think Dan could make it up, Mr. Dyke.'

'I rather thought you thought that.' But neither Toby's tone nor the amused expression in his eyes that went with it, told them what that comment meant.

When Dan had eaten a plateful of spaghetti they rose and left.

Darkness had fallen while they were in the restaurant, though there was still a russet tint of evening in the sky. It was a clear sky with a dusting of stars. The air in the streets was warm and still. Bare-legged girls and young men in open-necked shirts strolled along the pavements. From the direction of the pier, each note searing the evening's quiet with garish distinctness, came a clangour of brassy music.

It was not until they reached the car which Joanna had left in a cul-de-sac nearby, that Toby, looking round for the others, realised that George was missing.

'So he went to have his quiet think after all!' Toby swore hard and viciously. 'I ought to have known he was set on it. Never said where he'd meet me after it either. God knows what trouble he'll get me into. If I take my eye off him for a moment—'

'D'you mean, gone to have a drink?' asked Dan. 'What's the excitement?'

'Drink!' said Toby. 'I'd sooner have him on my hands screwed to the eyeballs than off on his own having one of his quiet thinks.' Muttering to himself, he pulled open the door of the car for Joanna to climb into it.

But Joanna, looking from him to Dan with a face that was suddenly drawn and miserable, said in a low voice: 'I don't really want to go home.'

Dan said: 'But you look tired as hell.'

'I don't want to go home,' she repeated.

A soft stir of air touched their faces. The music of the band grew louder, then faded again.

Toby slid a hand through her arm. 'I don't want to go home either. Let's go and listen to the band.'

Her smile was quick and grateful. They set off down the street towards the sea.

The fine summer evening had brought out of doors all the holiday crowd from the hotels and apartments of Asslington. Along the edge of the promenade coloured globes on strangely wrought pedestals shed gleams of rosy or amber or amethyst light over faces, bright dresses and white flannels. The band worked away industriously in the white-painted bandstand; there was dancing. The pier, spangled with little lights that outlined domes of fun palace and concert hall, floated above a motionless sea. A few people were bathing, the foam from their splashing shining whitely on the surface of the dark water.

Toby, Dan and Joanna, with arms linked so that the crowd should not force them apart, made their way slowly along the thronged promenade, then down some steps on to the shingle. They sat down at the water's edge, where the inch-high wavelets sighed quietly up to their feet. From the concert hall on the pier and from the bandstand behind them the latest dance music and one of Sousa's marches met and mingled in light-hearted discordancy. Some distance out at sea a ship was passing across their view, all lights ablaze.

Dan and Toby started making stones bounce across the water. Joanna lay back on the shingle.

'Of course I know I'll have to go home sometime or other,' she said presently.

'No hurry,' said Toby.

'No – no hurry,' she agreed.

'Just what's the trouble about going home?' asked Dan.

'Oh, nothing reasonable. But it's too quiet out there now. It feels choked to bursting point with – horrible thoughts and things.'

Frowning, Dan said: 'You don't want to give in to that sort of thing.'

'Equally,' said Toby, 'there's no point in trying to put up with more than one can stand. It only assists a crack-up later.'

'I don't know about that,' said Dan. 'I think there's often some point in it. The less you're ready to stand up to, the more helpless you become.'

'And who's going to mind if Miss Prees is a bit helpless?' The stone Toby had just thrown bounced more often and went a good deal farther than the last that Dan had thrown. Toby looked after it with signs of pleasure.

Dan's mouth hardened and he exerted himself for a better throw.

'She's going to mind it,' he said, 'when she realises it.'

'I doubt it,' said Toby. 'Helplessness is a perfectly reasonable condition at certain junctures. When one's mind's a bit numb it's a sensible precaution to rely on the minds and the support of others.'

Dan shook his head. 'She'll feel far better if she doesn't give in to her nerves. Don't you think so yourself, Joanna?'

'Sorry,' she said, 'I wasn't listening. What did you say?'

'Hell!' said Dan. His stone had just fallen *plonk* into the water a few yards from the shore.

There was silence. They sat in a row on the shingle, watching the slow, shining passage of the liner.

It was Dan who, some minutes later, remarked in a stifled voice: 'What a vile hole Asslington is!'

'D'you think so?' said Toby. 'I rather like it.'

'Indeed?' said Dan. 'You like Brighton, too, I expect – and Margate and Southend.'

'They have their points. The human spectacle, even at Margate and Southend, provides a certain amount of entertainment.'

'Can't say I've ever been entertained by it anywhere. Listen to the row of that filthy band – did you ever hear anything more fundamentally obscene? And look at that pier; look at all those bloody silly little lights. Look at that purple-skinned woman there, and that horrible fat man with his belly crammed with ten times too much food and his eyes rolling after every girl who's got a bit of bare arm or leg showing. Your human spectacle doesn't entertain me at all. Makes me feel sick.'

'Say,' said another voice, and George, looking pink and pleased with himself, squatted down on the shingle beside Toby, 'd'you know who you remind me of, talkin' like that? Couple of blokes I was with in Peru. We were—'

'George,' said Toby, rounding on him quickly, 'did you find it?'

'I say, have you been to Peru?' said Dan eagerly at the same moment.

George ignored Toby. He replied to Dan: 'I been everywhere. As I was sayin', we were out there, just the three of us – hadn't seen a soul for three weeks. We were campin', wonderful night, no one within fifty miles of us. These two blokes were doin' some piece of fancy travellin', goin' to write a book about it or somethin', and I'd hooked on because I was out of a job and they wanted somebody handy. Well, I overheard them talkin' to one another. One said: "I like the Arctic a lot better than the Antarctic, don't you?" T'other said: "Yes, you can't walk a mile in the Antarctic without coming across someone's footprints." Now I reckon you're like those two blokes; you're the Arctic type. Tobe here, he's an Antarctic.'

'Shut up,' said Toby. 'Did you find it?'

'Find what, Tobe?'

'The key you went to have a quiet think about. And did anyone spot you getting into the Gardens and poking around? Because the Gardens are closed – did you, by any chance, know that? Closed, not only because it's dark and Asslington doesn't like to take the risk that in the dark its Gardens might be used for immoral purposes, but because the police in their wisdom have closed them to the public, morning, noon and night. Anyone going in there is likely to land in a whole heap of trouble.'

80

'I ain't in any trouble,' said George with a sniff.

'Well, did you find a key under the window of Mr. Prees' room?'

George sighed. 'That's right. I found it.'

'And,' said Toby, thrusting his face towards him, '*did you leave it where you found it?*'

Even in the rosy glow from one of the globes of light at the edge of the promenade, which was casting its light over them all, they could see George's pink face turn noticeably pinker. It looked as if he did not intend to reply. Then he thrust a hand into a pocket, and bringing it out again, extended it to Toby. On the palm lay a small, silver key.

Toby gave a groan. He lay back flat on the shingle.

'Lord,' he said dispiritedly, 'what have I done to be landed with this? Tampering with vital evidence – removing, damn well pinching vital evidence. Just what nice yarn, d'you think, am I going to have to make up for Tingey?'

'But,' said Joanna, leaning forward and looking at the little, slender key that lay on George's palm, 'that isn't the key of the Haybox.'

George gave a chuckle. 'Course it ain't. This is the key of my es-cri-twah, where I keep the pictures of my best girls.' He pocketed it again. He turned on Toby. 'Askin' me if I'd left it where I found it! What d'you take me for – a fool?'

Toby growled angrily that that was a polite way of putting it. 'Anyway, was there a key there?'

'Yes,' said George seriously, 'there was. And that's rum, when you start thinkin' it over. It was in the middle of a patch of plants. And I never so much as picked it up, Tobe. I know a lot more than you do about how to discourage folks from wastin' their valuable time by thinkin' about me.'

Joanna said excitedly: 'But if the key was in the flower-bed, it means that perhaps Dr. Vanedden was right.'

'It means,' said Toby, getting quickly to his feet, 'that we're going along to speak to Inspector Tingey. And just for the minute that's all it means. We've got to learn a lot more about the meaning of Dr. Vanedden himself before we start letting comfortable theories rear themselves on the dubious foundations he supplies so snappily.'

81

Inspector Tingey, after inquiries at the police-station, was discovered having a late supper in the somewhat forbidding basement-kitchen of his home.

Mrs. Tingey, a flat-faced woman with bright, boot-button eyes and a complexion that looked as if it had been starched and ironed, was reluctant to let them come down the stairs to the basement, trying instead to usher them amongst the plush and seashells of the parlour. But Tingey's voice boomed up at them, telling them to come straight down. At a table covered with oilcloth, in the midst of a large tiled floor, they found him eating steak and chips.

He told them that he was heartily glad to see them, he rose and pulled forward chairs, he told Joanna he hoped she was well considering; but he gave her a hard stare as if he found her close-fitting black dress and small black flippancy of a hat a not altogether convincing version of mourning.

As the Inspector returned to his steak and chips Toby began with an abrupt question: 'Inspector, d'you happen to be acquainted with a Dr. Vanedden?'

There was a sudden cessation of the chewing movement of the powerful jaws. Knife and fork hovered above the plate. 'Vanedden, did you say? Yes, I've heard the name. Met him, too, I fancy. Quack doctor.' Tingey went on eating.

'Seems to me I've heard the name too somewhere,' said Toby. 'Perhaps someone I know had an inhibition removed by him, though somehow I don't believe it was in that connection. He lives in Asslington, I believe?'

'Got a week-end place down here. Lives in London. Practises in London. Has plenty of money, nice car, nice lady-friend or two, plays the cello, takes his holidays on the Riviera with one or other of the lady-friends. The doctor in front of his name don't signify a medical doctor at all, but though he don't conceal that fact, he isn't the one to emphasise it either.'

'You know, for someone who just happens to have heard his name, you seem to know quite a lot about him.' Toby kept a fascinated eye on the slow, rolling movement of the Inspector's jaws. 'Any special reason for that?'

'Any special reason for wanting to know?'

'Well, at the moment I do feel,' said Toby, 'that I wouldn't

82

mind knowing most of what there is to know about Dr. Vanedden.'

'Nor would several people. But then, that's the way people are.' More steak went into the Inspector's mouth.

'Dr. Vanedden,' said Toby, 'thinks he can explain the death of Mr. Prees.'

'Lord, the number of people who think they can do that,' said the Inspector.

'You're not interested then, in Dr. Vanedden's explanation?'

'Did I say I wasn't? I certainly *am* interested in what could have made a bright young fellow like you consult him on the matter.'

'I haven't done so up to the present,' said Toby. 'But Dr. Vanedden has appeared extraordinarily anxious to consult Miss Prees – or to get her to consult him – anyway to get her accept a certain view of things.'

Tingey turned to Joanna with a questioning look.

She said: 'Yes, he believes my father committed suicide.'

Tingey turned back to Toby. 'All right, M'Clusky, fire away.' Steak and chips continued to meet their destiny.

When Toby came to an end of the story which Joanna had told him in the restaurant, the Inspector, pushing aside his well-scraped plate and reaching for a pipe from the mantelpiece, said thoughtfully: 'So that's his idea – suicide with malice aforethought. Well, I dare say such things have been known to happen. But I wonder why Vanedden should take all this trouble, because even if the key does turn out to be somewhere that Mr. Prees himself could have hidden it, there are always the fingerprints on the revolver.'

'He thought,' said Joanna, 'that the police might be able to explain those.'

'Well, this policeman can't, Miss Prees. Your father couldn't have faked the fingerprints after he was dead, and if he'd faked them before he was dead, and if he'd faked them before he was dead and then let the thing off by some mechanism, he couldn't have removed the mechanism. So the idea won't hold water.'

'All the same,' said Toby, 'it might be worth looking for the key, mightn't it? Even if it weren't in any sense a proof of Vanedden's theory, it'd be rather interesting if you did find it, say, outside the window, as Vanedden suggested.'

83

'Maybe.'

'Come, come, Inspector, it'd be extraordinarily interesting. It'd make one wonder a lot of things.'

'I'm so used to wondering things,' sighed Tingey. 'For instance, why Mr. Dyke, whose acumen we all know such a lot about, thinks the key might be there.' Tingey's glance was singularly acute.

But Toby's face was bland and innocent, almost as bland and innocent as George's.

'Why,' continued Tingey, 'doesn't he take it as the gassing of a crackbrained busybody?'

'Simply,' said Toby gravely, 'that according to Miss Prees, Vanedden himself laid such singular emphasis on the probable presence of the key in the flower-bed outside the window – isn't that so, Miss Prees?'

Joanna caught the prompting in his look, and nodded.

'Hm,' said Inspector Tingey.

'I think,' said Toby, 'it might at least be worth your while to look into the matter.'

'Of course I'm going to look into the matter. I always look into everything. That's why I look as old as I do.' Tingey rose to his feet. 'Fact, I'll see to it right away.'

The others rose too.

'There's just one thing,' said Tingey.

They waited, while Tingey's benevolent gaze came round once more to Joanna.

'Miss Prees,' he said, 'do you happen to know the exact position with regard to your father's financial affairs?'

'I'm afraid not.' Then she asked: 'Why?'

'You wouldn't want me to go into that with so many people present, would you?'

'That doesn't matter. Please tell me why you asked.'

'Hm – and you're sure you don't know all about it?'

'Well, I know that he had his salary and a good deal of money invested.'

'That's just it,' said Tingey, stroking his moustache and keeping his gaze fixed upon her with its usual mild curiosity, 'he hadn't.'

'Hadn't?'

'Oh, dear, no.'

Her tired face reflected little but irritation at this new bewilderment.

Tingey said: 'He hadn't any investments, Miss Prees.'

'But he had.' Her voice jerked on to a note of nervous protest. 'His salary was seven hundred a year and I know we used to spend much more than that. D'you mean he was borrowing? Is that what the trouble was? Had he been getting deeper and deeper into debt? Was that it? Was that why he wanted to throw himself over the cliffs last night?'

'I don't know,' said Tingey, 'I'm sure I don't know.' His hand, still stroking his moustache, covered his mouth while he spoke; it partly muffled his words, giving his voice an odd quality. 'He certainly had other money besides his salary. He kept depositing large sums in his bank in notes – always in notes. That's odd, you know, about its always being in notes. Very few people do that, except people with little businesses, and even then there's usually a good few cheques amongst them. And he always seems to have used up the money as he went along, so that I'm afraid all that'll come to you under his will, Miss Prees, is his life-insurance money. Seems he didn't like investments – some people are like that. It's odd though – I mean that there's no sign at all of where all that money came from.'

Joanna did not look as if she had fully taken in what he had said. She suddenly wrenched off her little black hat, as if it were constricting her forehead, and pushed a hand through her thick, blonde hair.

Tingey went on: 'Er, how well would you say your father knew this Dr. Vanedden, Miss Prees?'

'I don't know, I don't know. I never even knew he did know him till yesterday evening.'

'Kept it quiet, did he?'

'Tingey,' said Toby sharply, 'what have you got on your mind about Vanedden?'

Tingey looked at him. 'What have I got on my mind?'

'Yes.'

The Inspector considered. 'Did you say, what have I got on my mind?'

'That's what I said. Who's Vanedden, or what's Vanedden?

The moment I mentioned him this evening you went glassy-eyed.'

'Did I now? Well, that reminds me. . . .' Tingey started rummaging in his pockets.

'Don't know why it reminds me. Mind makes funny jumps sometimes. Mine's always making funny jumps. Now where did I put it? . . . Ah, here we are. Never shown you this, have I, Mr. Dyke?' He held out to Toby a small photograph. 'That's a picture of my granddaughter, Mr. Dyke. Her name's Irene Dawn.' He beamed into Toby's face. 'Lovely little girl, isn't she?'

Toby took one glance at the grim-faced child in the photograph, then he handed it back. 'Come along, Miss Prees – come along, Moon. The Inspector doesn't feel like answering questions. Good night, Tingey, I'll be seeing you to-morrow, I expect.'

A very faint grin twitched at the lips under the Inspector's heavy moustache.

Toby, shepherding his party up the basement stairs, added over his shoulder: 'Child's a credit to you, Tingey – make a fine police-woman when she grows up.'

As the grin vanished and outraged scarlet spread over the Inspector's face, Toby and his companions emerged from the house on to the pavement.

It was on that same pavement, a short way down the street, that they came across Barnes, the caretaker.

He was standing on the curb, swaying a little dizzily, outside the lighted doorway of The Cap and Bells.

He saw them.

He said: 'Good evening. Good evening all.'

A wavering hand went up with a flourish to remove a hat that was not there.

'Shorry, Miss Preesh, can't take hat off. No hat. Like the letter. No letter. Letter definitely mishing. Told you about that this morning, didn't I? Told you about the letter being mishing. Hat mishing too. Shorry. Good evening all.' He raised his hand in a flourish again and started to cross the street.

But Joanna grabbed him by the arm.

'What letter, Barnes? What are you talking about?'

'Letter I told you 'bout. Mishing letter. Told you something was wrong, didn't I? Well, that's what was wrong. Letter gone.'

'But when? *When?*'

'When I come back from 'phoning the police. No letter on the desk, and Mr. Hyland and Mr. Weedon both standing there. Slipped me memory at first – couldn't think what was different. But that was what it was – hat mishing. No hat. Fancy no hat to take off in presence of dead. Good night. Good night all.'

5

A bright moon shone in a clear, night sky.

The headlights of the car, as it took Joanna back to her home along the road at the edge of the cliffs, merely yellowed the light that lay over heath and sea; there was no darkness for the beams from the lamps to penetrate.

The moonlight was so bright that here and there, adding an unfamiliar touch to the night's pattern of black and silver, the red of a roof was still to be seen.

George was driving the car. Joanna sat at the back beside Toby.

She had protested that she was not too tired to drive, but her gratitude had been clear when, without arguing, George had taken the driver's seat. She had not put much force into her question: 'But how are you going to get back to your hotel?' When Toby had replied: 'Grand night for walking,' she had let it go at that.

Dan had hesitated as if he too were considering the attractions of a drive and a five mile walk home through the moonlight, but suddenly he had said good night and had wheeled away from them down the pavement.

George seemed inclined to short bursts of rather sentimental song, but apart from that they covered most of the distance in silence.

At least four of the five miles of empty road, visible far ahead of them as a streak drawn like a chalkmark over a dim blackboard, were behind them before Toby remarked: 'An enigmatic nature, Tingey's.'

Joanna gave a start and said: 'I'm sorry – what did you say?' Her eyes, wide open, had been fixed on the margin of sea that showed above the cliff's curving edge.

'I said Tingey's a queer cuss. You don't know where you are with him.'

'No,' she said and sighed. 'You don't.'

'He knows something about Vanedden,' said Toby. 'It was there on his face the moment he heard the name. It surprised him too; it gave him something quite new to think about.'

She did not reply for a moment, then all she said was: 'What an unbelievably beautiful night.'

He studied her profile thoughtfully. Presently he asked her: 'Joanna, was that a shock he gave you about the money?'

'I don't know,' she said. 'I just don't understand it.'

'Perhaps it means you won't be as rich as you thought.' At her listless gesture he added: 'That thought doesn't worry you particularly?'

'I'd have tried to find a job of some sort anyhow,' she answered. 'I must have something to do.'

'What can you do?'

'Nothing very much. I can talk a few languages. I can type with one finger. I can wear clothes when I try. And I'm surprisingly good at getting engaged – to the wrong person.'

'Hm. Well, let's hope the life-insurance isn't one of those that are just meant to cover the cost of the funeral and to supply one or two mourners with respectable weeds. But in quiet and sober honesty – you aren't very much of a mourner, are you, Joanna?'

'I don't know yet.'

After another minute or two he started again: 'You really thought your father had considerable investments?'

'Oh,' she said restlessly, 'I don't know. I hadn't thought about it. I suppose so. I mean, it had never occurred to me he might have been getting all the money we spent in any other way. Where d'you think it can have come from? D'you think he was borrowing?'

'How should I know?'

She turned her head against the car's upholstery. Her eyes explored his face.

'All the same, you've got ideas about something, haven't you?'

'I know Tingey's got ideas about something,' he said. 'I shouldn't even be surprised if I know what the ideas are about.'

'What are they about?'

He gave a shake of his head. 'The thought isn't a pretty one – and quite vague. I think I'll keep it to myself for the moment.'

'Please tell me.'

Toby again shook his head. He was feeling for some cigarettes in his pocket when Joanna's hand took hold of his wrist.

'I want to know what those ideas are.'

'But listen—'

'It's all right, I can do a certain amount of thinking myself. I know a man doesn't get murdered unless he has an enemy. And one doesn't make enemies unless somehow or other one exerts power over somebody. And that – well, it's seldom a pretty thing to do. I tell you, most of the ideas I've had in my head to-day haven't been pretty ones; I can easily stand another.'

He said: 'Very well.' But he said it reluctantly, and was slow to continue. 'It's Tingey's idea, remember, not mine – that's to say, it's my idea of what Tingey's idea is. I think – but it's only something about his tone of voice and the look in his eye that made me jump to this conclusion – I think Tingey suspects that those large sums of money, all in notes, that your father deposited in his bank from time to time, were blackmail.'

The car swung to the right; it left the main road and proceeded more slowly over the rutted surface of the track that wound between the bungalows of the building-estate. George added one of his little bursts of song to the conversation.

'You know,' said Joanna in a quiet, unemotional voice, 'that's what I thought you were going to say.'

'But you don't mean you think—'

'– it's possible? After to-day how do I know what's possible and what isn't?'

'I shouldn't take it for granted, anyhow. There are other explanations.'

'Are they any more comforting?'

At that moment the car stopped. They had reached the gate of the bungalow.

'Were you very fond of your father, Joanna?' asked Toby.

'I'm afraid I haven't really been fond of him for a long time,' she replied. 'It's a relationship that in some ways goes very deep, and there's loyalty besides habit in it. But actually I distrusted

90

him – perhaps I almost feared him. And for some reason, recently, I've felt very sorry for him.'

'Say, Miss Prees' – George had turned in his seat and was looking round at them – 'would you mind tellin' me somethin'? Was your father ever in Egypt?'

It was so unexpected, her eyebrows made marks of interrogation over her eyes. 'Good heavens, why?'

'Was he ever?'

'No, he hardly ever went anywhere.'

'Oh well, never mind. I been kind of thinkin' about Egypt all the way out here – reckon it was the moonlight remindin' me of moonlight on the pyramids. There's nothin' like moonlight on the pyramids, you know, and the sand – sheikhs and all that – spices and vices. . . .' He turned away, muttering.

Toby and Joanna climbed out of the car.

They were standing in the road when a square of yellow light shone out at them suddenly from the bungalow. Someone had just switched on the light in the sitting-room. Its curtains had not been drawn; from where they stood they could see that Peggie and Gordon had just entered the room.

They saw Gordon drop into a chair. They saw Peggie cross to the window and reach for the cord at the side that drew the curtains together.

As the curtains shut out the view of the room Toby said: 'That young man was in the building, wasn't he, when the police arrived?'

'Yes,' said Joanna, 'he and Gerald.'

'I was just thinking of that key in the flower-bed. Suppose someone had taken that key from your father after he was dead, and then suppose someone suddenly had the panicky idea that the police might search him. Mightn't that be a reason for throwing the key out of the window?'

'You think it may have been Gordon who did that?'

'It may have been – though I don't know why he should take a key when he already had one.'

'Oh,' she exclaimed with a quick flare of anger, 'you keep coming back to Gerald! I tell you, that's absurd. If there's anyone on earth I'd trust —' But she checked herself. She turned to George and said ironically: 'If it interests you, Gerald Hyland was once in Egypt.'

'Was he now?' said George.

'Yes, in Cairo, for a whole fortnight. That's why he's written about sheikhs and pyramids ever since.' She laid a hand on the gate. 'Thank you very much for driving me home. I'll see to putting the car away. Good night.'

'Just a moment,' said Toby. 'You've told me a certain amount about the relationship between those two in there. Also you've told me a certain amount about the relationship between your father and Hyland, between yourself and Hyland, between your father and Miss Winnpole, between your father and Weedon. But I don't believe I've asked you yet about the relationship between yourself and Dan Moon.'

'Thank you for not asking.' She smiled at him. Then she turned, went through the gate and up the path.

Toby and George started on their walk back to Asslington.

It was before they were out of earshot that Toby said to George: 'Speaking of geography, George, whatever made you bring in Egypt? What does Egypt happen to mean to you?'

'Mice,' said George promptly.

'Mice?' A contemptuous comment followed it: 'Rats!'

Their voices faded as they disappeared down the road.

Too tired to bother about the car, Joanna left it in the road all night. She went straight to her room, undressed, and in her pyjamas and blue silk wrapper, settled down in front of the mirror to remove her make-up and to brush her hair.

She sat there face to face with herself for some time. Yet face-cream and hair-brush were used absent-mindedly and careless-ly. Her hands kept dropping into her lap and lying there listlessly while her gaze drove right through the white, express-ionless mask that hung in the glass before her to something far beyond it.

At length she lay down. But her tiredness was of the kind that brings no sleep along with it. Sleep was a long way off. There was a pricking sensation in her eyes and in her body a torpor that weighted her limbs with a dull, bruised feeling. But there was an over-sharpness and over-brightness in every image that passed through her mind.

It was about two in the morning when she rose, switched on the light and started to look for the box of sleeping-tablets.

Though her brain, in its exhausted wakefulness, had seemed to be functioning with unbearable clarity, as soon as she attempted to direct it to a particular object, every thought in it dissolved. Wandering round the room, she looked straight at the box of tablets several times before she realised that it was still where she had left it on the mantel-piece when she had taken it out of the pocket of her slacks the evening before.

She opened the box, took out two tablets and swallowed them, then lay down in bed again and put out the light.

She had been lying there for only a few minutes when she once more pressed the light-switch and got up hurriedly. She opened the box of tablets and stared at its contents with a muddled but deepening frown.

There were five tablets left in the box.

But yesterday, when she had given two to her father, the box had been practically full; it must have contained thirty or forty tablets.

Aloud she counted the five tablets. But thirty minus the two she had taken herself could not be made to equal five.

She shook her head, put down the box of tablets and went back to bed.

Shortly after that a cloud of sleep, heavy and soft, sank into her brain, seeping, as thick, yellow fog seeps in at the cracks of windows and doors, through her tired body.

Her drugged sleep was deep and dreamless.

It was past ten o'clock when Joanna woke, to find the morning misty as it had been the day before, with the same shimmer of blue penetrating the low-lying mist.

She had a bath and dressed and went to the dining-room. Coffee was waiting for her on a hotplate, and her usual grape-fruit and toast were on the table. Peggie Winnpole had had her breakfast already; Mrs. Searle came in to clear away her used cup and plate as Joanna went to her place.

Peggie herself came in before Joanna had finished.

She seemed to have no reason for coming, nor anything to say, but she lingered in the room, moving about, slightly altering the positions of ornaments, fidgeting with but not sitting down to read the newspaper.

When Joanna abruptly addressed her, she started away as if the sudden, sharp enunciation of her name had been a blow.

'Peggie,' said Joanna, 'you remember what I asked you yesterday evening?'

With clumsy fingers Peggie became very busy with rearranging the tangled sheets of newspaper. 'Yesterday evening? You asked me something?'

'Of course I asked you something, and you remember what it was. I asked you what reason my father had given for sacking you.'

'Did you? That explains it perhaps. I wouldn't *want* to remember anything connected with that. Forgetfulness is nothing but a desire to exclude from the mind some unpleasant experience. I've proved that again and again. Only yesterday—'

'Peggie, why did he give you the sack?'

'Oh —' Peggie let the newspaper fall to the floor. Her voice took its shriller note. 'You needn't worry, I'm going! I shan't stay a day longer than I need. I don't want to stay here, I want to get away. Even if I could get that notice cancelled, now he's dead, I shouldn't stay here. To-morrow, as soon as the inquest's over—'

'Don't be a fool,' said Joanna. 'I don't want you to go. But I do want to know what reason my father gave for sacking you. You needn't be afraid of telling me; I know it won't have been anything to your discredit. Whatever it was, I'm certain it was my father's fault that it happened; that's to say, I think he probably blew up about something you'd done, something perfectly normal and reasonable. In some of those moods he had recently he might have sacked you for sneezing.'

Peggie said in a low voice: 'You speak about him so coldly.' She added: 'I was very fond of your father, Joanna.'

'I know.'

'He was kind to me. There haven't been very many kind people in my life. But your father was always thoughtful and considerate. He was more than that. I never knew my own father, you know, and I've only very faint recollections of my mother. I was brought up by aunts and uncles. They were pious and narrow-minded; they used to take me to prayer-meetings and make me

94

testify. I suffered through it terribly, but of course repressed my knowledge that I did. I repressed all my feelings, I accepted everything I was taught, trying to find some way of expressing my nature through work – never anything but work. Of course I developed all sorts of inhibitions and a dreadful disharmony with my environment.' She was looking down, indeed her eyes were almost closed. Her voice had dropped to a monotone. Something in the way she spoke made it sound as if precisely those sentences had been said over and over many times already. Perhaps it was to herself she had said them, or it might have been that she was simply reproducing the self-exposures practised in the psychiatrist's consulting-room.

'Your father,' she went on, softly intoning the words, 'filled a great gap in my experience. At first I just assumed it was his kindness that made my whole life seem different. But then Dr. Vanedden explained to me that what had actually happened was that I had put him in the place of my father and for the first time was having an outlet for emotions I had never recognised.'

'You needed a doctor to tell you that?'

Peggie frowned quickly.

'Why do you always have to say things like that?'

Joanna drank some coffee.

'Anyway' – she put down her cup again – 'why are you going over all this? I know you were fond of my father. It isn't one of the things I have to have explained to me.'

'But it seems,' cried Peggie in a shrill voice that sounded as if it might crack into sobs, 'that I *have* got to explain – that's what I was coming to – that there are things I know about your father I'd tell to scarcely anybody. Certainly I wouldn't have told them to you; you'd never have understood. Whatever it was though, I'd have understood, I'd have been loyal, I'd never have betrayed him. Not so long as he was alive. Why, oh why, didn't he realise that? Even now it'd all be safe with me except that—' She gave a noisy swallow and pressed a hand to her chest.

Joanna waited.

After drawing one or two deep breaths Peggie added a few muffled words to her unfinished sentence: ' – except that now, for the sake of other people, I've got to tell the police.' She threw back her head. 'But I'll never tell you!'

Joanna said quietly: 'The police are the practical people to tell.'

'Oh, I don't want to do it,' said Peggie defensively. 'God knows I don't want to say anything to anyone. If only it could go into his grave with him . . . I thought perhaps it could, I thought at first I could sit back and say nothing. Oh, God, Joanna, it's a terrible problem I've had on my mind. For him, for you, for everyone, I've wanted to say nothing. Why should people have to know why he killed himself? Isn't it one of the really secret things in a person's soul why they go on living or why they don't?'

'But he didn't kill himself!'

'He did,' said Peggie. 'Didn't Dr. Vanedden explain—?'

'Oh, damn your Dr. Vanedden! You know my father was murdered. The fingerprints on the revolver—'

'You'll see, they'll be explained.'

Joanna sank back in her chair. She muttered: 'Well, I just don't understand it.' She seemed to sink into her own thoughts, losing herself in a bitter, bewildered dream.

Peggie stooped and picked up the newspaper from the floor. She put it tidily on the sideboard; she slightly altered the positions of some big white daisies in a jar; she fidgeted here and there as if she could not bring herself to leave the room. But at last she put her hand out to open the door.

That gesture caught Joanna's eye.

'Why, Peggie, your ring,' she said, 'it's missing.'

Peggie's left hand dropped to her side. 'Er – er, yes, I—' Patches of nervous red appeared on her throat and cheeks. 'I gave it back to Gordon. I just told him that at the moment I couldn't think about anyone but your father. He understood. Possibly we'll talk it over again later.'

Joanna nodded absently. 'Oh, by the way, there was something else I was going to say, Peggie. Was it you who removed a whole lot of sleeping-tablets from the box in my room sometime yesterday?'

'Well, I did take a couple. I saw them there and I've had so little sleep lately. I knew you wouldn't mind.'

'No, I don't mind. But you took rather more than two, didn't you?'

Peggie repeated: 'I took two!'

'You mustn't take more than two, you know,' said Joanna.

'They're pretty strong. They've got something to do with barbitone. I know, because I was there when Dr. Jones prescribed them for father. He said he mustn't take more than two, or three at the very outside.'

'I took two.' It was said with an unconvincing overemphasis. 'Anyway, they taste pretty horrible, so I wouldn't take more than I had to. I never can swallow things, you know, I always break them up in water. And besides—'

But just then the door-handle, on which Peggie's hand had been resting, turned in her grasp, the door opened, and Gordon Weedon looked in.

He saw Joanna, and said: 'Good morning.'

He and Peggie looked at one another, then Peggie slipped past him and went to her room.

The rather egg-shaped top of Gordon's head, covered with neat ridges of hair, gave a twitch.

He said with a diffident smile to Joanna: 'Poor Peg, she's taken it awfully hard, hasn't she? I think your way of taking it is simply wonderful. Of course Peg's a rather unbalanced, emotional type, isn't she? And she was frightfully fond of the old man. If it comes to that, we all were. Grand old boy – grand. Can't imagine what the place'll be like without him. Never seem the same again, I'm afraid. I mean, he'd got such a striking personality, and his knowledge – well, sometimes I used to feel that if only I knew as much as he did there'd really be nothing left for me to want. Appalling tragedy. The more one thinks about it the more one realises how appalling it is. Doesn't one?' His worried eyes, that seldom seemed to look at anything directly, snatched a glance at her face as if to see how she was responding.

She was not looking as if his words had moved her.

He coughed, and said: 'By the way, I slept in the sitting-room last night. It was so late and I thought Peg seemed nervous. Well, I'll be getting along now into town. Anything I can do for you there – I mean, any messages or shopping or anything? Count on me, won't you? I'd always do anything to help – glad to.'

He waited, but she did not reply.

Repeating: 'Well, count on me,' he wandered out.

Joanna remained sitting where she was for a few minutes, then she too left the room.

She left the bungalow. She walked down the road. She walked fast, doing her best to avoid the ruts which the sun by now had baked hard into ridges treacherous to the incautious ankle.

At a corner where a lane branched off from the road she passed a man who was lounging on the grass, smoking a pipe and reading a newspaper. He lowered the paper and stared at her steadily as she passed.

She walked still faster after she had passed him, and once glanced back over her shoulder.

He had risen and was strolling in the same direction as herself.

It was a hundred yards or so down the lane that Gerald Hyland's cottage stood. It had stood there for sixty or seventy years, a grey box of a dwelling, solid and unassuming, with slate roof and sash windows, a frowning stone porch and outdoor sanitation. Amongst the bungalows with their Tudor beams and gaudily coloured tiles, it looked like a dour old peasant woman who has somehow strayed into the company of tarts.

To-day a large black Cadillac stood at the gate.

Joanna did not bother to go in at the gate; she stepped over the broken-down wire fence that surrounded a patch of grass no different from the rough turf that covered the rest of the cliff top.

From an open window a peal of exuberant music reached her. Gerald Hyland's gramophone was pouring into the summer morning Purcell's Trumpet Voluntary. When, without knocking, she opened the door of the cottage and stepped into the low-ceilinged sitting-room, the little room seemed completely filled by Hyland's long legs and arms, which looked even longer, even more spidery than usual in the unfamiliar dark suit, and the gramophone's enormous horn. There was only just room in a corner for Dr. Vanedden.

Hyland did not switch off the record, he simply shouted at her above the music: 'Glad to see you, my dear. I was coming over myself later in the morning. You know Dr. Vanedden, don't you? He's a musician, he plays the cello.' He turned and beamed benignly at the little man with the high crest of silver hair, the chiselled features and the small, grubby hands. 'My God, how I envy him, actually being able to play an instrument.'

'Only in a quite amateur way, I assure you, Miss Prees.' The light, clear voice of Dr. Vanedden reached her easily above the jubilant sounds blaring out of the great horn. 'Only for my own pleasure. And as I play only in my own home, and as I live alone, it can safely be said, I think, that my pleasure is no one else's penance.'

'Ha, ha, that's good,' bawled Hyland. 'But remember you're going to play for me, Dr. Vanedden, I'm not going to let you forget that promise. And you won't forget about those books you're going to lend me, will you? Joanna, Dr. Vanedden's been telling me about his work. Marvellously interesting – and important, of course, desperately important in our present state of society. Never realised it before, never really given a thought to it. But Dr. Vanedden's enlightened me. I'm going to go into it thoroughly now. He's going to lend me some books. Perhaps I'll even be analysed myself.'

Dr. Vanedden's smile was deprecating. His reply was again addressed to Joanna: 'Mr. Hyland has an uncommon capacity for enthusiasm. In this rather cold world it has a very warming and encouraging effect.'

'It looks,' said Joanna dryly, 'like a remarkable case of what I believe is called transference.'

Dr. Vanedden laughed. There was roughness in the sound, disguised as joviality. He turned away and began looking through a pile of records.

Joanna said: 'There's a policeman or a detective or something out there. He followed me.'

Hyland started to say something, but as the Trumpet Voluntary came to an end just then, he leapt to the gramophone, asking: 'What shall we have next?'

Dr. Vanedden handed him a record. The next moment it was above the strains of *L'après-midi d'un Faune* that they had to do their talking.

Joanna went straight to the reason of her visit.

'Gerald, when you found my father yesterday, can you remember whether or not there was a letter on his desk?'

Hyland considered. 'I don't think so. Why?'

'Only that Barnes says there was.'

'Ah,' said Vanedden, leaning forward, 'a letter. I see what's in your mind. The letter that suicides leave behind them. So you *are* coming round to my view of the case, Miss Prees?'

99

'Not necessarily,' she replied. 'But Barnes the caretaker says there was a letter on the desk the first time he went in, and that it wasn't there later.'

'There wasn't any letter.' Hyland was definite this time.

'Are you sure?' said Vanedden. 'Because there should have been, there should have been. The confession, the self-justification, the apology . . .'

'There wasn't any letter,' said Hyland.

'I think there *must* have been,' said Vanedden.

Hyland sounded annoyed. 'There wasn't. It's Barnes' imagination. Why didn't he say something about it sooner if there was anything in it?'

'Because until a good many pints of beer had loosened his memory,' said Joanna, 'he only remembered that something was wrong, he couldn't remember just what.'

'Oh, that explains it then,' said Hyland breezily. 'Drunk. Frightful drinker, Barnes, same as the rest of his family. One of his brothers died of pneumonia contracted while he was sleeping it off in a ditch. I remember when they picked him out he was singing: "Wash me in the blood of the Lamb." Poor fellow!'

'There's a certain rather well-known proverb, isn't there, about wine and truth?' said Dr. Vanedden.

'Nothing in it,' said Hyland. 'I make up all my best stories when I'm a little over the edge.'

'Miss Prees,' said Dr. Vanedden, 'there must have been a letter. It's a psychological certainty. And what I should like to know is—' He picked another record off the pile and scanned its title. 'What I should like to know is, where's it got to?'

'Drunken maunderings . . . nothing in it at all,' rumbled Hyland angrily.

Dr. Vanedden regarded him in a slightly puzzled fashion. 'You seem, if I may say so, to have a great preference for the idea of murder as compared with that of suicide, Mr. Hyland. I find that interesting. Is it just the drama of it, the excitement, the sense of conflict? Perhaps. At all events, it's interesting. However . . .' He rose to his feet. 'It's my belief there are things Miss Prees would like to discuss with you if I weren't here, so—' He held out a hand to Joanna.

As soon as he had gone Joanna, switching off the gramophone without asking permission, inquired: 'What did he come for?'

'Come to think of it,' said Hyland, 'I haven't the least idea.'

'Didn't he ask you any questions?'

'Did he?' Hyland wrinkled his forehead. 'He saw the gramophone, you see, the moment he got here, and we started talking music. Then he started telling me about his work, and I got interested. Of course he's unorthodox; he's got quite his own approach to the subject and his own methods; he says the psycho-analysts are as down on him as the more old-fashioned sort of looney-doctor, or nerve specialist, or whatever they call themselves. But he wasn't at all bitter about it, in fact I thought he took a very commendably dispassionate view of the whole matter. I'm afraid I misjudged him yesterday – I'm sorry. Still, I really don't know what brought him. Perhaps he just felt that as friends of Edgar's we ought to know each other better. Seems that he knew Edgar more intimately than we realised. We discussed Edgar a bit—'

'You mean,' said Joanna, 'he asked you a whole lot of questions about him and you answered.'

'Well, he did ask me what ideas I had about his death, and so on, but really he talked a lot more about Edgar's attempt at going over the cliff than about his actual death. He wanted to know if I'd been expecting it, and what ideas I'd got on why it happened. Said it was interesting to him psychologically. I don't think any of his questions were merely inquisitive ones, or what you'd call in bad taste; he didn't want to know about Edgar's affairs – money matters, you know – or anything like that.'

'I see.' She looked down. Then her head came up and she looked straight at Hyland. 'But could you have told him anything about father's affairs?'

'What d'you mean?'

'Could you have told him anything about father's affairs, Gerald? Do you know anything about them?'

'Well, a certain amount, I suppose. Edgar consulted me once or twice. But why?' He sounded anxious. 'Has anything happened, Joanna? Is anything wrong?'

'Didn't you believe,' said Joanna, 'that father had a good deal of money invested?'

He looked as if he suddenly understood where her questions were tending.

'No – as a matter of fact, I didn't.'

'But then . . .'

'No,' he repeated, 'I knew he hadn't. But there's no need for you to worry, Joanna, he provided for you. I don't know what you expected – perhaps far more than there is. But myself, I don't think he did so badly for you. He insured his life for ten thousand pounds. The interest on that isn't a princely income, but you'll find it enough to give you a very agreeable sense of security in this uncomfortable world. Incidentally, it was on my advice that he did that. It was about two years ago; he told me one day that he was worried because he was afraid the genteel kind of education he'd given you hadn't really fitted you to make much of a success of earning your living, and he hadn't anything put by for you. So I suggested life-insurance. Some time later he told me that he'd acted on my advice, and that the sum you'd get when he died was ten thousand pounds. Can't think how he managed to rake up the premiums for that; beginning at his time of life he must have been paying out several hundred a year. Damn generous, I thought it. You know, Joanna, old Edgar had his faults, lots of them, but where you were concerned—'

'Gerald!'

The passion in her voice stopped him.

'Gerald, don't you know *anything* about money? Don't you know anything at all about how far it goes? I believe honestly you don't. I believe you could go into a shop and order a pile of records like that and not have the faintest idea that they'd cost you ten pounds – and I believe you could feed yourself on bacon and beans for a week and not know that your keep was less than ten shillings. Oh, heavens, Gerald – you knew that father's salary was seven hundred a year, didn't you? But you must have been able to see, from the way we were living, that we were spending two thousand or more. If you knew that he hadn't any money invested, what did you make of it? Where did you think it all came from? Or' – and she took a swift step nearer him – '*do* you know?'

'Goodness me,' said Hyland, his blue eyes staring with

astonishment, 'now that you put it like that, I see I never used my intelligence on the situation. No, Joanna, I haven't the least idea where it all came from. Matter of fact, I did think in a vague sort of way that he must be making a bit writing stuff for scientific papers. He once told me he did that. In fact, seeing how well he seemed to be doing out of it, I even thought I might try my hand at it myself – you know, you get an encyclopædia and copy stuff out of it in a nice, readable way, and then you give some obliging scientist a drink and get him to correct the worst howlers you've made – though I believe a good many scientific journalists don't think that last part of the operation's necessary, and still get away with it.'

'The sort of journals that printed father's stuff never pay anything at all,' she told him. 'All you get is the honour and glory of appearing in them.'

Hyland was going on: 'Certainly it's odd. It's damned odd. Why the devil did I never think . . . ? But I don't expect it's anything important. An examination of his bank book will tell you all you want to know about it.'

'An examination of his bank book, or it may have been an interrogation of the bank manager, told the police that father's been paying in large sums of money at intervals, all in notes, without a sign anywhere of where they come from. And what d'you think the police make of that? They think that someone may have been paying him blackmail.'

'Blackmail! *Blackmail?*'

She nodded.

In his bewilderment he turned to the gramophone and with fumbling hands set a new record going. But only a few bars to the Overture to *Figaro* had sounded in the room when Joanna switched it off again.

'Blackmail, did you say?' said Hyland. 'You know, that's really a remarkable thing. Because if you'd asked me I'd have told you ages ago that Edgar struck me as acting just as if he had something pretty grim on his conscience. Only I'd never have thought such a thing possible. . . .'

She leant her head on her hands.

After a moment Hyland stooped to look into her face.

'You aren't crying, are you, Joanna? You know' – he patted her shoulder – 'you mustn't let all this get you too badly. It – perhaps it isn't really as bad as it seems. I mean – you know, Joanna, I'd do anything for you. I mean that literally. Anything. I suppose I've lived very egotistically, generally speaking, just for myself and my own interests, and not cared for many people or gone out of my way to make them care for me. I was quite attached to Edgar, but I dare say that wasn't much more than habit; probably it just came from having known him most of my life. But I'm very fond of you, Joanna – no one's ever meant quite as much to me as you do. I – I mean it literally. Literally.'

She looked up at him and smiled.

'Yes,' he went on hastily, 'I'd really do anything on earth for you. Might make mistakes, of course; one can't always tell, can one, when one's simply making a damn foolish mistake. But always remember – always remember – that whatever I did I'd mean it for the best. However . . .' He cleared his throat. 'You know, you mustn't let this money business, whatever's at the back of it, upset you too much. If it turns out that Edgar was playing some queer game, well, you weren't involved in it. He's left you provided for. You've nothing to worry about.'

'Gerald, can I refuse to take that money?'

He gaped at her.

She repeated it.

'Eh? Not take it? Goodness me,' cried Hyland, 'not take ten thousand pounds when you haven't a bean! Don't be ridiculous. Where that money came from had nothing to do with you; Edgar kept you completely out of it all.'

'He didn't keep Peggie Winnpole out of it.'

He said quickly, 'What's that?'

'Peggie knows something. I'm not sure she doesn't know everything. She's going to tell the police. She won't tell me anything, because she seems to think that that's a way of getting at me. But at breakfast this morning she told me that she was going to tell something or other to the police because if she didn't people would be hurt by it. I think she—'

'Sh!' said Hyland sharply.

'But I think—'

'Sh!' He raised a warning finger. He was listening. Then he took a long stride to the window.

Joanna sprang to his side.

A few yards away from the window, stooping to pluck a harebell in the grass, was Dr. Vanedden.

He straightened, the flower held delicately between finger and thumb.

'Forgive me,' he said, 'for returning. I recollected, just after I'd started on my way, that there was something I wanted to ask you. I got so engrossed in our talk this morning that I quite forgot about it.'

He smiled at them. Something, it might have been irony, lurked in the smile.

'Well?' said Hyland.

'Can you tell me the address of Mr. Moon?'

With a slight hesitation, Joanna replied: 'Number five, Spencer Street.'

'Thank you.'

As he walked away, Joanna gave an uneasy wriggle of her shoulders.

'He couldn't have heard what we were saying from where he was, could he?' she asked.

'I don't think so. The only thing is...' Frowning, Hyland slammed the window shut. 'I could have sworn,' he said, 'that when I first looked out and he hadn't quite started stooping over that flower, he was walking *away* from the window, not towards it.'

6

During Joanna's absence Dan Moon had arrived at the bungalow.

He was in the sitting-room, standing looking at a book he had
taken from the shelves. From the vengeful dislike on his face it
might have been supposed that the book had been guilty of some
offence against him. But as, with a mutter of disgust, he thrust it
back on its shelf and looked round as Joanna came into the room,
the cloud of depression was still in his eyes and bad temper still
dragged at his mouth.

To his grim-sounding, 'Hullo,' she answered unenthusiasti-
cally, 'Hullo, Dan.'

'Those damn policemen won't let me into my lab. I've got
nothing to do.'

'Bad luck,' said Joanna.

'Why can't they let me in?' he demanded. 'What good's it
going to do them, keeping me out?'

She shrugged. 'Have a drink?'

'But look here, Joanna, why can't they let me in and get on with
some work?'

'I really don't know, Dan. They haven't told me.'

'Well, they did tell me, one of 'em did, a mean-faced chap in a
bowler-hat.'

'Then why ask me?'

'Because why the hell *can't* they let me in?'

She shook her head. 'Have a drink,' she repeated.

He muttered: 'Red tape, officialdom, that's all. It makes me
mad.' With the scowl still as sombre on his face and his lips
twisting bitterly, he fidgeted about the room. Signs of tiredness
under his eyes and something lethargic in the poise of his big

body made it plain that his nerves also had been suffering during the past two days.

With irritating clumsiness he managed to knock an ashtray off
the corner of a table on to the floor. As the thick glass thudded
on to the carpet he looked as if he would have liked to kick at it
like a child to vent his feelings.

Stooping to recover it, he grunted: 'Not seeing the new pick-
up to-day?'

'What new pick-up?'

'The one you had around with you yesterday.' His face had
gone red from stooping.

'I had two around with me yesterday. Anyway, what makes
you think I'm not seeing them to-day?'

'You've left all the extra off your face.'

'That was for the journalists and photographers, not for them.'

'One of them's a journalist.'

Joanna gave a laugh.

Dan scowled and sat down opposite her.

'Look here, Joanna,' he said, 'I'm worried.'

She raised her eyebrows.

'I'm worried about you,' said Dan. 'I've never known anyone
who was quite so good at getting their life into a thoroughly
unnecessary mess. Really, I'm worried.'

'I could see something was worrying you,' she said. 'I'm glad
that's all it is.'

He retorted: 'I don't like messes. They're unnecessary.'

'I expect,' said Joanna, 'Peru's in a mess. Those South American places always are. Perhaps you won't like Peru.'

'What's Peru got to do with it? We're talking about you.'

'When are you going to Peru, Dan?'

He waved Peru aside. 'Let's talk about one thing at a time. You
know what I mean. You're always doing this stunt of picking
people up. It's natural, you're quite attractive. But you haven't any
discrimination, you never seem to have the slightest idea of what
you've got hold of. I mean, look at that divinity student – and
then flying to the opposite extreme with that advertising artist.
Just anyone who turns up'll do, if that's the mood you happen to
be in. But now that you're all on your own, with no one to keep
an eye on you, what d'you think's going to happen to you?'

107

'Oh, the worst – definitely.'

'No, this is serious. I've been thinking about it ever since last night. Actually I don't see why one should bother about people who are such darned fools, but for some reason one does. I really shouldn't like to see you make a mess of your life.'

'Talking of discrimination,' said Joanna, 'it occurs to me that in nearly every restaurant I've been to with you, you know the Christian name of the waitress.'

'Well, why shouldn't I? Besides,' said Dan, 'I don't really mean I think you ought to behave like a plaster saint. But I think you ought to show you know what you're doing. Then more responsible people wouldn't have to bother about you.'

She gave a little giggle. Yet her gaze, meeting his, was oddly hard and concentrated.

Peremptorily he changed the subject. 'About your father, Jo . . . Oh, I know you don't want to talk about it – though God knows what else one can talk about; death always takes charge of a situation, even though talking about it and thinking about it, when one can't arrive at anything, only make one feel as if some wretched clock had got ticking in one's brain, just a meaningless tick, tick that's got to go on till the damn thing's run down. But, Jo, there's something I want to ask you.'

'Go ahead, Dan.'

He cleared his throat uneasily. 'Suspicion's a funny thing. Ever noticed how easy it is, when you lose something, to think the window-cleaner or the man who came to put the geyser right must have pinched it? Drop any irrelevant grain of suspicion in a person's mind and up comes a huge, hideous weed that strangles all their natural sense and generosity. You and I've known each other a good time. . . . Somehow, though, I don't think we've ever known each other really well. You've always thought me an awful fool, and I've always felt that you . . . Well, anyway, I don't suppose either of us has ever got to the point of feeling sure where we stood with the other. . . .'

'Dan, are you trying to get around to asking me whether I suspect you of having something to do with the murder of my father?'

He cleared his throat again. 'I – I just thought I'd like to know – what you thought. The police have been making such a song about those pods.'

108

'But have I done anything to make you think I thought . . . ?'

He picked up a match-box to fiddle with. 'I never know what you're thinking – that's the trouble.'

'I'm sorry, I hadn't realised that. And I hadn't realised you felt we didn't know one another. . . .' Her eyes, as she raised them to his face again, had the same hard concentration as before. 'I suppose that's why you keep telling me I don't know what I'm doing. The funny thing is, I've always thought I did, that I knew it perfectly well. And if – other people don't—' Her voice faltered. 'Well, if other people don't that's their fault, isn't it? What about a bathe?' She sprang to her feet.

The tide was high.

When they reached the beach by the steep path cut into the side of the cliff only a few yards of shingle lay exposed between the boulders at the foot of the cliff and the little frill of foam at the edge of the sea. Hot sun and a soft breeze mingled to give a naked skin the most enchanting of summer caresses.

They swam far out to where it was deep and the sunshine, flowing down into the water, seemed to be held there in a softly stirring, green-gold coolness. Overhead, almost at the limit of sight, a gull hovered, its wings making a faint, white glitter in the blue.

Joanna turned over on her back. She watched the gull. As she lay there, almost motionless, balancing with slight movements of her hands, the look of thought disappeared from her face; it grew placid and still as the bright sea itself. Presently the gull disappeared; only deep, shining nothingness arched above her.

'Joanna, what do you believe is the real function of the scientist in the modern world?'

She gave a crow of laughter.

Dan, splashing somewhere near her, asked: 'What's funny about that? It's a question I've been trying to arrive at a definite answer to for some time.'

'I'm sure it's a most serious question. The time, the place – and you yourself, Dan – that's all that's funny.'

Dan said no more until all at once he exploded: 'Hell!'

Lazily she inquired: 'What's the matter?'

A pause, then Dan answered: 'Nothing.'

'But—'

'Can't I say hell if I want to? I say, Jo, shall we swim round the point?'

'I feel much too lazy.'

She heard him swimming about. But she had closed her eyes; the water carried her gently. Then something soft slid against her, and as with a gasp and a splash she wriggled aside, a large jellyfish, its swaying transparency veined with purple, drifted past her like a remarkable flower. Turning round to speak to Dan again, she could not see him. Then she realised that he had started for the shore.

Striking out after him, she saw what it was that had made him curse and probably also suggest swimming round the point.

On the beach, at just about the spot where she and Dan had left their towels, two figures were sitting.

The presence of Toby Dyke, with his big, inquiring nose and raised question-mark of an eyebrow, and with George as usual at his side, brought death, doubt and suspicion close to them again.

Joanna, sitting down on the shingle, rubbing herself with her towel, said: 'By the way, Mr. Dyke, it appears that when Barnes is drunk he has visions. I asked Gerald Hyland this morning whether there was any letter on the desk when he went in and found my father, and he said there wasn't.'

'Well, we'll go and ask Barnes about it when he's sober, shall we,' said Toby, 'and see if the vision persists?'

'But Gerald said—'

He cut her short: 'This isn't a time to take anyone's word at its face value.'

'Gerald Hyland,' said Dan, rubbing salt water out of his hair, 'is an old humbug. I'd never believe anything he said.'

Toby Dyke looked interested.

'He's an old fool,' said Dan, 'completely dishonest with himself, lives in a world of day-dreams and fake. Look at his novels – romantic wish-fulfilment. Look at all his crazes – if they don't indicate self-deception and general instability I'd like to know what does?'

'Ah,' said Toby Dyke. Then he turned his head and looked at

110

Joanna, waiting for what her reply might be to this attack on Gerald Hyland.

Joanna did not say anything. But when Dan was not looking she gave him a thoughtful stare. When she looked away again she was frowning, and her lower lip was caught between her teeth.

It was not until the afternoon that they were able to interrogate Barnes once more about the letter he claimed to have seen on the desk, for it was not until about three o'clock that they found him. Looking for him at the herbarium, they had been told by the constable who turned them away from its doors, that he was not there. He was not at home either. At that point Dan had left them, saying he was going back to his room to do some writing. At last, strolling rather aimlessly along the promenade, they discovered Barnes on a bench, drowsing in a stupor richly perfumed with beer.

When Toby's hand fell on his shoulder he sat up with a start. Before they had had time to comment, he told them aggressively that he was perfectly sober.

'But I ain't got nothin' to do, that's the trouble,' he said peevishly, as they arranged themselves along the bench beside him. 'They won't let me in to clean up. Now why the hell shouldn't they? It ain't good for a bloke to turn him loose with nothin' to do. But I ain't drunk, and you needn't think it. I ain't hardly ever drunk, because I can stand it, see? My missus says I come home drunk last night, but that's her exaggeration. I wasn't drunk – I can stand it.'

'You weren't drunk and incapable, certainly, nor even drunk and disorderly,' said Toby, 'but just drunk and a bit confused, eh?'

'Eh? What d'you know about it? What are you gettin' at? I wasn't drunk.'

'Don't you remember meeting us last night?'

Barnes turned and looked at him.

'You'd something to tell us about a letter,' said Toby. 'Don't you remember?'

Barnes pulled a short, dirty piece of string out of his pocket. He put one end of it in his mouth and chewed it. His eyes were full of far-away thoughts.

111

'Maybe. Maybe I remember the letter. But I don't remember tellin' anyone about it.'

'It's the letter that matters, not the telling.'

'Matters how?'

'To the police.'

'I don't care about the police. They won't let me in to get on with my work. That's what I tell my wife when she goes on at me, I say I got to have somethin' to do, and they won't let me in to get on with my work.'

'Still,' said Toby patiently, 'do you remember a letter?'

'Oh, yes, I remember a letter.'

'Where?'

'Right on the desk. And then not there when I come back presently. Someone took it to post it – Mr. Hyland or Mr. Weedon maybe.'

'Hm, maybe.'

Barnes looked round at him once more. 'Reckon I'd like to know what you're thinkin'. You got a funny way of sayin' things.'

Toby gave an absent nod.

'Course,' said Barnes, 'you wouldn't post a letter without it had an address on it, would you?'

One of Toby's eyebrows shot up. 'It had no address?'

'No – no address.'

'Sure of that?'

'That's right.'

'What makes you sure?'

'Well,' said Barnes, 'it catches your eye, a plain envelope does.'

'You're sure it wasn't just an unused envelope with nothing in it?'

'Am I tellin' you there was a letter there or ain't I?'

'And whereabouts was this letter – I mean where on the desk? Was it in front of the old chap as if he just hadn't written the address on it yet?'

'No,' said Barnes, 'it was propped against the inkpot, sort of facin' to the door. The desk itself sort of faced to the door, if you see what I mean, with Mr. Prees sittin' behind it. The letter looked as if he'd put it there so's anyone comin' in would see it first thing.'

'I see.'

George murmured: 'Funny to leave a letter like that an' not write on it who it was meant for.'

An elbow jogged Toby's. He turned his head and Joanna whispered: 'D'you think all this is to be trusted? Is he really sober?'

'He's sober all right. He's had some drink, but' – he grinned – 'remember, he can stand it.'

'Then you believe in this letter in spite of Gerald?'

Toby shrugged his shoulders. 'I'm curious to know whether or not Tingey's going to believe in it.'

'But I can't understand . . .'

'You aren't the only one,' he told her.

'No, Miss Prees, you aren't the only one.'

They had run Tingey to earth in the herbarium. On stating that it was Tingey they wanted to see, they had been allowed into the building. In the same room where he had questioned Joanna, seated at the table on which was spread out a collection of torn scraps of paper, odd lengths of string, cigarette-stubs and other articles that might have come out of a wastepaper-basket, he had been doing some writing when the constable showed them in.

He had listened to Barnes' story.

'No, Miss Prees, you aren't the only one who doesn't understand what it's all about.'

He looked tired and irritable as a man does when he has been thinking hard but has next to no material on which to do the thinking.

Turning to Toby, he went on: 'I'm grateful, Mr. Dyke, for that tip about the key. Here it is, you see. One of our chaps found it in the flower-bed, just like you said. Funny that, your knowing where it'd be. Anyway, it helps to cast what you might call a vivid darkness on this murky problem. And now I'm grateful to you for bringing Mr. Barnes along. You're being a lot of help. 'Tisn't your fault if everything you do only makes me see through the glass a bit darklier. Or – is it?'

Toby straddled a chair.

'What d'you mean, Tingey?'

'You wouldn't by any chance *want* to see me get all tangled up in this case, would you, Mr. Dyke?'

113

'I don't know what put such an idea in your head.'

'No more do I, really. Only you do seem to be taking a rather personal interest in some of the people connected with it, and then . . .' Vaguely the sentence faded out. Tingey's gaze came to rest broodingly on Joanna.

She was looking at the assortment of oddments on the table. Nothing there appeared to make sense.

Toby said impatiently: 'Be your age, Inspector. You know Miss Prees wants this cleared up as much as you do.'

'Cleared up, yes – but then there are different ways of clearing things up, aren't there, Mr. Dyke? Take the matter of this key, for instance.' Though he spoke to Toby, his eyes still dwelt on Joanna. 'It's in the flower-bed. Now would you say that was cleared up or wouldn't you?'

'Of course not. When you know who threw it there and why—'

'Ah – and how Mr. Dyke came to know just where it'd be – then we'll know a lot.'

With a blank shake of his head Toby replied: 'As it happens, that'd tell you very little. If you knew what made Dr Vanedden suggest it was in the flower-bed, perhaps then you'd know a lot. But I'm not even sure of that. I think it's quite possible that Vanedden just guessed at the key being in the flower-bed. You see, if one believed in his theory that Mr. Prees killed himself in such a way as to have someone blamed for his murder, and in creating evidence to support this had concealed the key, then the flower-bed would seem a very probable place for the key to be in. I don't see any real reason for assuming that Vanedden was drawing anything but a legitimate inference – making a good guess, that's to say.'

'Hum,' said Tingey. 'Miss Prees, what d'you think about it?'

She glanced up from her puzzled study of Tingey's wastepaper siftings.

She said hesitantly: 'I don't know. I can't really believe my father would do a thing like that – I mean purposely leave such a peculiarly horrible kind of trouble for other people.'

'But perhaps that part of it was only secondary. He might have had some other reason, mightn't he?'

'What reason?'

'Oh . . . some good reason,' said Tingey vaguely.

114

'What about the fingerprints then?' she asked. 'Have you found a way they might have been faked?'

'Not so far.'

'Then there can't be anything in the theory, can there?'

'Good – I'm glad you like evidence better than theories, Miss Prees.' He gave her his slow, kindly smile. 'Now sticking to evidence – I wonder if you can tell me something. When you returned to the herbarium, as you told me, shortly before eight o'clock, and tried to get in, pushing at the door and leaving your fingerprints on it, did you notice anyone who saw you there, anyone who could corroborate your statement – *that you didn't get in?*' Very gently he put the question. He was like a still life of gentleness and kindliness.

A protest broke from Toby.

Joanna turned rather white. She said fumblingly: 'My finger-prints – on the door?'

He explained: 'Yesterday morning you were kind enough to leave me a very nice impression of one finger in that wax there. So there's no doubt they are your fingerprints on the door.' He nodded towards the electric embedding-oven that stood on the bench against the wall.

In the hard wax in one of the dishes was the clear mark of the finger-tip that Joanna had pressed there.

Her voice shook slightly on the first word as she answered: 'B-but d'you mean you think I've got something to do with it all?'

'If I did,' he replied, 'I should have warned you that anything you said might be used in evidence. . . . No, all I'm asking is whether anyone saw you at the door.'

'I don't know whether anyone saw me or not. I didn't notice anyone. I suppose I was too worried to be thinking about anything like that.'

'That's a pity. Dear me. . . .' Puffing out his cheeks, he let them deflate in a sigh. 'I wish I knew whether you put that fingerprint there on purpose or not, and if on purpose, just what was in your mind.'

'I'm afraid I hardly knew I was doing it.'

'You know,' said Toby Dyke in her ear, 'you needn't answer questions like that if you don't want to.'

115

But she shrugged that aside impatiently, as yesterday she had shrugged aside a similar caution from Hyland.

'And I suppose, Miss Prees,' said Tingey, 'you've never possessed a key like this one we've found in the flower-bed?'

'Never.'

'As I thought, as I thought. This key's very puzzling, you know. I've been sitting here thinking about it, trying to keep count of all the different things it might mean. I was making some notes about it when you came in.' Tingey pulled towards him the writing he had pushed aside when they entered. 'It might mean that Vanedden was right, as to its having been Mr. Prees himself who threw the key there, though to my mind the fingerprints on the revolver make nonsense of that. Then it might have been someone on whom that key, if it had been found, would have been suspicious. All the people who work in this place have a key like it anyway, so on the one hand they wouldn't need this key, and on the other, if for some reason they'd taken it and it was found on them, they could always swear they'd had a duplicate made of the one they had already. So it doesn't look as if the murderer was one of the people who work here. On the other hand, the key was manifestly taken from Mr. Prees *after* he was dead – so whoever took it got into the herbarium without using it. That suggests they owned a key themselves. But then it's possible, isn't it, that they got in without using a key at all, that's to say that Mr. Prees himself came down and let his murderer in at the door and took him along to his room. In that case the murderer, after doing the shooting, took the key because he wanted to be able to get into the herbarium again later. And then he became afraid he might be searched, so he flipped the key out of the window into the flower-bed. That's possible, that's quite possible. But there's still another theory.' Tingey looked up from his notes. 'Suppose the murderer's a very clever man who reckons that if he flips the key into the flower-bed some clever detective is going to come to the very conclusion that I almost did – namely, that the murderer's someone who *has* got a key. Now' – he looked at Toby – 'which of those theories d'you like best, M'Clusky?'

'I'm not in a fit state to like any of 'em, Tingey. I don't know enough.'

'Well, I'll tell you something in confidence – I don't like any of 'em myself.' The Inspector gave his notes a dispirited push. 'In fact, I'm inclined not to attach much importance to this key at all. And as for this letter that was or wasn't on the desk – as you say, I just don't know enough.'

Barnes cleared his throat. 'Cross me heart, the letter was there.'

The Inspector sat frowning, drumming with his fingers on the table.

Barnes began again: 'Cross me heart—'

'Miss Prees,' said Tingey, 'd'you think Mr. Hyland would cross his heart that the letter *wasn't* there?'

'Look here, Tingey,' said Toby, 'why not ask Gordon Weedon? He was the next to come into the room.'

'And hope that we'll get more truth out of two liars than one?' Tingey gave him a pitying smile. 'I never expected to hear a thing like that from you, Mr. Dyke.'

'Why assume that Weedon's a liar?'

'Because I happen to know that he is one.'

'You *know* it?'

'That's right.'

'Come on, come on, Tingey' – Toby hitched his chair up nearer – 'out with it. What are you keeping to yourself? What d'you know? Think how useful I've been to you. Perhaps I'll go on being useful. Tell us what you've got on Weedon.'

Tingey replied slowly: 'It's true you have been useful. . . . Well, I don't mind telling you this – Mr. Weedon isn't very good at making facts match up. He tried to explain certain of his actions yesterday in such a way as to – well, to put it mildly, cast doubts on his veracity.'

'Why bother to put it mildly when you've just said he's a liar?'

'Um, yes. You see, Mr. Dyke, it's like this. Mr. Weedon's land-lady says that her 'phone rang at about a quarter past seven. She answered it, and a voice, very agitated, asked for Mr. Weedon. She went up and roused him and Mr. Weedon came down in his dressing-gown. She didn't hear much of what he said, but then suddenly he yelled out: "My God, don't do that!" The next moment he was bolting up the stairs, and in another couple of minutes he was down again, dressed, and dashed out. Well, Mr. Weedon admits all that, and says it was Miss Winnpole who rang him up. Now that won't hold water for a moment. First, your housekeeper, Miss Prees, says Miss Winnpole never made any call that morning. The exchange says the same. Miss Winnpole says she did ring him up, but what with her being his fiancée and his having had plenty of time to tip her off, I reckon we don't need to pay too much attention to that. Besides, the exchange managed to trace a call put through from the herbarium to Mr. Weedon's lodgings at seven-thirty.'

Joanna stiffened. 'From the herbarium – from my father?'

'That's what it looks like – unless it was his murderer.'

'But,' said Toby in a puzzled way, 'was it a man's voice or a woman's that the landlady heard?'

'Ah, that's just it, she says she's not sure, it might have been either.'

'My father's voice was rather high,' said Joanna thoughtfully.

'But if it wasn't Mr. Prees, if it was the murderer,' said Toby, 'Weedon knows who it was.'

'Just so,' said Tingey.

Toby gave a whistle.

'Well, when I put all this to Mr. Weedon,' Tingey went on, 'he sticks to it it was Miss Winnpole rang him up, and that all he did when he dashed out was go for a long walk. Which is silly, you know – very silly.'

'D'you think he came up here?' asked Toby.

'Well – somebody did.'

Joanna shuddered.

Toby said: 'But it was Weedon who only the evening before saved the life of Mr. Prees.'

'I'm not saying he didn't. I'm only saying, in certain circumstances he told a lie.'

'I see. Well' – Toby hitched himself off his chair – 'thanks for talking. I think we may as well be getting along. Really, it's a pity it was Weedon who did the life-saving act the other evening. He'd do very nicely as a suspect.'

'Hrrmph.' It was George, diffidently drawing attention to himself. 'Er – this is a very nice collection of stuff you've got on this table, Inspector. Does any of it mean anythin'?'

Tingey gestured at the scraps of paper, cigarette-stubs, matches, pins and ends of string. 'Take a look for yourself.'

'F'rinstance' – George pointed at a torn-off corner of an envelope with part of an unused three-ha'penny stamp sticking to it. 'What about this?'

'It came from the floor in Mr. Prees' room. Now you know as much about it as I do,' said Tingey.

'Where's the rest of the envelope?'

But just then an exclamation broke from Joanna. It was followed by a crash as, in springing to her feet, she overturned her chair. As they all looked round at her they saw that she was gazing up at the fanlight over the door.

Through the fanlight a pair of bright eyes were staring down at them. Set in deep, bony sockets, they looked as if they were peering out of a skull.

Even as Toby and Tingey looked, the eyes disappeared.

Joanna gave a self-conscious laugh. She picked up the chair.

'I'm frightfully sorry. It startled me, seeing those eyes like that. Of course it's only Gerald – no one else'd be tall enough to look in over the door. Hullo, Gerald' – as the door opened – 'you've just given me an awful fright.'

But Gerald Hyland, coming into the room, took no notice of Joanna. A couple of his long, spidery strides brought him face to face with Tingey.

He said: 'I've come to tell you something of the utmost importance. I've remembered – there *was* a letter.'

Tingey said: 'I think Mr. Hyland and I had better talk this over.'

The others took the hint.

But before they reached the door, Hyland was already plunging through his explanation. It came with a rush and an expansive gesture: 'Memory, Inspector, can be a great deceiver. It keeps dealing one blank cards, absolute blanks – that's to say, that's what they look like – blanks, complete blanks. Yet the pattern's there on them all the time, only' – he radiated enthusiastic earnestness at Tingey, who looked a short, squat man beside him – 'it's in invisible ink! You know all about invisible ink, of course; you heat it and then it shows. Well, that's how it works with these blanks that memory hands out to us. You heat

119

them, perhaps with anger, or desperation, or drink – different things work at different times, naturally, and with different people. Suddenly the whole thing's plain to you. Well, Inspector, I don't know what made it happen this time with me, but I know – there *was* a letter.'

Toby, George and Joanna, outside in the passage, were still followed by Hyland's harsh voice, each word audible through the open fanlight.

'Isn't it lucky I remembered? Probably it's something vital to the elucidation of all this. It might so easily have remained buried deep below the level of consciousness until it was too late. I'm terribly forgetful; every one will tell you so. If I hadn't had that flash of vision – for that was how it happened, a sort of vision – I suddenly *saw* poor Edgar sitting there, with the revolver on the floor and the letter propped up against the inkstand in front of him . . .'

With a hand on her shoulder, Toby was pushing Joanna along the passage.

'But that means,' she said, 'that perhaps there may have been something in Dr. Vanedden's theory.'

'Whatever it means, it doesn't mean that.'

'But don't you see,' she said, 'my father wrote that letter, as people who kill themselves nearly always do, and—'

'Don't *you* see, my dear, innocent young thing,' said Toby, pushing her on, further from that communicative fanlight, and himself speaking softly, 'that if your father wrote a letter saying his death was his own doing, he wouldn't then have thrown the key out of the window and done conjuring-tricks with his fingerprints in order to make it look as if his death were someone else's doing? That letter doesn't fit with your Dr. Vanedden's theory at all.'

She considered. 'No . . . I suppose it doesn't.'

'Certainly it doesn't. But you're missing the really interesting point. The interesting point, Joanna' – he showed his teeth in a grin – 'is that your candid friend, Gerald Hyland, forgot that letter, then had a vision and remembered it.'

'You mean you don't believe him?'

'I don't believe in visions.'

Angry-eyed, she said: 'You keep coming back to Gerald.'

'He keeps doing such odd things.'

'But you yourself know, better than anyone, that he couldn't have been there at the time my father was shot.'

'Ye-es.'

'Are you changing your mind about that? Are you beginning to wonder if he's got a double who cooked the liver and bacon for your breakfast, or whether it wasn't all done by mirrors?'

He smiled at her tone. 'You know, I wish I had someone with as much belief in me as you seem to have in that long-legged crank. I've got no one but George to believe in me, and George is subject to moods of scepticism which can be very trying. Meanwhile I'd—' He broke off. 'Where *is* George?'

He was not in the passage with them.

Joanna said: 'I expect he's gone to have a quiet think about something.'

He turned on her. 'Now don't let's have any of that. You and I had better be careful to remain friends if we want to get anywhere. If you're annoyed with something about me, say so, but don't just vent your feelings of distrust by making that particular kind of suggestion – it gives me the jitters.'

'Why d'you keep venting your feelings of distrust on Gerald?'

'Why does he do such damn suspicious things?'

'Aren't you forgetting your friend's story about the wet Saturday afternoon in Manchester?'

'Listen!' said Toby. 'Can you look me in the face and swear there's absolutely nothing suspicious – making the utmost allowances for Hyland's idiosyncrasies – in the way he forgot that letter, then remembered it?'

She had a try at doing it. She failed.

They had reached the street. With a dusty-looking film spread over the sky, the summer afternoon was settling into a tired stupor of heat. The air that fell on their faces smelt of orange-peel and petrol.

They paused on the steps outside the Gothic entrance.

'Your friend Hyland,' said Toby, 'wants a verdict of murder. It's a funny thing to want, but he wants it like hell. He hates the idea of suicide. The first time that letter's mentioned he says no, there wasn't one. Why? Because, like you, he leapt to the conclusion that the presence of a letter supported the idea of suicide – people expect suicides to leave letters behind them. But then he does a bit of thinking – and contrary to all appearances, I believe Hyland's capable of quite a lot of thinking – and bearing in mind the key and the finger-prints, he suddenly realises that a letter giving the whole game away makes no sense at all. As soon as he's arrived at that, he comes charging along to say that there *was* a letter.'

She answered stonily: 'That's just a hypothesis.'

'Ah, you don't know what I can do with a hypothesis!'

'No – it's complete guesswork. You don't really know anything about it. And I do know something. I know – and I'm not going to qualify it by agreeing that it's something one can't ever really know – one can, I do! I *know* the kind of man that Gerald Hyland is.'

'What a nice girl you are, Joanna. There's not much faith, hope or charity in this world, but you've got lots of them all.'

'There's not much horse-sense either, but I've got some of that too.' She was turning away. Yet she stopped. 'Anyway, was there a letter?'

'I think so. Both Hyland and Barnes supplied the detail that it was propped up against the inkstand. I don't think they've had a chance to consult on the matter.'

'That might be a coincidence.'

'My dear girl,' he said in exasperation, 'the rising of the sun day after day might be a coincidence.'

'You don't much like being argued with, do you? What became of the letter?'

But through the doorway behind them at that moment came George. Toby rounded on him, demanding where he'd been.

Sniffing the sultry air, George halted in the doorway, then came down the steps towards them. Joining them, he observed thoughtfully: 'Shouldn't wonder if there's another storm presently.'

'George, where've you been?'

'Just been havin' a word with Mr. Barnes, Tobe. What are we goin' to do now – have some tea?'

'What were you asking Barnes?'

'Here, can't I have a quiet word with a chap without havin' to tell you all about it? Lucky you and I ain't married; you'd be the sort of wife who always read my letters.'

Toby rapped out the question: 'George, what were you asking Barnes?'

George sighed. 'Just somethin' about pods, Tobe. I was wonderin' whether they'd had one of those parcels of pods from Egypt, like Mr. Moon told us about, any time recently. Seems there was one last week. I thought I'd like to take a look at it, but somehow Mr. Barnes and me we couldn't seem to lay our hands on it. And then I was askin' him—' George paused reflectively. 'I was askin' him whether they was troubled with mice in the herbarium.'

Toby exploded with a couple of fierce words.

'There,' said George, 'I knew you wouldn't be interested. And it's all right, they aren't. I reckoned probably they weren't, but I just had to make sure.'

'Mice in the herbarium – bats in the belfry! I don't know what the hell's come over you. Anyway, tea isn't a bad idea. What about some tea, Miss Prees?'

They had started walking along the pavement.

She asked as before: 'What about that letter? What's become of it?'

'Look here, suppose we drop the subject of that letter,' said Toby. 'Like Tingey, we don't really know anything about it.' He sounded bad-tempered. When they reached a café he turned abruptly in at the door and led the way to a corner table.

But Joanna did not sit down. She stood with both hands resting on the back of a wickerwork chair.

'Do you think Gerald removed the letter?'

'Does it matter what I think?'

'You do think so.'

'Sit down and have some tea. Haven't you learnt yet that very few people's thoughts are worth taking seriously?'

'You've got ideas about that letter. Why won't you tell me what you think? Is it because it's something to do with Gerald Hyland and you know I won't believe you?'

He said: 'In God's name, why can't you sit down and make up your mind whether or not you want buttered toast?'

'I don't want buttered toast. I want to know what you're going to do about that letter.'

123

'I'll tell you. I'm going to have a quiet think about it.'

She made a sound of disgust and turned to go. Then she came back again.

'When you have a quiet think, does it mean the same kind of thing as when George has a quiet think?'

He gave a laugh, leaning back in the wicker chair. 'Be intelligent, Joanna,' he said, 'and grasp the fact that I'm not talking. You know, there are all sorts of occasions, quite intimate ones sometimes – I believe they even happen between husband and wife – when one has to reconcile oneself to a person not talking. Why not put in a little practice at it now? Actually there's something I'm thinking about much harder than I am about that letter.' He dropped his voice slightly. 'I'm thinking about one of those blank cards that memory's dealt out to me. You know, I liked that metaphor of Hyland's. I'm trying to see whether or not some plain, hard thinking will bring up that invisible ink he talked about. I'm inclined to think something shadowy is just beginning to appear – and if you want to know what it's all about, the answer's Vanedden. I believe I've remembered where I've heard his name before. I'm not certain; I'll have to verify it. But there was something about two young women. One died in a motor-accident, the other committed suicide, and both, I believe – this is the thing I've got to check up – were patients of a Dr. Vanedden.'

'And?' she added, as he did not continue. 'There's some more to it, isn't there?'

'Yes – and both took drugs.'

'Drugs!'

The waitress broke in on them. She demanded what they wanted, and took Toby's order for tea. As she whisked a few crumbs off the table and emptied an ashtray, she stared curiously at Joanna.

As the waitress went away Toby leant forward and laid a hand on Joanna's arm.

He tried to put reassurance into his voice. 'Don't look like that, Joanna. It's only an idea, you know. I've got to check it; I may be quite wrong. And even if I'm right about Vanedden – and it does explain Tingey's attitude to him, doesn't it? – it may have nothing to do with your father. It may all be a coincidence.'

124

'Like – like the sun rising day after day!' She gave a hoarse little laugh. 'Those sums of money in notes . . . drugs . . . oh, it's horrible!'

With a jerk she shook his hand off. As she walked out of the café her wide, dark eyes had almost the blank look of blindness.

7

Outside the heat was stupefying. The blue-black sky seemed to be slung only just higher than the chimney-pots. No breath of freshness came from the oily calm sea. The street was busy, but its noises made only a brittle crust of sound over a sinister stillness.

She hurried along.

Down a turning beyond the herbarium was the boarding-house in which both Dan and Gordon had rooms. It was one of a row of bow-fronted buildings, each plastered in a different colour. If their façades failed to harmonise, their interiors sang in a thin, cracked unison the same song of comfortless gentility. Unmarried members of the herbarium staff nearly always lived at Number Five; once, possibly, some good reason had existed for this arrangement.

As Joanna was hurrying down this street a small figure with a crest of silver hair emerged suddenly from Number Five, ran down the steps and darted into the large, black Cadillac that stood in the road.

As the Cadillac drove off Joanna saw an odd thing happen. Another car that had been drawn in to the kerb moved off after it.

Joanna had passed this car without paying any attention to it; now as it passed her she caught a glimpse of the man who sat at the wheel. It was the same man she had seen that morning, sitting on the grass near the bungalow, reading a newspaper, smoking a pipe, the man who had got up and strolled after her as she went to Hyland's cottage.

There was grimness on Joanna's face when she rang the bell of Number Five, and when the tired-eyed landlady came to the door, she asked if Gordon Weedon were in.

But the landlady's reply was lost in the thud of swift feet on the stairs as Dan Moon came down them at a run. He jerked to a startled standstill when he saw Joanna.

'I was just coming to look for you!'

She answered: 'I'm looking for Gordon. There's something I want to ask him.'

Both spoke in matter-of-fact tones; both were too excited to note the excitement of the other.

Dan said: 'I don't think he's in. Come upstairs. Vanedden's just been here. I was going looking for you to tell you about it. It's given me an idea.'

'But where's Gordon? It's something awfully important.' However, she was following him up the stairs. Mrs. Brandon, the landlady, shambled off.

'With Peggie, I expect,' said Dan. 'Jo, did you see Vanedden just now?'

'Yes – and the man following him.'

He looked round. 'What man?'

'The man I thought was following me this morning when I went to see Gerald. But Vanedden was at Gerald's cottage then; it may have been Vanedden he was following all the time; it's true I didn't notice him anywhere when I left Gerald's cottage.'

'You didn't say anything to me this morning about a man following you.'

'It didn't seem important. I thought he was just a policeman keeping an eye on me.'

'Is he a policeman?'

'Probably.'

They reached the second floor. As they went into Dan's bed-sitting-room Dan went on: 'Jo, that man Vanedden knows something – and he's trying damned hard to find out how many other people know it. That's what he was here for just now, and I bet that was why he was out at Hyland's place this morning.'

The pressure of heat in the room was almost intolerable, though both windows were wide open. The sky was such a low-slung, solid blackness that inside it was almost dark. It was an untidy, shabby room, furnished haphazard from the second-hand dealers, though its proportions had a sober, pre-Regency stateliness.

127

'Vanedden arrived here about half an hour ago,' said Dan, going to the window and trying to breathe some air into his lungs. He was wearing flannels and a shirt, the shirt clinging to him damply, while his face was pale and strained with the heat. 'He started straight in asking me what I thought had been the cause of your father's attempt at suicide. I told him I hadn't an idea. He talked about other things, made me talk about my job and so on, but he kept coming back to that – why had your father tried to kill himself? I said sorry, I couldn't oblige, and about the third time I said it I started getting a queer impression that he was pleased I couldn't oblige. After a bit I felt absolutely certain of it; he wouldn't have liked it at all if I'd been able to tell him anything – in fact, what he'd come for was to check up that I didn't know. And I can tell you, with him sitting looking at me, never taking those queer eyes of his off me, and asking the most sympathetic questions possible about just what a botanist does and why, I felt rather glad I couldn't tell him anything. I've a feeling that if I'd dropped a single hint I knew anything, I might still be sitting in that chair there, oozing nice red blood over the carpet. Jo – what's the matter? You aren't listening.'

'Yes, I am.'

'You aren't.'

She murmured: ' "... oozing nice, red blood over the carpet." That's what you said, isn't it? I'm listening all right.'

'What's the matter?' he repeated.

She did not look at him. 'How long have we known each other, Dan?'

He considered: 'Off and on, three years. As a matter of fact – from my point of view they've been three rather unsatisfactory years.'

'Why?'

'Oh – nothing seems to have turned out quite as I intended. This – this job or anything. Peru's a bloody silly scheme really, but it's better than anything else I can think of at the moment.'

'I thought perhaps – now that father was dead – you might have stopped thinking of Peru.'

'Well, I don't know. . . . But why not tell me what's up, Joanna? You're looking white and queer.'

'I've had a shock, Dan.' Slowly she drew a fingernail along a

128

crack in the paint on the window frame. 'It's funny, I always thought I was the sort of person who was rather good at standing shocks, not the Peggie Winnpole kind that goes to pieces straight away. And this is a shock I ought almost to have been expecting. Everything pointed to something of the kind. Yet ever since I heard it I've been feeling shaky and sick inside. Then when I got here, seeing that man Vanedden . . . Anyway,' she added in a low voice, 'there's something I've made up my mind about. I'm not going to take that life-insurance – I'm not going to take *any* of it.'

He said: 'Well, that's your own business.'

She went on: 'It was Toby Dyke suddenly saying he remembered where he'd heard the name Vanedden that did it. He'd heard it in connection with some girl who was killed in a motor-accident, and another who committed suicide. Both were patients of Vanedden's, and both took drugs. Drugs, Dan!' Her voice made one of those sudden, betraying changes of pitch. 'D'you see what that implies? D'you remember how the Inspector seemed to know an extraordinary amount about Vanedden? Well, they must suspect Vanedden of being the person who supplied the drugs, only they can't have been able to prove that he did. But that must be why they've got a man watching him now – and somehow or other, you see, in a way none of us could understand, Vanedden was connected with my father, and somehow or other also, my father kept getting hold of large sums of money in notes, which came from God knows where. D'you see what it all means? I don't know at all how the thing arranges itself in detail; I don't know if my father had something to do with getting hold of the drugs, or with distributing them, or whether he simply knew about Dr. Vanedden and was forcing him to pay. It doesn't matter much – somehow all that money came from drugs, cocaine or something, stuff that makes people go off their heads and kill themselves, and go driving cars in such a crazy way that they smash themselves to bits. . . . Drugs are things that degrade people and then destroy them. And my father . . . No, it doesn't matter, it doesn't matter at all where he comes into the pattern. At the very least he knew of it, and put all the money he got out of it into a life-insurance for me – for *me!*'

129

'Hi!' His hand gripped her above the elbow. His voice was rougher than usual. 'You aren't taking that money, you've just said so. Right – that's all there is to that.'

'But Dan, don't you see, these last few years – everything I've had—'

'For God's sake!' His hot, earnest face glared down at her. 'Didn't he pay for it himself, Jo, didn't the whole thing get him so badly in the end that he tried to kill himself? Because that's why he did it, it's perfectly clear now. But look here, you're not to let on to Vanedden how much you've sorted out. That man's dangerous, and if he knew—' Dan broke off as a sudden vivid whiteness blazed in the room. 'That was lightning,' he said.

Almost at once came the thunder.

Joanna said quietly: 'I don't know if father paid for it or not. Is anything ever paid for?'

He swung away from her and threw himself down in a chair. 'That's not the sort of thing I've got opinions about. All I care about at the moment is that you shouldn't think you've got to try to pay for it.'

She was silent. Then she spoke restlessly: 'I wonder if Gordon's come in yet. I want to see him.'

'We'd have heard him if he had,' said Dan. 'His room's next door. What d'you want to see him about?'

'I wanted to ask him—' She paused again as the lightning came, slashing open the shadow that enclosed them. 'I wanted to ask him about the letter Barnes said he saw. Toby Dyke's making something important out of it. I don't understand what, I only know he's trying to drag Gerald into it somehow. And that got me badly frightened. If anything happened to Gerald . . . Can it, d'you think, when he couldn't have had anything to do with it all? But Toby Dyke never seems to think about anyone else. I wish I'd never gone to him yesterday. I don't know why, I thought he was to be trusted.'

'I told you, you don't know the first thing about people; anyone can take you in.' Dan's eyes were full of disquiet. 'Go on and tell me more about the letter.'

She told him of that afternoon's interview with Barnes, of the interview that had followed with Tingey, of Hyland's change of opinion, of Toby's comments.

While she was speaking a few big drops of rain fell. They fell dead straight, and the sounds they made as they struck the street were as sharp as if it had been a handful of gravel falling.

Dan drew a hand over his sticky forehead. Lightning and thunder were coming in quick succession. The air felt as if it might solidify in the lungs.

Suddenly, as if with one tearing crash that tautly suspended blackness over their heads had burst, the rain smashed down in a dense, hissing torrent.

Joanna, as she finished speaking of the letter, came away from the window. She wandered restlessly about the room, waiting for Dan's comment.

He said after a moment: 'I suppose Barnes might have invented it all.'

'But Gerald's said now he saw the letter too.'

'Only after he'd had time to think about it.'

'D'you mean you think the same about that as Toby Dyke does?'

'I don't know. It's – odd, his remembering it like that afterwards. I should think either he must have known all the time that the letter was there, or else it was never there at all. I don't mean he mayn't have had some excellent reason for answering as he did.'

Her mouth became a hard line. 'Why are you all so certain that Gerald's a liar?'

'I didn't say I was certain.'

'Oh, why dither about it? You've made up your mind.'

'Well, you must be remarkably uneasy yourself, or you'd be more inclined to laugh about it instead of taking it so seriously.'

'I haven't felt very inclined to laugh at anything during the last two or three days.'

'Oh, blast the whole business! For God's sake, let's get our minds off it.'

'What's the good of that?' She was back at the window, where a faint coolness was coming from the downpour. 'You know, I'm finding it quite interesting, seeing the way people react at a time like this. Drop any odd, irrelevant grain of suspicion in their minds and up it comes at once in a huge, horrible weed that chokes out all their natural sense and generosity – you were quite right when you said that. People don't seem to have any real standards of what's probable and what isn't.'

He chewed a thumbnail, looking sullen and irritated. 'Well, there's one thing I'd like to know,' he grunted, 'and that's whether you ever kidded yourself, even for a moment, that either of those two poor fish you got engaged to mattered to you one-tenth as much as your sacrosanct idiot of a godfather, or whatever he happens to be.'

'Dan!'

'Did you?' he asked interestedly.

One of her fists clenched. 'Why, why do I ever try talking to you? I ought to know by now it isn't any good. The same thing always happens; first you start abusing someone I'm fond of, and then when you've had enough of that you start abusing me.'

'All the same, I'd really like to know if you ever believed you really cared for either of those two poor—'

'Don't!' she shouted at him. 'Don't call them poor fish!'

'Well, what else were they? Your advertising man mightn't have been so bad, but that divinity student—'

'I'll tell you something about my divinity student.' She advanced on him with twitching fingers. 'He never went swimming with me and when we were a hundred yards from the shore asked me what I thought was the function of the scientist in modern society. And he never took me out to dinner and sat silent for about two hours and then looked deep into my eyes and asked: "Joanna, what *is* True Democracy?" And he never—'

'Hell!' cried Dan, jumping to his feet. 'I didn't want to ask you that! I wanted to say something quite different. And then next morning you told me you were engaged to that creeping Jesus in a dog-collar, and so I was damn glad I hadn't said what I'd been going to say, and—'

'Oh, how I hate an unintelligent lie!'

'If you hate unintelligent lies you'd better get busy hating your dear old friend Hyland, because—'

'There, you see! You're trying again to get at me through someone I'm fond of. There's nothing as mean as that. It's the meanest, cheapest way there is of getting at a person. You've always done it, you've always criticised everyone I like.'

'Like that man Dyke, I suppose? I was just getting at you, was

I, when I told you you hadn't the faintest idea who could be trusted?' Glaring at her, with lightning and thunder to punctuate the sentence, he demanded: 'Well, when are you going to announce your next engagement?'

'What, to – to Toby Dyke?' Astonishment, for one instant, wiped the anger from Joanna's face.

But as Dan turned away, red-faced, towards the empty grate, picking up a match-box and beginning to break it to pieces, she turned abruptly on her heel. As she left the room she heard a movement behind her as if Dan were following. First she hastened, then she hesitated. But Dan did not appear.

Joanna went on quickly down the stairs.

Once more that evening Joanna saw the black Cadillac.

It was just after she had left the bus by which she had returned from Asslington to the bungalow. She had descended out of the bus into the storm and had gone a dozen yards down the track that led through the building-estate. Soaked already, with her clothes clinging to her and her hair flattened to her head, she was almost blinded by the sting of the rain. She heard a car coming, but until it sent up a wave of grey-white mud that washed over her shoes she did not raise her head to look at it.

Then she saw the long, black car and Dr. Vanedden crouched over the wheel.

Peering through the streaming windscreen, he was forcing the car forward as fast as it could travel over the ruts and slime. There was something strange in his attitude, something tense and desperate. As the car lurched on to the high road he opened the throttle. The Cadillac raced away into the obscuring rain.

When Joanna, in shoes squelching mud, reached the bungalow, she found the door standing open.

Inside all was quiet. There seemed to be nobody about. On the tiles in the hall a pattern of damp footmarks crisscrossed from door to door. They were such small, neat footmarks that only the feet of Dr. Vanedden could have made them.

First they led into the kitchen, then into every single room in the bungalow. The door of each room stood slightly ajar. It gave the whole place a strange air of forsakenness.

Like the footmarks, Joanna went first to the kitchen, looking for

133

Mrs. Searle. But there was no Mrs. Searle. A note on the kitchen table explained her absence. The note informed Joanna that Mrs. Searle did not like the atmosphere of crime in which she found herself, and had departed with apologies to stay with her sister in Asslington.

It was almost dusk in the kitchen. Twilight had come an hour ahead of its time, the daylight smothered by the darkness of the storm. Only the flashes of lightning showed up how the small, neat feet had come a few steps into the kitchen, then gone out again and into the sitting-room, out of the sitting-room and into the bedroom that had been Joanna's father's.

Joanna followed the track of them, her own shoes making damp prints alongside the others.

Swiftly, with the tightness of alarm about her lips, she went from empty room to empty room.

It could have been only her own shrinking nerves that imposed on each room a sense of unnatural stillness. Nothing was out of place, nothing was unfamiliar. When the lightning flashed, sharply coloured glimpses of the books on their shelves, of the flowers in their vases, leapt at her out of the dusk. Yet, entering one room after the other, she was as tautly poised as if from behind each door she expected some horror to spring out at her.

But the horror that waited for her was not of the kind that lurks behind doors or jibbers in dark corners. It was a quiet, sleeping horror.

Quiet and sleeping, in a room with drawn curtains and air that reeked of eau de cologne, lay Peggie Winnpole. She lay on the bed, on top of the crumpled counterpane. Her crumpled cotton dress was tossed over a chair, her shoes had been dropped on the floor. She was wearing her kimono over a limp, lock-knit petticoat. With one arm crooked under her head and the other hanging down so that the hand just brushed the floor, she was lying rigidly still. She was very pale. She was so pale and still she might have been dead.

But it was not death, it was sleep.

Yet when Joanna, suddenly trembling violently, sprang to her side and started shaking her, Peggie's eyes did not open. Even cold water dashed in her face did not make them open. Her name, shouted in her ear, did not make her eyelids quiver.

134

Joanna stood away from her, staring at this inert, impenetrable sleep with horrified, frightened eyes.

Then she began to notice things.

First there were the footmarks. They went from the door to the bed. From the bed they started towards the dressing-table. But the carpet, unlike the tiles of the hall, had rapidly absorbed the damp from the soles. Before they reached the dressing-table they had faded out, and there was no sign of the route by which Dr. Vanedden had left the bungalow.

Then there was the glass that stood on the bedside table. Peggie's spectacles lay beside it, also a damp handkerchief. There was a little liquid at the bottom of the glass, and in the liquid some scraps of a white, powdery substance. There was a spoon in the glass.

When Joanna saw the glass, the deposit of white powder and the spoon, she wasted no more time in attempting to waken Peggie. She ran to the sitting-room. She picked up the telephone. She had the word 'police-station' quivering on her tongue.

But there was something wrong with the telephone. Not a click, not a buzz, sounded in the instrument she held against her ear. No operator addressed her.

Slowly Joanna put the telephone down. She was suddenly cold and shivering inside her drenched clothes.

Though the storm had passed its peak when for the second time that evening Joanna plunged out of doors into the crashing rain, the thunder was still rattling like giant's dice round the dark cup of the sea.

It was difficult to run on the slithery road. Cutting between two empty bungalows, Joanna tried running on the squelching turf instead. It was a little easier than on the road, yet twice she fell before she reached Gerald Hyland's cottage.

That he was not in she knew before she got there. If he had been in there would have been a light in one of the windows. Bursting in through his back door, squelching through the scullery into the sitting-room, she snatched up his telephone. Ghostly in the dusk, the huge horn of his gramophone reared over her head. The shadows, oddly shaped, oddly overlapping in the small, packed room, crowded up to her.

As, panting, she gasped, 'Police-station' into the telephone, one of the shadows stepped forward and stood at her side.

She gave a sharp cry.

But the shadow only said: 'I'm frightfully sorry. I didn't realise you hadn't seen me.' Out of a swarthy face with a beak of a nose, dark eyes gleamed down at her.

She said: 'You – you startled me. What are you doing here?' But then she turned to the telephone again, and into the ear of a constable in Asslington poured the story of what she had seen. She demanded a doctor, an ambulance, and Inspector Tingey.

Toby Dyke moved away from her side. A match spurted in the dusk as he lit a cigarette. A second shadow stirred in the room. It was George, coming through the door that led straight on to the steep cottage staircase. The plump little man had a completely soundless way of moving, as if he were light as a bubble.

Something passed from him to Toby. It showed white for an instant between their two hands, then disappeared into one of Toby's pockets.

Joanna jammed the telephone back on its stand. 'Where's Gerald? What are you two doing here?'

Toby replied: 'Let's be getting along to the bungalow. If I've understood your message to Tingey correctly, that woman oughtn't to be left alone, even if there's nothing much we can do for her.'

'I had to leave her, I had to get at a telephone.'

'What's wrong with your own?'

'I don't know. Perhaps the storm's done something.' She stooped and looked at a knee she had grazed in falling. 'Where's Gerald?'

'I don't know,' said Toby.

'Does he know you're here?'

'I hope not.'

'Then what are you doing here?'

He took hold of her by the arm. 'We ought to get back to the bungalow as soon as we can. It oughtn't to be left a moment longer than necessary with no one to keep an eye on things. You can tell me all the things you didn't tell to that policeman when we get there, and I'll tell you what George and I have been doing here. But we oughtn't to waste time.'

'All right,' she agreed.

'Are you up to another dash through the rain?'

She nodded.

'Come on then, let's get going.'

Peggie's condition when, a few minutes later, the three of them came into her bedroom, appeared to Joanna just the same as when she had left her. Leaving Toby staring grim-faced at the sleeping woman, Joanna went to her own room to change out of her wet clothes. When she came out again, dressed in a skirt and jumper, she found him in the hall, looking at the criss-crossing of the footmarks. There were unusual lines about his mouth.

He said to her: 'I'm not a doctor. I don't know much about medicine. But I've seen a few people die. I think they'll have to do some remarkable things at the hospital to pull that woman round.'

'I wish they'd hurry up and get here,' she said, shivering.

'Joanna,' he said, 'I want you to talk, and talk quickly. They won't be long getting here. Tell me, have you any idea what poison she could have got hold of?'

'Yes, I think I know.'

'What was it?'

'What were you doing in Gerald's cottage?'

'Come on, come on,' he said, 'let's not waste time. Let's get as much of this straightened out as we can before the whole place is filled up with policemen and doctors and ambulance men. What d'you think it is she's taken? What's the white stuff in the glass?'

'Tell me first, what were you doing in Gerald's cottage?'

He frowned with impatience. 'Checking an alibi, if you've got to know.'

'Whose?'

'Hyland's, of course. I've been saying that he didn't leave the cottage before we did that morning. But that doesn't mean we were with him the whole time. He was up long before we were, cooking breakfast and so on. And part of the time all we knew of his being about was that he kept putting records on the gramophone. Well, I wanted a look at that gramophone; I wanted to see if it had a mechanism for changing the records by itself.'

'It hasn't.'

'I know it hasn't. But I couldn't know that until I'd taken a look at it, could I?'

'You could if you'd asked me.'

'I'm afraid' – his voice had an unpleasant edge to it – 'I mightn't be particularly inclined to believe anything you told me about that man if you thought the truth might endanger him.'

'What was your friend George doing upstairs? I saw him hand you something – something white – when he came down.'

'He was looking for a handkerchief I'd left under the pillow!' He was fuming. 'Joanna, did you come to me yesterday asking me to help you or didn't you?'

She said stubbornly: 'It wasn't a handkerchief he handed to you when he came downstairs. It looked like a piece of paper.'

'Joanna, the police will be here at any moment. Are you going to tell me what you know about that poison?'

'But I don't see what need there is for you to know any sooner than the police – and I know you aren't being honest with me about what you were doing in Gerald's cottage.'

'My dear girl, I want to do some thinking. Thinking! And I've got to think quick, because I know some things that the police don't know, and I've got to make up my mind before they come just how much of what I know I'm going to tell them.'

'Why don't you tell them the truth?'

He gave her a steady look, and something like a smile twitched at his lips. 'Because,' he said, 'you came to me and asked me to help you. I'm trying to help you.'

There was a silence.

Suddenly, on his noiseless feet, George appeared between them.

'There's nothing wrong with the telephone, Tobe,' he said. 'You pick it up and wait, and then after a bit the operator sings out: "Half a mo' – just let me finish my chapter," all same as usual.'

Joanna's face blanched. 'But it was dead – absolutely dead when I tried it!'

All at once there were cars, splashings, footsteps, voices outside.

Toby said: 'Hell, the police!'

Joanna said: 'Thank God, the doctor!'

138

The doctor was helpless. A few minutes after his arrival Peggie's breathing ceased.

Joanna, with Toby and George, waited in the sitting-room while policemen came and went, while orders were given, while Tingey did some thinking.

They sat silent.

The dead woman had meant nothing to Toby or George, while Joanna had felt for her a contemptuous, uneasy dislike in which resentment at the knack Peggie had had of drawing to the surface all that was least generous, least gracious in Joanna's nature had had its part. But death is a silencing fact.

The rain went on. The dusk became darkness.

Though Toby several times seemed about to say something, it was Joanna who actually spoke first.

'The telephone *was* out of order.'

'I believe you.'

She searched his face. 'Are you sure that you do?'

'Oh, yes. The question is, will Tingey?'

'Why shouldn't he?'

'Because he entertains certain very grave doubts about you.' At the look of surprise on her face, he added in exasperation: 'Oh, God, I wish you'd got your wits about you!'

She bit her lip.

He went on: 'I don't want to talk about it now the police are here. We might be overheard. Before they came it'd have been a good idea to go into it all – now it's a rotten one.'

She said no more. Presently Tingey came in. Joanna had to tell him everything from the beginning.

She told him, not only of her glimpse of Dr. Vanedden driving past her in the rain, but of how she had seen him come out of the boarding-house in Spencer Street and of Dan Moon's theory about the reason for that visit.

But Tingey said: 'We won't go into Mr. Moon's ideas at this stage, Miss Prees. Just tell me what actually happened.'

So she picked up the thread again at the point where the Cadillac had driven by, splashing her with mud.

'I came straight up to the bungalow,' she said. 'I'm not sure why, I expected something to be wrong. I think it was Dr. Vanedden himself who made me feel like that; he looked terrified – as

139

if he were running away from something. By the way, there wasn't any sign of that man who'd been following him.'

'Never mind about him,' said Tingey. 'Go on.'

'Oh, then did you know about him? It was someone to do with the police?'

He only waited for her to go on with the story.

She continued: 'I found the door open, and I saw all those footmarks. I followed them. I was careful not to let my own get mixed up with them. They went into the kitchen first – it looked as if he'd gone as far as the table and read Mrs. Searle's note and then gone out again – and then they came in here.'

'I saw the note,' said Tingey.

'Well, I didn't see anything wrong until I came to Miss Winn-pole's bedroom. Then I – I found her. At first I thought she was just asleep, and I tried to wake her. But I couldn't. It wasn't possible. I got frightened. I—' She made a short break in the staccato senten-ces. 'I knew there was something very much the matter. Then I saw the glass with the spoon in it and the fragments of white powder. And then I knew what she'd done. She'd taken an overdose of some sleeping-tablets. . . . I warned her about them this morning when I found a whole lot of them missing. I—' Again she stopped herself to take careful command of her voice. 'I'm afraid I'm telling this very incoherently – I'd better go back some way. You see, my father had some sleeping-tablets prescribed for him by Dr. Jones. I'm not certain of just what was in them, but I know they were something to do with barbitone. I know that's dangerous. I heard Dr. Jones telling my father that he mustn't ever take more than two at a time. Well, the night before last my father asked me to give him a couple. I did, and then something made me slip them into my pocket. I was afraid, I suppose, that father might try again to kill himself. Later I put the box on the mantelpiece in my room. And then last night I couldn't sleep and I took a couple of them myself. But I found the box was almost empty. The night before there must have been thirty or forty tablets in the box, but last night there were only seven. I worried about it a good deal. In the morning I asked Peggie if it was she who'd taken them. She said yes, she'd taken two. I was sure she'd taken more, so I told her about their being dangerous and that she mustn't ever take more than two, and she went on insisting that she hadn't –

140

but she did it in that awfully emphatic way that always makes one sure a person isn't telling the truth. I felt certain she'd got the rest of them somewhere. Then I forgot all about it until I saw the powder in the glass this evening. You see, Peggie was one of those people who can't swallow tablets; she always broke them up. She'd used the spoon for that, I suppose.'

'Now please be very careful, Miss Prees,' said Tingey. His tone was remote and severe. 'You mentioned that spoon before. You maintain, as I understand it, that when you first entered Miss Winnpole's room this evening, there was a spoon in the glass on the bedside-table?'

'Yes,' said Joanna.

'Then what did you do with that spoon, Miss Prees?'

'Do with it?'

'I'm asking you, what did you do with the spoon?'

She was puzzled. 'I left it there, of course, I didn't touch anything.'

'Then why isn't it there now?'

Bewildered lines on her forehead deepened.

Toby put in quietly: 'There was no spoon in the glass when I got here.'

'But there must have been. I . . . Oh, I don't know. I don't believe I ever looked at the glass after we got back from the cottage. I really don't remember if the spoon was there then or not. But I know it was there when I first found Peggie. I sort of noted that that was what she'd used to smash up the tablets. I *know* there was a spoon there.'

Tingey's face said nothing. 'Well,' he said, 'what did you do next?'

She told him of her attempt to telephone and then of her dash to the cottage. But she paused expectantly for his objection, and when it came – 'But there's nothing wrong with the telephone now; I used it to ring the police-station as soon as I got here' – she merely looked at him silently.

Tingey made some notes.

She put a question to him: 'Would you mind telling me, did Miss Winnpole see you to-day, or try to see you?'

'Not to my knowledge,' he replied. 'Were you expecting her to do so?'

141

'She told me this morning she was going to,' said Joanna. 'She told me she was going to tell you all the things she wouldn't tell me. You see, I think she knew quite a lot. I believe she knew the reason why my father tried to commit suicide, and the reason why he was murdered.'

'Not very safe things to know – perhaps,' said Tingey.

'And there's something I think I ought to tell you,' said Joanna. 'I was in Mr. Hyland's cottage this morning, telling him about it, when suddenly we realised that Dr. Vanedden was just outside the window. I'm not sure if he heard what we said, but I think he might have done. And I couldn't help thinking – you know how those footmarks of his started from Peggie's bed towards her dressing-table. . . . Well, was he starting a search in case she'd left a letter to you, telling you all she knew? And if there wasn't one, did he think she must have already posted it, and was that why he was looking so terrified as he was driving away?'

'You're jumping to a great many conclusions, Miss Prees.' Tingey was a sterner-faced man to-day.

Toby murmured: 'So Hyland as well as Vanedden knew of Miss Winnpole's intention to spill it all. . . . By the way, Tingey, going to tell us now what you know about Vanedden? Matter of fact, I think I've got there on my own. Drug-distributor – isn't that the trouble?'

A constable came in. He said: 'Weedon's out here, sir. What shall we do with him?'

Tingey rose to his feet. 'I'll come.' He turned to Toby. 'Always been quick at smelling things out, haven't you, Mr. Dyke – you and McClusky here? But we've no evidence against him. Don't you forget that. It's true there were two or three cases, women – heroin the stuff was. The women were all patients of Dr. Vanedden's, but none of them ever said a thing to give him away. We never traced any transactions or source of supply. But we've kept an eye on him ever since.' His dour gaze shifted to Joanna. 'I reckon your father could have saved us a lot of trouble if he'd been so minded, Miss Prees. I don't know how he got on to it in the first place, but it looks as if he were another of the people who have queer, individualistic ideas of what they've a right to do with their knowledge. Well, he paid for it. But,' – and now his gaze swept the three of them – 'as you all seem to be giving this problem a lot of thought, there's something I may as well tell you. Dr. Vanedden didn't murder Edgar Prees or Peggie Winnpole. At the time when Edgar Prees was killed Vanedden was having an early morning dip, and then spent an hour or more tinkering with a little motor-boat he's got; there are several men from the bathing-tents and whelk-stalls who can swear to that. And at the time when Miss Winnpole must have swallowed those ground-up tablets – assuming for the moment that the autopsy will bear out your theory, Miss Prees – we had a man of our own keeping an eye on him. Vanedden got away from him because our man had a puncture, but until about three-quarters of an hour before the time when we received Miss Prees' telephone message from the cottage our man can give an exact account of what Vanedden was doing. And Miss Winnpole took more than three-quarters of an hour to die. So whatever other ideas you may have about Vanedden, you can knock him off your list of possible murderers.'

Toby leant forward. 'Are you certain Peggie Winnpole was murdered?'

'Always asking for certainties, aren't you, Mr. Dyke? At your age you ought to know better.' Tingey had gone to the door. It was with an unfamiliar grimness that he added over his shoulder: 'Suppose you and Miss Prees have a try at working it out together.'

Joanna's chair scraped against one of the bookshelves as she pushed it back and rose.

'He doesn't believe me about the spoon and the telephone,' she said.

Toby Dyke shrugged his shoulders. 'Anyway, he's feeling uncommonly serious. It's one of the first times I've heard him talk without bringing in Irene Dawn.'

'I think I can do some of that working out he suggested,' she went on. 'Someone must have got into the bungalow while I was at the cottage and removed the spoon and also removed whatever it was that was stopping the telephone working. I expect there was a wad of paper or something I didn't notice jammed in so that the receiver-rest didn't move. I think I know too why the telephone had been fixed like that. It wasn't to stop me getting through; I dare say I wasn't even expected. It was to stop Peggie getting through. She might have had time to realise, before she really went under with the poison, that there was something the matter with her, and have tried to get hold of a doctor. And I think I know also why the spoon had to be moved. Peggie was poisoned by taking too many of those tablets – but she didn't necessarily mean to take too many; she may have thought she was only taking two or three. Someone else had broken them up for her; smashed up in water, she wouldn't have known how many she was taking. But the wrong person's fingerprints would have been on the spoon. I dare say the glass itself could have been wiped clean and then Peggie's hand put round it, but it would have been very difficult to do the same with the spoon; people don't hold spoons simply with two fingers, they keep shifting the fingers about; there'd be a smudging and overlapping it'd be very difficult to fake. So the spoon had to be removed.'

Toby said: 'You've got it all very pat, haven't you?'

'I've the advantage,' she replied, 'of knowing it's true that the spoon was there and that the telephone wouldn't work.'

'As a matter of fact,' he said, 'I believe you.'

'I wonder why.'

'For the simple reason that Dr. Vanedden's footsteps went first into the kitchen. Didn't it seem to you odd that they should do that? Think – he arrives at the bungalow, he knocks, nobody answers, he goes in, and then he goes straight to the kitchen. Why?'

'Did he hear something?'

'I think so. There was someone in the kitchen. But whoever it was went out on hearing Vanedden. When Vanedden saw your housekeeper's note on the table he concluded it was she whom he'd just heard leave.'

'And how do you know it wasn't?'

'Listen, those footsteps were still damp when we got here, weren't they? They hadn't been there long? Very well, if Mrs. Searle had left just as Dr. Vanedden arrived, you'd have met her, wouldn't you, walking along to the bus? But the person he heard in that kitchen never left the bungalow; he waited outside the back door. As soon as you left he came inside again, put the telephone right, removed the spoon and cleared out.'

144

'Why didn't he leave footmarks all over the place?'

'Probably left his wet shoes on the mat.'

'And where did he go to?'

'We'll be able to start deducing that when certain people hand in their alibis.'

Joanna was stooping over a bowl of flowers. They were wilting; they had been there for some days and no one had thought of giving them fresh water.

'We're explaining it all very nicely between us, aren't we?' she said. As she touched a fading rose several crimson petals dropped on to the table. 'Now suppose we go back a bit. Why does Tingey entertain grave doubts about me?'

He reached out for her arm and drew her towards him. He spoke in her ear. 'I've told you, this isn't the place to have a showdown. If you'd kept up with it all you'd be the last person who'd want me to talk about it where it might be overheard by policemen – at least, I think you would be. I wonder . . . I wonder how love, affection and all that, and your sense of justice balance up in you. I wonder what you'd do, for instance, if you knew that—' His voice dropped lower still. 'I wonder what you'd do if you knew that a friend of yours had committed a crime?'

But she did not have to answer.

The door opened.

White-faced, shaking, with hands groping ahead of him and with small steps which he was so careful to keep in a straight line that he might have been drunk, Gordon Weedon came into the room.

8

Gordon took hold of the back of a chair. He sat down heavily. He still had on his dripping mackintosh, and his hair in the rain had sprung into little tight curls.

He turned his white face to Joanna. There had been tears in the eyes.

'She's dead, Joanna!'

Joanna answered something.

'She's dead!' he cried. 'I don't understand it, I don't know what's happened, they won't tell me anything except that it's some sleeping-tablets that did it. Did she kill herself or did somebody do it to her? I don't understand. I never thought she'd kill herself. I knew she felt she hadn't anything to live for once your father was dead, but I didn't realise it meant all that. Of course I knew I could never make it up to her. I knew she cared for him in a way she'd never care for me. I didn't mind that. After all, what am I? I'm nothing. I never shall be. I'll never amount to anything. I'm one of those people no one ever takes any notice of. I'm dull and uncertain of myself and don't bother about creating a good impression. Peggie never really loved me, and now she's dead, and I don't understand it!'

Toby tapped Joanna on the shoulder. He had filled a glass with whisky from the decanter on the table. He put it into her hand. She held it out to Gordon.

Gordon coughed over the whisky and hit himself on the chest, then drew a deep breath and sat staring straight before him. His lips moved as if a torrent of words were still pouring through them.

All at once he jerked his head round to look sharply at Joanna. 'Do you understand what's happened?'

'No, Gordon, I don't.'

'Did she kill herself?'

'We – we don't know.' She took the glass away from him.

'That's what they said out there. They said they didn't know. I didn't believe them. Police never tell you anything you want to know. It's their way of exercising power over you. You have to tell them everything, everything – but when you ask them a question they say they don't know. It isn't fair – when you're suffering – when you've had such a shock that you don't know what you're doing or saying. Well, I'm not going to answer any more questions at all. They can ask me anything they like, I shan't answer. I don't care what it makes them think. It doesn't matter to me what anyone thinks. I've lost everything that mattered to me, and if they take away the rest I don't care.'

'Gordon, what are you talking about? For heaven's sake don't behave like this.' She glanced at the decanter of whisky, as if pondering the wisdom of giving him some more.

He said in a low voice: 'I'm sorry. I know I've gone to pieces. But that's the kind of person I am. I can't help it, I just go to pieces. You know, she broke off our engagement this morning; after all this time . . . She was very sweet and kind about it, and I thought perhaps it'd come right, but now it can't. We can't ever talk it over. . . . Joanna, was she murdered?'

Toby replied for Joanna. 'Miss Prees has told you, we don't know.' He put firmness and authority into his tone, and it seemed to have a steadying effect on Gordon. 'The possibility has to be considered. If you'll think clearly for a moment you'll realise that Miss Winnpole was the person who had the most intimate knowledge of Mr. Prees' affairs. With that knowledge she may very well have been a menace to somebody. On the other hand that knowledge itself may have been too much for her to face.'

'Oh, God,' muttered Gordon, 'it was all that old devil's fault. I wish I'd let him go over the cliff the other night, then perhaps this wouldn't have happened. He always made use of her, got everything he could out of her. She did twice as much work for him as he'd any right to expect. I always thought that was why she kept having those frightful headaches. And then he goes and chucks her out!'

'I suppose,' said Joanna curiously, 'you don't know precisely *why* he sacked her?'

'Oh, yes, I know that.'

She kept her excitement out of her voice. 'Why did he?'

'What d'you think? What would it be? It was because she tried to save him some trouble, of course. That's just the sort of thing he'd sack her for, isn't it? As a matter of fact, if she'd asked me about it beforehand I could have told her she was being a fool. I knew he wouldn't stand it. But I don't suppose she'd have believed me.'

'But what was it she'd done?'

'Oh' – he seemed impatient with the subject – 'she just dealt with some post for him while he was away with that bad throat last week. She opened a letter or something.'

'But, good heavens, that was something he hated – always. She must have known that. He couldn't stand anyone interfering with his post, or tidying things up for him, or touching anything that belonged to him. Really, she must have known it. I wonder whatever made her do it.'

'I told you, if she'd asked me about it I'd have told her not to. But all the same, that he'd go and sack her straight off like that – well, I could hardly believe it when she came and told me about it.'

'Reckon it's true all the same.'

This comment, coming from George, who was sitting on the edge of a chair in an attitude of diffidence and discomfort, made Toby and Joanna look round at him in some surprise. But Gordon only stared at the carpet.

'Fact is,' George went on, 'when I was chattin' with Mr. Barnes this afternoon he told me he'd heard a bit of what went on between Mr. Prees and Miss Winnpole the day she was sacked. Seems the fanlight over his door was open. Matter of fact, it was noticin' the way Mr. Hyland's voice carried through the fanlight made me think of askin' Mr. Barnes if maybe he'd heard anythin'. And he had, but not much. But he says Mr. Prees was goin' for her for havin' opened somethin' or other. And then – well, then, he said, Mr. Prees and Mr. Weedon had a go at one another.'

Gordon laughed hollowly. 'Oh, yes, I made up my mind on the

spot I wasn't going to stand it. I told her to leave it to me. I told her to leave it to me. I told her I'd damn well see he changed his mind about it, or else—'

Joanna interrupted: 'Oh, was that why she said what she did when you brought father in from the cliffs?'

'I don't know,' he answered. 'What did she say?'

'She said: "Oh, my God, Gordon, what have you done?" '

'Did she? I don't remember. Yes' – he laughed again – 'I suppose she was afraid I'd been putting that or-else into practice. Of course, there wasn't anything I could do really. I could point out to him what a rotten, inhuman thing he'd done, but that was all. I say, Joanna . . .' He looked at her dully. 'I don't mean to speak like this about your father. I – I'm sorry.'

'Go on,' she said shortly.

'But I've nothing particular to say. I say, thanks awfully for that whisky; it does seem to have done me good. I was making an awful exhibition of myself when I came in here, wasn't I? I'm sorry.'

Toby Dyke had strolled forward. 'What happened when you pointed out to Mr. Prees what a "rotten, inhuman thing he'd done"? Did you make no impression?'

Gordon puckered his brows, 'What's this – another interrogation?'

'Not if you don't want it to be.'

'I've had enough questioning. Out there just now, before I'd had time to recover from the blow or anything – it wasn't fair. I'm not going to answer any more questions. Not that I mind your knowing – I don't mean that. You were asking did I make any impression on him? Of course I didn't. I don't suppose I should have at the best of times, and that night he was definitely queer. I sort of realised it and started worrying. Really worrying, you know, in spite of what I've just been saying about him. I was – well, I did admire him, respect him – and that evening he seemed so definitely queer. So when I saw him start to walk home of all things, I decided to follow him. I—' He finished vaguely: 'I did follow . . .'

Toby, with a harsh lack of sympathy in his gaze, was glowering at the dainty cupids that supported the clock on the mantelpiece.

149

He said to them: 'But I don't understand it – I simply don't understand where the death of Peggie Winnpole fits in. Unless . . . Unless it's repeating the same pattern, strengthening it, darkening the main lines . . .'

'What are you mumbling about?' asked Joanna.

Toby turned round. 'Weedon, who rang you up yesterday about a quarter past seven?'

Gordon replied fretfully: 'I told you, I don't think people ought to keep on asking me questions just at the moment. I told you, I don't think it's fair. I don't mean I mind answering. But I don't think it shows much understanding. I mean, I can't really think clearly.'

'Has the quality of your memory been impaired?'

'I – I don't know.' Gordon's hands fumbled up and down the arms of his chair. 'I don't suppose so. But I know I wouldn't put much faith in my own judgment at the moment. Some people can keep their heads clear through anything; I wish I was like them, but I can't help it if I'm not.'

'If your memory hasn't been impaired, can't you remember who rang you up yesterday at about a quarter past seven?'

'Anyway,' said Gordon, on a weak note of protest, 'why do *you* keep on asking me questions? I don't know what it's got to do with you.'

'If Miss Prees put the same question to you, would you feel better about it? Would her desire to get as rapidly as possible at the truth about the death of her father and of Miss Winnpole seem less unsettling than mine?'

Joanna leant forward. 'Gordon, who was it rang you up yesterday morning?'

He looked at her in silence. Then, with a slight sigh, he surrendered to the steadiness of her gaze. 'But I went into all that with the Inspector, Joanna. It was Peggie who rang up.'

'The exchange says no call came through from the bungalow.'

'Oh, good heavens, you know what they're like on this exchange.'

She agreed dubiously. 'Yes – pretty bad. But all the same . . .'

'Anyway' – his pale cheeks had flushed – 'it *was* Peg speaking!'

Toby took up the questioning again: 'Weedon – your landlady says that you shouted into the telephone: "For God's sake, don't do that!" – or words to that effect. D'you feel like giving us any explanation of that?'

Gordon gulped. 'No,' he said, 'Why should I?'

'Only that you'll leave us with the impression that you may have been saying that to whoever murdered Edgar Prees.'

Gordon's eyes bulged slightly.

'And the fact is,' said Toby, 'even if you were discouraging the idea of murder, even if you said "don't do that" to someone who'd just said to you: "I'm about to bump off the curator," your keeping quiet about who it was makes you an accessory.'

'But I tell you, it was Peg who rang me up, and I said "don't do that" because she'd just told me she'd made up her mind to pack her things and leave for London straight away. She said she couldn't bear staying now that Mr. Prees was angry with her. Then I got into some clothes and went dashing out because I wanted to make sure of stopping her. But somehow . . . well, once I got outside I started thinking it mightn't be such a bad idea if she did go away. And, my God, how I wish she had! I changed my mind and didn't go out to the bungalow; I went for a long walk instead.'

Toby said sternly: 'The call was from the herbarium; there was no call from the bungalow that morning.'

'Aren't I telling you you're all wrong? Why are you certain I'm a liar?'

'Because you're such a rotten one – you won't face it when the facts are too strong for you.' With a mutter of impatience Toby flung himself down in a chair.

After a short silence Joanna said: 'Gordon, don't mind if I ask just one more question.'

He gave a soft, bitter laugh.

'Just one,' she said. 'When you got to the Haybox yesterday morning and went into my father's room, did you notice a letter in a blank envelope on the desk?'

'No,' he said shortly.

'You didn't – you're quite sure?'

'I didn't.'

She looked dismayed.

Toby said: 'It's all right, for once he's speaking the truth. I know all about that letter. When Weedon came into the room there was no letter on the desk – that's correct. But that doesn't mean there can't have been one there earlier. As a matter of fact' – he lowered his voice – 'there had been one. I take back my doubts about your friend Hyland's vision. It was a perfectly good one. Only he didn't communicate the whole of it to Tingey. He kept back something rather important.'

'Well?' she asked sharply.

'Well, Joanna, what he kept back was that when he saw that letter there he happened to pocket it.'

For a moment there was only disbelief on her face.

Then she spoke stiffly: 'I suppose you've got reasons for saying that.'

He put a hand into his pocket. 'Take a look at this.' As they came round him he drew out of his pocket a white envelope. It had been torn open. Holding it carefully by the very edge, he slid out of it a piece of paper. He unfolded the paper.

It was a single sheet of note-paper. It had a few lines written on it. There was no date, it was not addressed to anyone in particular. Starting off abruptly about half an inch from the top of the page, in a small, precise handwriting, the words ran:

> *My death is my own doing. I believe in my right to commit this act. I ask nobody's pardon. As I have explained, I have lived for others and not found my sacrifices appreciated. If my life was for their satisfaction, my death is for my own. Let there be no undue demonstrations at my funeral. Speaking as one whose interest in flowers has always been scientific, I should prefer an absence of floral tributes. Death is welcome. – Edgar Press.*

'Is this your father's handwriting, Joanna?' Toby held the letter out towards her.

She made a show of reading it once more. Low-voiced, she replied: 'I think so.'

'That's something that'll have to be checked.'

'Where did you find it?'

'George found it when he was upstairs in the cottage. It was in the breast-pocket of the flannel jacket Hyland was wearing that morning when he went into Asslington. I thought it'd be there. He's been wearing a dark suit since your father died, but I thought he was much too untidy-minded to have changed over the contents of all the pockets.'

'But look here,' Gordon broke in excitedly as Toby started refolding the letter, 'why haven't you handed this over to the police? This'll change everything for them.'

'I'm going to hand it over to them – only I'm going to do some thinking first.'

'But I'm sure it's illegal to hang on to it!' cried Gordon.

'I'm afraid it is.'

'It's suppressing evidence!'

'Well, don't make such a noise about it. I tell you, I've got to do some thinking about it.' Suddenly his fingers, busy returning the letter to its unaddressed envelope, moved swiftly; the paper crackled as he thrust it back into a pocket.

The door opened and Tingey came in.

Tingey said: 'I imagine, Miss Prees, you won't be too keen to spend the night here alone.'

She replied: 'I hadn't thought about it.' Reluctantly withdrawing her gaze from the pocket into which Toby had crammed the letter, she turned to face Tingey.

He seemed anxious for her to leave. He said: 'I know I shouldn't like a daughter of my own to stay here alone.'

'Ah, but what about your granddaughter?' cried Toby, giving him a clap on the shoulder. 'Myself, I'd trust a child with a face like Irene Dawn's to look after herself in any circumstances.'

'You aren't serious, Mr. Dyke,' Tingey replied stolidly.

'Well, I expect I could sleep at the cottage,' said Joanna. 'That might be the best thing to do.'

'Mr. Hyland's, you mean? I sent over to fetch him,' said Tingey, 'but he hadn't come home.'

'He'll be home later.'

Tingey looked uneasy. 'You don't happen to know where he is?'

'I haven't seen him since this afternoon,' she answered. 'But I know I can sleep there all right.'

Obviously relieved at her decision, which left him in charge of the bungalow, he went out again.

Joanna went to her bedroom. She collected a few things for the night. She put on a raincoat and changed her shoes. With her

153

belongings in a small, leather case, she reappeared in the sitting-room, and accompanied by Gordon, as well as by Toby and George, set off for the cottage.

They blundered their way through the darkness. Hyland had not yet returned. Switching on the light in the sitting-room and dumping her case, she said: 'I think I'll make some coffee. He won't mind.' She left them in the sitting-room. Plugging in the electric kettle in the kitchen, she hunted out cups and saucers, and sugar and milk from the disorderly cupboards. She put five cups on the tray. But by the time the coffee was made there was still no Hyland.

They drank the coffee and passed up their cups for more. Cigarette-smoke drifted on the air, but only an occasional word was spoken. Toby's face had the hardness that goes with concentration, George looked as if he were having difficulty in keeping his eyes open, Gordon's white face was ravaged with emotional exhaustion.

Still Hyland did not come.

It was Joanna who returned to the subject of the letter. 'All the same, why didn't you give it to Tingey?'

Toby heaved himself off the cramped little settee where he had been sitting. He said: 'Earlier this evening I asked you a question. You didn't answer it.'

'What question was that?'

'I asked you what you would do if you knew that a friend of yours had committed a crime.'

'Was that what you meant then – Gerald's removing that letter?'

He shook his head. 'That was only a part of it.'

Her coffee-cup rocked slightly as she set it sharply down. 'Oh, heavens, I wish he'd come.' Then she asked, prodding at some grounds in the cup: 'What's the rest of it?'

'You haven't answered my question yet.'

'What would I do if a friend of mine had committed a crime?'

'That's right.'

'A friend – someone I trusted?'

'Exactly.'

'I think I'd wait and ask him why he'd done it – and what was behind it.'

154

'That's what I thought you'd say.'

'Well?'

'Hyland doesn't happen to be a friend of mine,' said Toby, 'but he's certainly a friend of yours. And if you remember, when you came to me yesterday evening wanting me to help you, I agreed to do so, or at any rate implied that I would. So your friends, for the moment, shall stand as mine – that letter can stay in my pocket until Hyland gets here.'

But even when the coffee left in the jug had grown cold, when George had dropped into a doze, and the cigarette-stubs in the ash-tray had grown into a pile, there was still no Hyland.

Toby had become restless.

'I don't know that we ought to leave you here if he isn't going to turn up,' he said. 'Why not come back into Asslington with us and take a room somewhere?'

'Oh, he'll turn up sometime.'

'What d'you think he's doing?'

'Putting a trunk-call through to the Dalai Lama to ask his opinion on the love-life of boa constrictors . . . Really, it might be absolutely anything. One never worries about Gerald.'

'But I don't like the idea of leaving you here alone.'

'I never mind being alone.'

'I think you ought to come back to Asslington.'

Gordon said wearily: 'There's an empty room at our place. Mrs. Brandon'd put you up.'

'That's a very good idea,' said Toby.

'Oh, don't bother about me,' she said, 'I tell you, I don't mind being alone. Besides' – her face was troubled – 'I don't much want to go to Spencer Street. I'd a sort of row with Dan this afternoon; I'm not keen on seeing him.'

Toby took no notice of her objections. 'Come on, let's get going. Hi, George, suppose you wake up and collect the car from up the road. Miss Prees is coming back to Asslington.'

Yawning and blear-eyed, George staggered to his feet.

'Right y'are, Tobe. Only why couldn't you think of it a bit sooner, eh? Reckon if only your brain'd work a bit quicker sometimes the pubs wouldn't so often be closed.'

Mrs. Brandon was able to fit Joanna in in a room on the top floor.

She brought in a jug of hot water, put clean towels on the rails, told Joanna that breakfast was at eight punctually, and wished her good night.

A few minutes later there was a tap on the door.

'I say,' said Gordon, 'you haven't had anything to eat, have you? It's no good trying to get anything out of Mrs. Brandon at this hour, but I've got a tin of soup and some biscuits and things in my room. And I can make some tea, or some more coffee if you'd like. I've just told Dan you're here, and – about Peg. He's in my room now, heating up the soup. He said I wasn't to ask you to come down without telling you he was there, in case you're angry with him still, or something. I wish you'd come. It's – easier somehow if I don't have to sit alone and think about it.'

'All right,' she said, 'I'll come. And thanks for the soup; it's a good idea.'

She followed him.

It was a dreary little supper. Joanna and Dan were not at ease with one another, and though Gordon had asked for company he met the attempts at talk made by the other two with unresponsive silence. His protuberant ears had a hot, nervous redness; in his eyes there was an over-alive intensity of thought. He kept chewing his fingernails. Dan and Joanna sat with him for about an hour, then Joanna, whose head was drooping with weariness, said good night and rose to go.

After a moment Dan followed her.

She was halfway up the stairs to the top landing, when he looked up at her over the banisters.

'You know, Jo, I've been thinking. Wasn't it pretty stupid of us to flare up like that this afternoon?' he said hesitantly. 'We ought to be getting past that sort of thing.'

She yawned. 'Ought we?'

'Well, oughtn't we?'

'Oh, I don't know. It comes in handy sometimes, having someone to let it loose on – temper, and so on, you know.' Another yawn muffled the words.

'I don't agree. I think it's time we learnt to treat each other rationally.'

'What's the point of learning something new like that when you're just off to Peru?'

156

'I'm not off to Peru.'

'You're—' Suddenly her eyes looked as if all the sleep had been shaken out of them. 'You're not going to Peru? But – why not?'

'I always thought it a rotten idea.'

'Why, has someone else mapped all the vegetation already? Or d'you think you won't like the food? Or are they going to have a revolution or something?'

'Listen, Jo—'

But Joanna, with a stiffening of her muscles, hissed at him sharply: 'Sh!'

'You see, I've—'

'Sh! Listen – there's someone in your room.' She came a step down the staircase.

Dan's movement was so quick, so noiseless, that whoever was in his room could have had no warning. The door was suddenly flung open, and Dan charged into the darkness inside. The beam of an electric torch met him in the eyes. It dazzled him for a moment, then it vanished. Light feet padded softly on the linoleum.

As Dan made a rush after the sound of them, Joanna, at the door, pressed down the light-switch. But nothing happened; Dan had long ago arranged things so that the light was worked by the switch at his bedside. He himself had not wasted time groping for it. In the darkness, dodging furniture with the certainty of old acquaintance, he chased the intruder.

Bed-springs sang and groaned as someone leapt on to the bed. There was a thud as feet came down again on the other side of it. Then someone pushed past Joanna and went racing down the stairs. As she spun quickly to catch a glimpse of him, she saw a short, plump form that moved as lightly as a bubble, a pink, grinning face turned back for a moment over a blue-clad shoulder, an eye that winked. With the slickness of a fish diving into a crack in a rock, George swooped down the stairs and out of sight into darkness.

Dan, giving it up, switched on the light by the bed. 'Did you see who it was?'

Gordon had come out on to the landing. 'I heard a noise – whatever's happening?'

Doors up and down the staircase were opening.

157

The voice of the schoolmistress on the second floor was demanding shrilly: 'Is it a fire?'

Mrs. Brandon was crying from the depths: 'What is it? What is it?'

The curate who was in Asslington for his health was calling: 'Please nobody get excited. Leave it to me – I'll deal with it.'

Joanna whispered: 'It was that queer little man, George.'

'He's been searching my room.' Dan was looking round at the open drawers with socks, shirts and ties hanging out of them, at the books jerked off the bookshelves on to the floor, at the pictures taken down from the walls, at the soot in the fireplace – for even the chimney, it seemed, had had its swift examination.

The voices up and down the staircase were still clamouring. Dan went out on to the landing.

'It's all right, Mrs. Brandon, it's just a visitor of mine remembered he had a train to catch and had to leave in a hurry.'

Peevish comments accompanied the closing of doors. Joanna and Gordon came into Dan's room and looked at the disorder.

'But what was he looking for?' Gordon sounded shaken and nervous. 'I don't like it.'

Dan picked up an odd sock from the middle of the floor. 'D'you think I do?'

'He's got no right to do a thing like that. I should tell the police about it.'

'I'm darn well going to.'

'Haven't you any idea what he was looking for?'

'Look!' Joanna was picking up books and putting them back on their shelves. She straightened up, holding out a piece of paper. 'I think he must have left this on the dressing-table, and it fluttered down to the floor. It tells you what he was looking for.'

Dan grabbed the piece of paper.

In a large, clear but uneducated handwriting, the words were written upon it:

Sorry to make your room in such a mess, mate, but I had to look if you had the pods here.

Without comment Dan handed it on to Gordon.

Gordon shook his head over it and handed it back to Joanna. 'D'you think he's – he's perfectly normal?' he asked. 'It doesn't make any sense at all, does it? It sounds like the act of a lunatic to me. I wonder – d'you think that's why that man Dyke always keeps such a close eye on him? Is he – well, I don't want to make unpleasant suggestions about anybody, but d'you think perhaps he isn't quite all there?'

Dan, tumbling shirts and ties back into a drawer, muttered: 'Well, he'd better look out for himself when I catch him.'

As soon as Gordon had gone, Dan slammed a drawer shut and crossed to Joanna's side.

'Jo, you've got some idea about all this, I can see it on your face.'

She inserted a book on statistical methods next to the latest Agatha Christie.

'Not really an idea, Dan.' She sat back on her heels. 'George keeps coming back to those pods, that's all. This afternoon he asked Barnes if a parcel of them had arrived recently. It seems one arrived last week, and now isn't to be found. And also...' Frowning, she searched her own thoughts. 'I'm just remembering something. D'you remember yesterday evening in that restaurant when you were telling Toby Dyke about why you were so mad with my father? You were telling us about the pods, and how they were always so mutilated when father gave them to you that you could never tell much about them. You used the phrase that it looked as if he'd let mice get at them. Well, ever since then, George doesn't appear to have been interested in anything but mice. He even went to the trouble of asking Barnes whether or not there are mice in the Haybox – or so he says. I think what he meant was that he was thinking about the pods and why they were mutilated.'

'But why should he be thinking about the pods?'

'I don't know.' She stood up and stretched tired limbs. 'I told you it wasn't really an idea. But there's another thing I'm just remembering. Last night he suddenly asked me if father'd ever been in Egypt. Those plants you've been working on come from Egypt, don't they?'

'But what if they do?'

'Oh, I don't know – heavens, I hope I'll get some decent sleep to-night, but I don't feel awfully like it. I feel all on edge. Dan, have those pods any possible connection with heroin?'

159

'None whatever.'

'You couldn't make it from them in some way?'

'Heroin's a derivative of morphine, which is the active principle of opium. You're exceedingly ignorant, Joanna.'

'But the pods themselves, have they nothing at all to do with opium?'

'Definitely nothing. And I told you they aren't really pods at all, they're sort of gourds. The plant they grow on sprawls along the ground, something like – well, something like a vegetable marrow.'

She was still pursuing her thought. 'Could heroin have been packed up in the tin they came in?'

'It always goes through the Customs.'

She sighed. 'Oh, dear, it doesn't seem to make sense, does it?'

'I don't know, perhaps it does. At least, perhaps it makes sense of George's actions, if not of the thing as a whole. After all, he might be just as ignorant as you, and be making a guess that heroin was derived from *Citrullus colocynthus*, or he may not have realised about the tin going through the Customs. But why did he leave a note to tell me what he was looking for? That seems to me rather queer. You know, I've an idea that this show to-night was just a stunt for putting the wind up me somehow.'

'There's one other thing that's occurred to me. . . .' She had got to her feet and had crossed to the mirror. Her sentence was broken off by her surprise at the pallor and tiredness of the face she saw there.

'Well, go on,' said Dan.

'You see,' she said, 'according to Gordon, Peggie was sacked because she opened some post of my father's. Well, that's something I don't comprehend at all. She knew what he was like – she knew it much better than any of us. I know she knew how he blew up if anyone touched or interfered with anything of his. Honestly, I can't see her opening a letter addressed to him. But suppose it wasn't a letter. Suppose it was simply a parcel of plants from Egypt – plants she knew you needed. She'd think of it as addressed to the Haybox in general, not particularly to father. And if father happened to be away ill—'

'You're perfectly right! There was a parcel, and I actually suggested to her she might open it. But that's the last I heard of it.

I forgot all about it because I suddenly got the letter from that Russian, and it put everything else out of my mind. I went up to London to check the thing up at the B.M. . . . But still, it doesn't help, you know.'

'Anyway, where's that parcel got to now, Dan?'

'I haven't an idea.'

'And if you had, I don't suppose it'd get us anywhere.' Discontentedly she stuck a cigarette in her mouth. 'Well, good night, Dan. If I don't go up to my room soon, Mrs. Brandon will think you're keeping bad company – I've a horrid feeling, though, I'm just going to lie awake and go on thinking. I wish I could stop it, and do some constructive thinking on my own future instead. That's as perplexing a problem as any. You know, I'm beginning to realise that people like Peggie have got something on people like me. It's a great pity it didn't occur to me two or three years ago to work hard and get myself properly trained for something. I'm tired of messing about.' She grimaced and the cigarette went into the fireplace. 'I've been smoking too many of these things the last couple of days – my mouth's like sandpaper. Good night,' she said again.

'Jo . . .' Sitting on the edge of his bed, his elbows on his knees, squeezing his mouth up between two sets of knuckles, Dan was studying the pattern on the rug between his feet. 'There's something you might tell me.'

'My brain feels as if it had been minced for cooking,' she replied. 'I don't think I can do any more thinking about pods, dope or murder.'

'It's about that man, Dyke. Was I just making an awful fool of myself this afternoon, throwing him up at you, or – wasn't I?'

She gave a little gasp of laughter.

He waited, then said: 'You haven't said I was, so I suppose I wasn't.'

'Oh, that doesn't follow at all.' Light and unreal, her voice had a sudden tremor in it. Her hand groped for the door-handle, groped blindly, could not find it. 'Whatever I thought, I wouldn't call you a fool to your face.'

'You're always doing it,' he pointed out. 'And I don't know . . . perhaps I am one. Look at the mess I made over those pods – don't suppose I'll ever live that down. All the same, I keep

161

thinking we ought to manage to be reasonable with one another. . . . I'm a pretty reasonable person. The trouble is, I've always been scared out of my wits about what you thought of me. I wish I could get straight about it. It's queer, I don't usually worry much about what people are thinking of me; that's why I get on with them all right, I suppose. . . .'

'Dan!' She had found the door-handle by now. Holding on to it hard, she spoke with a quick rush of words: 'I – I think I'm going to start being reasonable now. I'm going to tell you just what I think of you. If that isn't any use to you, you can – you can keep out of my way for the next few days, and after that I expect I'll be going away somewhere, so it won't matter. The fact is – Dan, I'm in love with you! I – nearly always have been, I didn't really want my advertising artist or my divinity student, I wanted you, but you wouldn't seem to realise I'd got anything but conversation, and – Dan! . . . Dan! . . . Dan, will you please let me finish?'

She never did finish.

Muffled, interrupted, she managed to add a detail or two to her explanation. For instance, about the function of the scientist. . . .

But Dan was not very interested in the details.

9

It was another misty morning.

It was more damply, densely misty than those that had gone before. The tide of a silent, enshrouded sea edged slowly over the shingle. In the small island of visibility that each person carried along with him, everything was coated in dull silver.

Objects were so closely hidden that when, at the distance of six feet or so, they suddenly revealed themselves, it was sometimes with an odd effect of shock. Certainly it was a shock when the grey nothingness suddenly solidified into the form of Inspector Tingey. Peering, listening, he was standing at the gate of Hyland's cottage.

He said: 'Ah, good morning, Miss Prees, I thought it might be you.'

There was something disturbing about the way he said it.

But there are certain conditions in which the mind functions slowly. Joanna was in such a condition this morning. She had slept little, she was very tired, yet a drowsy, glowing calm pervaded her. She was not disturbed by the Inspector's tone. When she put her hand on the gate, it slid wetly under her fingers. Brightly she said: 'Good morning.'

Standing aside to let her through the gate, Tingey told her: 'If it's Mr. Hyland you're looking for, he hasn't come in yet.'

She stopped in the gateway. 'D'you mean not since last night – or just that he went out for something this morning and hasn't come back?'

'Not since last night, I'm afraid. His bed hasn't been slept in.'

She went up the path. There was someone in the cottage; she heard a movement as she pushed open the door. But it was only Toby Dyke.

As soon as he saw her he replied to the question on her face: 'No, he isn't here.'

She looked round the cramped, untidy room.

'Of course, he often does this kind of thing,' she said. 'With Gerald it's nothing to worry about.'

'That's right,' said Tingey, 'I'm sure it's nothing to worry about.'

'Oh, no, it's nothing to worry about,' said Toby Dyke.

'It *isn't* anything to worry about.' She perched on the arm of a chair. 'Where's your little friend George? Did you know Dan had a visit from him last night?'

'Did he? No, I didn't know.' Toby sounded irritable.

'Where is he?'

'I don't know,' he snapped at her.

'What, is he missing too?'

'Looks like it. . . . Oh, there's never any need to worry about *him*. He always turns up again, even if he's done twelve months in the interval. Where are Moon and Weedon?'

A shade of trouble crossed her face. 'I – I don't know. They'd both gone by the time I got up. I expect they've gone back to work at the Haybox.' She did not sound quite satisfied with her answer. She had not been satisfied with it when she had first offered it in answer to her own disappointment at not finding Dan waiting for her when she came down to breakfast.

'So everyone's missing,' said Toby.

'I can tell you who's missing,' said Tingey, reconnoitring the gramophone, some records and a mess of fishing-tackle. 'I reckon it won't be for long though – we're bound to catch up with him. Vanedden.'

'Vanedden! I thought you were keeping an eye on him,' said Toby, 'or didn't your man manage to pick him up again yesterday afternoon?'

'He picked him up all right. Vanedden simply went home and stayed there. It was an hour or so ago he gave us the slip. He went for a dip in the sea as he always does, swam out into the fog – and never came back.'

Joanna exclaimed: 'You don't mean he's drowned!'

'No, Miss Prees, that's just what I don't mean. Because his motor-boat is missing too. He must have made up his mind

164

about it last night and got it planned in advance. Of course he was relying on a fog coming up, but anyone who was used to the weather here could have counted on that. He simply swam out until he couldn't be seen, then had someone pick him up with the motor-boat.'

'Then he had someone to help him,' said Toby.

'That's right.'

'An accomplice who helped him with the murders?' asked Joanna.

He looked at her curiously. 'Oh – you like that idea, do you, Miss Prees.'

'Like it? No, I . . . What d'you mean? Of course I don't like it.'

'Hmmph,' said Tingey. He sat down. He was not in the best of tempers this morning.

Toby straddled a chair facing him. He asked in a bored tone: 'How's Miss Winnpole's murder coming along?' It sounded as if he were dutifully making conversation.

'Who said it was a murder?'

Toby's eyebrows went up. 'Well, well,' he said, 'wasn't it?'

'I asked, who said it was a murder?'

'Plenty of people feel inclined to say it.'

'Just so. And if we accept the testimony of Miss Prees about the spoon and the glass, then it probably was one.'

Toby's quick glance at Joanna surprised an expression of dreaming contentment on her face. She seemed to feel its inappropriateness for it vanished the moment she realised he was looking at her.

'Are you sticking to your story of the spoon and the telephone?' he asked her.

'Of course.'

'Well' – he turned back to Tingey – 'why don't you believe her?'

Tingey shook his head. 'No, Mr. Dyke, there are some things I don't want to discuss with you. At the inquest the evidence will all be brought forward in the proper way. I don't want to be unfair to anyone. If I went on you'd only turn on me and say I was trying to trick Miss Prees into damaging admissions. And, mind you, I've never said I didn't believe her about the spoon and the telephone. Maybe there *was* a spoon in the glass, maybe

165

the telephone *was* out of order. I'm not saying, I'm not even hinting that she wasn't telling the truth. But . . .' And he sighed. 'I'm afraid it'll be very difficult to convince a jury of it.'

Toby seemed nervous. He was biting the inside of one cheek. He seemed annoyed that Joanna's attention had strayed again into absent-minded serenity.

'I don't know what you're working up to, Tingey,' he said, 'but you're making some unholy mistake.'

'Well, I wish I were,' said Tingey, 'but there you are – that's life. The times when one wants one's own estimate of the probabilities to come out right, it's the other fellow who's got the right horse.'

'You haven't got the right horse this time, Tingey. I could show you that if only you'd talk.'

'No, Mr. Dyke, I tell you it wouldn't be fair. If you like I'll ask Miss Prees just one question – and mind you, Miss Prees' – he eyed her gravely – 'you've no need to answer this question if you don't want to. But it's something I'm curious about. It'd be interesting to know just what was in your thoughts when you did it.' He leant a cheek on one hand. A tinge of wistfulness had got into his gravity. He said very gently: 'Why did you throw the key out of the window?'

'You see,' said Tingey to Toby after a long silence, 'we have Miss Prees' account of her actions that morning. She took her father to the herbarium, she left him there. Now she was gravely troubled about him. His condition undoubtedly suggested that suicide might still be in his mind. Well, she drove away, she left the car at the car park, she walked along the sea-front. She walked back again, she had a cup of coffee, she sat on a bench. We've checked all that; it's all just as she said; there were plenty of people who noticed her. Next she says she went back to the herbarium. She says she pushed and knocked at the door, but couldn't get in. She says she went back to the bench and sat on it a bit longer. Now . . .'

Tingey had picked up a paper-knife from Hyland's table. He scraped one of his cheeks with its blunt edge.

'Now,' he said, 'it's a funny thing, we've not been able to find anyone who saw that. Nobody saw her banging on that door and

166

then coming away again. Of course I know that doesn't necessarily mean it didn't happen precisely as she says; it doesn't necessarily mean she found the door ajar and slipped inside. Yet that's what might have happened, isn't it? She might have found that the door wasn't really closed although from a little way off it looked as if it was; she might have seen that the street was empty with no one to notice if she did just pop inside. She might have gone up to her father's room and found him. . . .' Tingey paused.

'Go on, Tingey,' said Toby grimly.

'Found him writing a letter,' said Tingey, 'declaring his intention of committing suicide, or perhaps holding a revolver at his own head. She might've . . .'

'Go on, go on.'

'She might've tried to get the revolver away from him, mightn't she? There might have been a struggle. She might have got her hands on it, knocked the trigger . . .'

'What a twisty rat you are, Tingey. Why don't you say what's really in your mind?'

'But I'm saying it, Mr. Dyke.'

'You aren't. You're making out a nice case for manslaughter; you'll go on that she then realised her own fingerprints were on the revolver and that she might find herself in the very worst kind of trouble; that she then wiped off the fingerprints and pressed her father's on instead. Yes, that's the way your case for manslaughter goes – but it isn't what's in your mind.'

'I really don't see what call you've got to say that, Mr. Dyke – and I don't see what call you've got to call me a rat.'

Toby's open hand came down with a smack on the table. 'Because what's in your mind all the time is that she went up there and shot her father in cold blood. Murdered him. That's what you're going to try and show at the inquest. You know that if she believed her father was really determined on suicide, then she'd a motive for murder.'

'Aren't you going a bit fast?' said Tingey. 'I never asked—'

'You asked what made her throw that key out of the window. You believe, I suppose, that she took the key off her father's chain and threw it out of the window, and then came and told me an unlikely story about a theory of Dr. Vanedden's according to which that key was very probably to be found in the flower-bed; that she then persuaded me to go to you and tell you just where to look for it—'

'Mr. Dyke, Mr. Dyke,' pleaded Tingey, 'you're going too fast! It's true that's the way I reasoned that bit out, but—'

Toby's palm again slammed the table. 'You're wrong from start to finish. But if you believe it was Miss Prees who threw the key out of the window, then you believe she killed her father on purpose. The fingerprints on the revolver might have been part of a clumsy attempt to make an accidental shooting look like suicide, but the key in the flower-bed could only have meant that she wanted this death recognised as murder. And you know that killing her father would have been no use to her unless his death was recognised as murder. Manslaughter! – I tell you, you are a dishonest rat, Tingey. You believe she went up there, shot her father, then deliberately pressed his fingers on to the revolver *in the wrong places*, and threw the key out of the window – all to make sure that she inherited the ten thousand pounds life-insurance which would never come to her if her father's death turned out to be his own doing!'

'Stop!'

It was Joanna.

They turned to her with slightly dazed expressions, as if she had suddenly materialised there in the room with them, instead of having been there all the time.

Tingey scraped the blunt paper-knife up and down his cheek; he might have been desperately attempting to make up for an inadequate shave that morning.

'Oh, dear,' he said, 'oh, dear, I never meant to bring all this up at the moment.'

Joanna had bright patches on her cheeks. She was on her feet.

'I don't know which of you is wrong or why, or – or what either of you really think. But it all seems to me to make nonsense. I think the best thing'll be if – if I simply tell you what really happened.'

'The best thing'll be,' said Toby, 'if you keep your mouth shut.'

'I don't think so.' She was breathing fast. 'I think the only thing is to tell the truth. I – I'm sorry, Inspector, I didn't tell it before. I've been wishing I had. I'd have felt better if—'

'Miss Prees' – he checked her – 'I really think Mr. Dyke may be right that it'd be best for you to tell me nothing whatever. I've told you, I don't want to take an unfair advantage. At the least, think very carefully indeed before you decide to say anything.'

'I *have* been thinking,' she said.

Toby Dyke was biting fiercely on a knuckle.

She said: 'I've thought a lot, and I'm sure the only thing to do is to tell you just what I actually did that morning. Well, when I went back to the herbarium that morning, the door, as you suggested, wasn't quite closed. I didn't look round to see if the street was empty, because of course it seemed to me a perfectly natural thing to do to go in. I've been in and out of the Haybox ever since I was a child. I – I did go in. I – went upstairs.' She was speaking slowly, as if thoughtfully selecting each word in its turn. 'I found my father. He was dead. There was a letter there, saying he'd killed himself. Of course I realised that meant I shouldn't inherit the ten thousand pounds I'd – been expecting. Well, I haven't any other money, and I didn't see quite how I was going to set about earning it, and so – you see, I did polish the revolver, and I did deliberately press my father's fingertips on to it in the wrong places, and I threw the key out of the window, and I pocketed the letter. . . . In fact, I faked his suicide to look like a murder faked to look like suicide. But . . . well, there was something I didn't reckon on. I sort of forgot, I suppose, that where there's a murder there's always a hunt for a murderer. I forgot about the suspicions, the fear and everything. I didn't – I don't want anyone to suffer for what I did. Even if I don't get the ten thousand pounds . . .'

Tingey smiled faintly. 'You certainly won't get that, Miss Prees.'

Consternation and incredulity were making Toby's face oddly naïve. 'Well, I'm blowed . . .'

Tingey laid down the paper-knife. He was still smiling. 'I'm very glad you've told me all this,' he said. 'It's about the way I'd reckoned it out for myself. And it may be possible, for a certain reason, not to take a too serious view of your action. But there's

169

still something I don't understand, something that doesn't fit in with what you've just told me. You said you forgot that where there's a murder there's always a hunt for the murderer; you said you'd rather forego the money than let anyone suffer unjustly. Very well. But if that's so' – he leant towards her – 'why, at the time, did you try to put the blame on Gordon Weedon?'

'But I didn't.' Yet her eyes, at that moment, lost their candour. They evaded his; they looked down.

'Ah, but you did – and only the evening before, Weedon had saved your father's life at considerable risk of his own.' Tingey looked harder now, less ready to listen sympathetically to explanations. 'You prepared evidence, didn't you, while you were up there in the herbarium, to show that Weedon had been up there that morning? Perhaps you knew that he had been up there; I think it's quite likely that when you were approaching the place you saw Weedon suddenly come out and go walking off up the street.' Taking no notice of her quick shake of the head, he went on: 'As I understand things, your father telephoned Weedon and told him he was going to kill himself; that was a kind of revenge on Weedon for having interfered the day before. Weedon said: "For God's sake, don't do that!" and raced round to try and stop him. But when he got there your father was already dead. Now perhaps you didn't see him come out; perhaps he merely struck you as the easiest person to put the blame on. That's the sort of thing that happens to people like Weedon – those weak, indeterminate folk, they always get blamed for everything. Pathetic, really, when you come to think of it, considering they're pretty often brave and unselfish.'

'But what did I do?' she broke in, suddenly angry. 'I didn't put any blame on anybody.'

'Miss Prees, are you going to deny that while you were up there in your father's room it occurred to you to go into Weedon's room and switch on that electric oven-affair with the little saucers of wax in it, that you waited until the wax was nicely melted, then switched the thing off again – that you then went away, and when you came back and I was questioning you in that room, you deliberately pressed a finger into the wax to demonstrate to me that the wax was still softish, in other words that the oven had been on not long ago, and that therefore somebody – since the room was Weedon's, most probably Wee-don – had been in there that morning?'

Sucking in a slow breath through parted lips, Joanna stared at the Inspector.

'This has gone off the rails,' muttered Toby. But he waited for what she had to say.

She said it abruptly: 'No – that's something I won't stand – being blamed for something as thoroughly mean as that. I – I never even thought of Gordon while I was up there. I don't mind admitting that I tried to defraud an insurance company; lots of people would do that if they got a chance. But certainly I didn't go plotting to get someone I know quite well hanged for a murder.'

'Then tell me why,' said Tingey, 'did you press your finger into the wax? You looked as if you knew it would be soft, but how could you know it would be soft if you didn't know the oven had been on?'

'Ye-es, I did sort of know it'd been on. . . . Perhaps – why, of course!' Her face brightened. 'Of course that was it. The smell of Xylol! You see, when you want to make sections of plants, you embed them in wax. But if you simply melt it you don't get the material properly impregnated. So you dissolve the wax in Xylol and then it's all right. Well, Xylol's got an awfully strong smell while it's hot – don't you remember the smell in the room that morning? – and it hangs about, gradually getting fainter, for a few hours afterwards. Well, I don't know anything much about botany, but I do know that when there's that smell of Xylol then somebody's been melting wax, and you can poke your fingers in it and mess it about. I used to love doing that when I was a child; I used to make my father furious.'

'Hmmph,' said Tingey.

Toby's sudden laugh rang out. 'You know, I never knew you had it in you, Joanna. You've been giving me surprise after surprise this morning. I don't know whether this stuff about Xylol's true or not, but it's mighty ingenious. And so's the rest of it. I almost believe you've got the Inspector to swallow it.'

Tingey was shaving his cheek with the paper-knife again. 'Oh, Mr. Dyke,' he said gently, 'really, come now. . . .'

'You mean you don't believe me?' said Joanna quickly.

'No, Miss Prees, I don't.'

'You mean about the Xylol? – because you've only to ask Dan Moon or – or Gordon or any botanist.'

'No – not about the Xylol.'

'Then . . .' Her voice dropped. It grew stiff and strained. 'You *do* think I went up there and shot my father?'

The paper-knife scraped up and down his cheek.

Toby rapped out a couple of curses.

'This can't go on,' he said. 'We've got to clear it all up. It's true, Tingey, Miss Prees has spun you a fantastic string of lies, but she'd a simple and quite characteristic reason for doing it. All the same, I'm not going to have you sitting there brooding on how she murdered her father. She didn't murder her father. What's more, nobody murdered her father. Edgar Prees wasn't murdered. And Peggie Winnpole wasn't murdered. Nobody's been murdered. And I can prove it to you.'

As Joanna, realising what he was about to do, sprang towards him with a protest, he drew out the letter that George had found in the pocket of Gerald Hyland's jacket.

He laid it down before Tingey.

'The place to begin, of course,' said Toby, 'is the attempted suicide. That was an important part of the pattern, the key to the whole thing. Edgar Prees wanted to kill himself. He couldn't face life any longer – he wanted to die.'

He had sat back comfortably; his long legs were woven between a pile of gramophone catalogues, a table-leg, a wireless set and a typewriter.

'You remember, when Gordon Weedon saved his life that evening on the edge of the cliff, Prees called it "devil's work." Those were the actual words he used for it – 'devil's work.' We can make a good guess, knowing what we do now, at what had brought him to such a state of mind. At some time or other he'd got himself involved in Vanedden's drug-traffic. I don't know how, nor just what part he was playing in it. It'll be much easier for you, Tingey, than for me, to find out all the details of that. It seems to me most probable that having somehow got to know of what Vanedden was up to, he was using his knowledge to extract large sums of money from him. If you can't quite see how

172

the highly respectable curator of the herbarium attached to the famous Asslington Botanical Gardens ever came to embark on such a course, I think I can explain it to you. A friendless, arrogant man with a deep conviction of his own rectitude, it provided him with two things he had lacked all his life – excitement and power. Excitement and power that he could enjoy while he went on sitting in his armchair at home. He scarcely had to lift a finger to promote the scheme; it just functioned for him. At first, I imagine, he experienced nothing but sheer enjoyment from it. He had knowledge that other people hadn't – not only of Vanedden but of himself. He knew what a sham he was, and it must have given him a good deal of amusement. But unfortunately for him, he wasn't a man who was totally free from a conscience. From the time that the money started coming in he had to convince himself that it wasn't for himself he was wringing it out of Vanedden, while letting Vanedden go on with his dirty trade. It was all for his daughter. Everything he did was so that she could have money, luxury, and a fine start in life. He was selling his immortal soul for his daughter – that's how he managed to persuade himself he felt about it. He was committing a selfless crime, taking the guilt on himself but conferring the benefits derived from it on another. I'm certain he succeeded in feeling a hell of a suffering martyr because of it.'

Joanna stirred. But leaving no time for her to speak, he went straight on: 'The necessity, however, for that make-believe, the fact that he couldn't just sit back and take the funny business for granted, shows that there was a dangerous split in his nature. Vanedden could dish it all out to you in fancy terms, I expect. But the fact was, the old man's conscience kept gaining on him and upsetting him. When that happened, what he wanted was reassurance from his daughter. She had to show him that it was worth it. Hence his hysterical demands for gratitude; hence the wild exaggeration of his disappointment in her when, at the advanced age of twenty-two or three, she hadn't yet achieved great things. She was turning all his endeavours to barrenness and waste – he began to come near hating her.'

'You know,' Joanna's low voice put in, 'I believe that's right; I believe that is what had happened to him.'

173

'As we know,' said Toby, 'he'd been working up, during the last few months, to a complete breakdown. The conflict was too much for him; he cracked. But suicide wasn't only the natural climax to his own despair; it was a subtle act of vengeance on his daughter. I can remember very clearly that evening, after we'd brought him home, how he looked at her and said in his cold, deliberate voice: "I owe nothing to anyone." With those words he was stating his own rejection of all her claims upon him; he was casting her off. An important part, to him, of his suicide, was that it would leave her penniless.'

Tingey nodded and murmured agreement.

'Now,' said Toby, 'if you think of what happened on the morning when he died, if you think of his actions before he disappeared into the herbarium, aren't they obviously the actions of a man whose mind is still bent on suicide? Personally I never had any doubt that whatever might actually have happened inside the herbarium, his intention in going there was to get hold of his revolver and kill himself, this time in a place where no one could interfere with him. And yet someone, so the evidence seemed to say, did interfere with him. Murder interfered with him. It was an almost incredible irony – and most people found it incredible. You remember how everyone has kept trying to produce explanations so that the evidence of the wrongly-placed fingerprints and the key in the flower-bed could be ignored, and a verdict of suicide, which seemed so much more natural in the circumstances than a verdict of murder, could be returned.

'I've just said "everyone" kept trying to produce explanations. . . . That isn't quite correct. One person was stubbornly averse to any suggestion of suicide. That person also, I realised, wouldn't have been at all pleased if Edgar Prees had succeeded in dying by his own hand. I knew that person couldn't have been the murderer; while Edgar Prees was being shot, he was cooking liver and bacon for my breakfast. But Hyland did have a few minutes alone with the dead body of Prees. . . .'

He smiled suddenly at Joanna. 'You must have thought all this out yourself since I last saw you,' he said, 'or you wouldn't have had your own explanation ready.'

'Yes,' she said, 'I thought it out last night. I got thinking about what it really meant, finding that letter in Gerald's pocket.'

174

'Exactly. You see, Tingey' – Toby looked back at the Inspector – 'I don't know if you happen to have noticed it, but Joanna Prees means more than anything in the world to Gerald Hyland. He'd do almost anything for her. I say almost – I don't believe he'd actually go the length of committing a murder for her. But certainly he'd no hesitation about faking a suicide to look like murder, so that she could inherit her ten thousand pounds. And he did have those few minutes by himself with the dead body of Prees. Barnes was telephoning for the police, Weedon hadn't come in yet. Hyland hadn't much time; he must have done his thinking pretty quickly, and acted quickly too. He'd the revolver to wipe clean and then to mark again with the fingerprints in the wrong places, and the key. . . . I don't think he really knew what he was up to with the key. Perhaps he began by thinking he might simply remove it, and then, thought perhaps that might be dangerous; anyway, throwing it out of the window added to the general confusion. And then there was the letter. As a matter of fact, until Barnes started talking about the letter, my ideas about Hyland were very conjectural. I knew it was possible for him to have performed these actions, I knew he was the kind of person who was capable of having done them, I knew that he was acting queerly, that his friendliness towards George and me had turned to nervy suspicion, that he was excitable, and that he seemed to find the idea of murder much less upsetting than the idea of suicide. But with the letter I got to something concrete. You see, suppose there had been a letter, then it must have been Hyland who removed it. And what would Hyland have done with such a letter? Would he have destroyed it? I thought not. He showed no signs of being a vicious man, but only a some-what over-individualistic and ill-balanced one. He would not, I thought, want someone else actually to be convicted for a mur-der that had never happened. I decided he would have kept the letter – and being obviously a man of uncommonly untidy and unmethodical habits, he would have kept it, I thought, in the same place where he first happened to put it. On this reasoning I searched for the letter in the pockets of the grey flannel suit that he'd been wearing that morning in the herbarium. Well, that's where I found it. You've got it there in front of you, Tingey – and you've got the answer to this case.'

'Hmmph – and what about Miss Winnpole then?'

Toby began to look bored. 'Just a repetition of the same pattern.'

'Suicide faked as murder – but why? And d'you mean it was Hyland who tampered with the telephone and removed the spoon from the glass?'

'I think,' said Toby, 'it was Peggie Winnpole herself who tampered with the telephone, at least in the first place. She knew when she took those tablets that she wouldn't die at once, and that if anyone found her they'd telephone at once for a doctor. So she jammed something into the telephone so that the receiver-rest got stuck and so that if anyone tried to ring up they wouldn't get through. After all, suicide in her case, just as in Prees' case, fits the probabilities very much better than murder. She was a neurotic, suicidal type anyhow, and she'd just suffered some blows that would have unsettled a much more stable person. I believe she'd somehow learnt, not only what Prees had been doing, but of Vanedden's activities too. The two human beings she'd looked up to most and relied on most had suddenly been revealed to her as criminals. But if it was she who jammed the telephone, it was Hyland, I think, who removed the obstruction. I think he was in the bungalow at the time when Vanedden arrived. Probably he'd only just got there – his gumboots, I expect, were on the back doorstep; that's why he left no wet footmarks. When he heard Vanedden's car drive up he went out by the back door again to avoid a meeting. After he'd heard Miss Prees go running off to his cottage he came in once more, examined the telephone to see why it hadn't worked when Miss Prees tried to use it, found the paper or whatever it was, removed it, removed the spoon from the glass—'

'But why?' The question broke from Joanna like a protest.

'That's right, why?' said Tingey.

'I told you – the pattern, the same pattern. He thought it'd strengthen it, make it clearer. Instead, of course, it only caricatured it. That's where people of Hyland's type always go wrong. They haven't any sense of proportion in anything. Perhaps his abnormal height's a part of the trouble; he's out of proportion himself. But you see, he was afraid from the start that Vaned-

176

den's unlikely theory might be believed, and a second murder, he thought, would suggest that there really was a murderer roaming around—'

'Inspector!' Breaking in before Toby had had time to finish, Joanna spoke in anxious haste. 'Inspector, when I told you it was I who faked the fingerprints and all, you – you said there was a certain reason why you thought you needn't take a too serious view of my actions. Does the same reason hold now that you know it was Gerald, not me at all?'

Tingey blinked. 'You and Mr. Dyke, you go at things so fast,' he said. 'Perhaps it does. We'll see. It's true he did try to defraud the insurance company of ten thousand pounds. . . .'

'What is the reason?'

'Simply that there isn't any ten thousand pounds.'

She gave a slight gasp. Yet the expression that succeeded the surprise on her face looked like relief.

'But I don't understand,' she said quietly.

Tingey explained: 'Your father had been paying his premiums for two years. But for anything to be paid up on them he'd have had to pay them for three years.'

The door was burst open.

Out of the mist, dressed only in swimming-shorts, and dripping with water, came Dan Moon. There was blood at the corner of his mouth and blood on his arm in a curious gash that looked as if teeth might have torn it. There was a strange whiteness about his face, a look of dazzled horror. Holding on to the door frame, he tried to subdue his gasping for breath.

'We've got Vanedden!'

Tingey leapt to his feet.

'We've got him – but we couldn't stop him – we couldn't stop him killing Gordon. We saw it – oh, my God, we saw it – and we weren't in time!'

George had Dr. Vanedden's motor-boat.

He also had Dr. Vanedden.

He also had the tin containing the dried specimens of *Citrullus colocynthus*. He showed Inspector Tingey the locker in the motor-boat where he had found it.

He also showed Inspector Tingey what else was in the motor-

177

boat. Hunched in it, with bloodied, battered face and broken skull, was the body of Gordon Weedon.

Like Dan, Gordon had been wearing swimming-shorts; his skin was wet with sea-water. He looked as if a great, ruthless thumb had come down upon him and crushed the life out of him.

But it was the small, delicate, dirty hands of Dr. Vanedden that had done it. Using a jagged piece of rock, they had smashed down on to Gordon's head, smashed again and again, until Gordon had sunk beneath the water.

'And it was only then that I got there – got hold of him – Gordon, you know. If George hadn't come up in the motor-boat that devil'd have got away. . . .' Shivering, as if he were frozen to the bone, with his teeth chattering, Dan was pouring out to Joanna his story of what had happened that morning.

The fog steamed around them. They had not followed the others to the beach. He had stopped her at the head of the path when Tingey and Toby went racing down it. The edge of the cliff was there, a few feet ahead of them; of rough grass with its coating of dull silver, of slippery chalk there was no more, but only a soft grey sea of mist a hundred feet deep.

'His face, Joanna – I've never seen anything like it. I've never seen real evil before.' Dan's fingers felt like claws of steel digging into her arm.

She said: 'You'd better come back to the cottage, Dan, and get some clothes on.'

'All right,' he said. But he did not move. 'They'll be coming up here. They'll bring Vanedden. I'd like to see his face again to make sure it's human. That's – that's quite stupid of me, I know, but it's how I feel. You go back to the cottage, Joanna.'

'But what happened? Go on – go on and tell me.'

'You see, George turned up early this morning. He was in a tearing hurry. He said Vanedden had just gone in swimming and would I follow him? I asked why the hell, and he said there was such a thick fog, anything could happen in it. I asked him why the hell didn't he follow Vanedden himself if it seemed to him important – he went red in the face and said he couldn't swim. So I went. I went where he pointed, though I couldn't see

178

anything, and didn't see the point of it all, and couldn't hear anything. And then – I realised suddenly it came from that diving-raft sixty or seventy yards out – a scream, Joanna. God, it was horrible. I raced for it, and there was Gordon slipping off the raft into the sea, his face just a red jelly, and Vanedden hitting at him. . . .'

'Do come back to the cottage, Dan. You're freezing.'

'I couldn't do a thing for him, Jo – I tried, I did all I could.'

'Yes, of course you did. Oh, do come back to the cottage.'

'He was dead, you see, when I got him. And when I got near, Vanedden tried to do the same trick on me. Then the motor-boat came up, Vanedden's own motor-boat, with George in it, and he tackled Vanedden. He got him down on the raft all right, and strapped up his wrists and ankles, and shoved him into the motor-boat. Then we got Gordon in. I thought we'd go straight back to the shore, but George said there were a good many people about already, so we came up the coast a bit instead, and brought the boat in here. I got a shock when I saw you there in the cottage. I mean, thinking of your seeing what Gordon looks like. . . . But I'm glad you were there, Jo! It's good to have you to keep one's eyes on, instead of – that face.'

'But what was Gordon doing there on the raft? What was Vanedden doing?'

'Well, George told me a certain amount on the way here. It seems that late last night Gordon went downstairs and tele- phoned. George was still in the house. When he ran downstairs after searching my room he didn't go out; he just banged the front door and then hid somewhere. I suppose he meant to go on and hunt Gordon's room for the pods or something. Anyway, when Gordon came down to the telephone, George heard all he said. Gordon was ringing up Vanedden and making an appointment to meet him next day. George couldn't make out where, because it seemed to be Vanedden who fixed the spot, and Gordon just said it was a good idea, nobody'd see them there. You see, Vanedden must have known already this fog was coming up and told Gordon to meet him on the raft. . . . Then Gordon said, just before he rang off: "You've been caught up with, Vanedden – you're going to have to pay for what you've done." '

'But—'

'He'd realised, don't you see, that it was Vanedden and his beastly drugs that had really killed both your father and Peggie? Gordon meant to have some sort of reckoning – and that was why Vanedden murdered him. . . . By the way, the pods were in the motor-boat. We found them in the locker while we were bringing the boat round.'

'Yes – *but what have the pods got to do with it?*'

He pulled her closer to him. 'I've been awfully stupid about them, Jo. I've been working on those damn things for a year, and it never occurred to me. . . . After all, what *are* pods? Sort of containers, aren't they? – seed-containers. And these, well, I told you they were sort of gourds really: they're quite big things – as big as my fist almost. The heroin was inside the pods. It was sewn up in little bags, and then the pods were sealed up round them. That's why the pods had always been mutilated when your father handed them over to me. At the Customs they looked inside the tins, but not inside the pods. They were used to the tins coming through, and going to a respectable place like the herbarium—'

'Dan, look, they're coming!'

Up the cliff-path, through the mist, dark figures were advancing.

But there were only three figures. Down below on the beach, George was still keeping watch on the body of Gordon Weedon. It was Tingey and Toby who were coming up the path, with Vanedden between them.

Joanna had a glimpse of Vanedden. A glimpse to be remembered. His cold, grey eyes were as detached as ever, his skin was its usual smooth parchment-colour, the dark eyebrows were slightly raised. His concern with the situation appeared to be an entirely impersonal one.

But the glimpse was over in a moment. As, between Tingey and Toby, he reached the top of the path, he made a sudden, leaping movement.

Their hands lost him.

Over the edge of the cliffs went the small figure with the crest of silver hair, to drown in a soft grey sea of mist, a hundred feet deep.

There was something impersonal even about the cry that was torn from him as he fell.

Tingey had gone.

Toby and George had gone.

Through the lifting mist, singing in a hoarse, jubilant voice, came a tall, striding figure.

'Well, well,' said Gerald Hyland, coming into the cottage, 'congratulations!'

Joanna and Dan disentangled themselves.

Hyland's hands rested on their shoulders. His blue eyes beamed with affection.

'This is grand, you know, simply grand. I tell you what – I've just had a good idea – I'll give you a wedding-present. And I'll give it you straight away. I don't mean I won't give you another when it actually comes to the point, but I'll give you one now, to celebrate, so to speak.' He gestured: 'My gramophone – you can take it.'

'But, Gerald—'

'Oh, and the records, too. You'll find there's nothing so soothing and stabilising as good music. Not that it's really in my line, of course – matter of fact, it goes right over my head, it's no good pretending it doesn't. And besides, I haven't an inch to turn round in here. Besides, now that I've found something that really is in my line, something that's just what I needed to give my life some value, some fullness, I shan't have time for that sort of thing any more. You see, from now on I'm going to do some work for humanity – that's bound to take up a lot of time, isn't it? Incidentally, that's what I was doing last night. Of course you weren't worried, were you, at my not coming back? . . . No, I knew you wouldn't be. Actually I was sitting with a most remarkable group of people, meditating. That's the work I'm going to do for humanity – I'm going to sit and meditate and increase my consciousness. And when I've increased my consciousness enough I'm going to start to work on my self-consciousness. You see, when enough people have done that, the whole world becomes a better place – that's obvious, there's no need to argue about it. Wonderful, wasn't it, running into one of the people in the group? It was quite by chance; we met in a

181

pub and got talking. Then he took me along, and we all meditated away until late into the night. Then I went home with him and we talked till morning. . . . Anyway, for God's sake, take away that gramophone, and I hope you'll both be very, very happy.'

EPILOGUE

'You know, George,' said Toby Dyke, one day in his flat in London some months later, 'there's just one thing that sometimes worries me about that Asslington affair last summer.'

'Eh?' said George. He was lying on his back on a divan with a newspaper over his face. It was not long since he had eaten a large Sunday dinner.

'I said, there's one thing that sometimes worries me about that Asslington affair. What was it that poor chap Weedon was doing in the herbarium the morning Edgar Prees shot himself through the head? Weedon never admitted he'd been up there, but clearly he had. There was the smell of Xylol in his room, the soft wax; that embedding-oven had been turned on sometime that morning. Had he simply been up there early, doing some work, and was he then afraid to admit it? . . . George!'

George's breath lifted the newspaper with a soft, fluttering sound.

'George, wake up and listen!'

'I'm listenin',' said George thickly. 'You said, what was Weedon doin' in the herbarium that mornin' when old man Prees was shot. Why, he was shootin' him, of course.'

'I said, wake up, listen!'

'That's right,' said George, 'shootin' him. 'Twasn't a suicide faked to look like a murder faked to look like a suicide; it was a murder faked to look like a suicide faked to look like a murder faked to look like a suicide – and, of course, it was Weedon who done it.'

'Look here, will you stop talking in your sleep and listen!'

George puffed at the newspaper and shifted it a little to one side. One eye looked over the edge.

183

'Tobe,' he said, 'you and me are friends, we been through a lot together, you done more for me than I can count. And I swear to you, I'll never give away to anyone but yourself just what a rotten detective you are.'

'For the Lord's sake—'

'Rotten. Oh, I know all that stuff about Hyland faking the fingerprints; that was all perfectly right. And Hyland did think it was a suicide he was coverin' up. But that was because Weedon had left it lookin' like a suicide.'

'But the motive, George. You know he hadn't any. He'd shown he hadn't any. He'd cause for rancour, all right, but he'd shown that didn't weigh much with him—'

'I know, I know, by savin' Prees' life at the risk of his own. But he might have been savin' it *for* somethin', mightn't he? – remember Prees called it devil's work? And then, somethin' might have happened between that night and the next mornin' to alter his view of things, mightn't it?'

Uneasiness gleamed in Toby's sunken eyes. 'Hm, possibly, but—'

'The fact is, you never paid enough attention to those pods, Tobe. What I reckon happened was this; those pods arrived, Miss Winnpole opened the parcel, spotted somethin' fishy about them and found the heroin. It was a pretty big blow for her, but she didn't give the old man away; she tackled him instead, and got the sack for her pains. Well, when that happened she told her fiancé about it – and Weedon certainly didn't feel about it the same way she did. What he saw was that he'd got the old man in his grip. He went along and told him so – told him he'd got to share the proceeds and all that – and that was just the last straw for Prees, whose nerves had been goin' anyway. He sets off for the cliffs and tries to make an end of it. And Weedon stops him. Why? Well, Prees is promising to be a nice source of income, isn't he? And at that stage Weedon doesn't know there's anyone in it but Prees. He doesn't know about Vanedden, and if Prees dies there's an end of the whole business. And Prees knows all that and calls it devil's work. See?'

George had sat up on the divan. He was sitting cross-legged like a chubby pink idol.

He went on: 'But Prees is a man of character; he never could

184

stand bein' interfered with or givin' in to other people; he isn't goin' to let Weedon get away with it. So next mornin' he goes along to the herbarium to shoot himself. But first he rings up Weedon and tells him he's goin' to do it – and what's more, he tells him he's just written a letter to the police tellin' them the whole thing; maybe he even said he'd told them about the part Weedon thought he'd like to play in it. Well, Weedon yells out: "My God, don't do that!" – and sprints round to the herbarium. He gets there just as Prees has put the address and stamp on the letter and is goin' to set off for the letter-box outside. Weedon'd got to get hold of that letter. He tries to grab it, but his strength ain't up to much, he can't do it – and he sees the only way to stop it being posted is to shoot the old man. He snatches up the revolver and does it. And then, of course, he arranges things to look like a suicide, and then he takes a look at the letter. . . .'

Eyeing Toby gravely, George gave a slight shake of his head. 'You never set about these things in the right way, Tobe. That letter – you never did enough thinkin' about that letter either. You never said to yourself why was it in a blank envelope? That's one of the things that struck me as real queer from the start. People scarcely never leave letters around for other people without puttin' their names on them. And then there was that torn bit of an unused stamp stuck on to the corner of an envelope that Tingey found on the floor. And then there was the letter itself; don't you remember the way it started off abruptly right up at the top of the sheet? Is that the way a man like Prees would start a letter? You bet he wouldn't. He'd start off with somethin' nice and pompous and self-important: To the Chief Constable of the County of . . . You know the style of thing. No, Tobe, that letter you found was only the second – or, for all I know, the third – page of the letter Prees had written. The rest had been destroyed. Weedon had destroyed it. But seein' how the last part about the death bein' Prees' own doin' was on a separate sheet of paper, he put that into a clean envelope and left it on the desk. He was too smart to try forgin' Prees' handwritin' on it – he knew he couldn't do it. So he just left the envelope plain. He'd have been smarter still, of course, if he hadn't put it in an envelope at all, but had left the sheet just lyin' on the desk. Still, we all make mistakes sometimes or other – eh, Tobe?'

Toby, sitting hunched in his chair, gnawing a knuckle, grunted.

'Well,' George continued, 'I reckon it was just then, when he'd arranged everythin' and had just got ready to go, that he heard Barnes arrive. Must have been a nasty moment for him. So he slipped into his own room and hoped there'd be a minute when he could get downstairs and out. But there wasn't; Barnes went and took it into his head to clean that corridor and the entrance-hall that mornin'. So Weedon was stuck – and realisin' he was stuck he thought it'd be best if he tried to make his bein' there look more or less natural. So he simply started some work, switchin' on that oven and goin' ahead with whatever those chaps do when they're workin'. He didn't get his chance to slip out until after Hyland had turned up and sent Barnes off to telephone. Then instead of tryin' to slip out of the place and maybe get spotted by someone just comin' in, he went straight into Prees' room and claimed he'd only that minute got there.'

Toby grunted again. 'And what about Peggie Winnpole?'

'I reckon she guessed most of it,' said George. 'I don't know though – maybe she didn't. But her breakin' off her engagement to Weedon, it must have meant somethin', I should think. Anyway, Weedon knew she'd made up her mind to let on to the police about the heroin: I dropped a question or two to Miss Prees and I found out Weedon was in the bungalow the mornin' Miss Winnpole said she was goin' to tell the police all she knew. He overheard – or perhaps she even told him. So in the afternoon when she said she was goin' to try and have a sleep it was probably him who suggested she should take some tablets to make sure of it – and it was probably him who smashed them up for her in the glass of water. Remember Miss Prees sayin' how, smashed up like that, she'd never have known how many she was takin'. Well, then he jammed up the telephone so's she couldn't get through if she thought there was somethin' the matter with her before she'd gone properly off, and then he waited around. Of course it was him that popped in after Miss Prees went runnin' off, and took the spoon out and washed it and put it back where it belonged, and put the telephone right again. And then after a time he came back and put on his show of woe. He had to do that. He was soaked with the rain, so he

186

couldn't go home and pretend he'd never been out; and too, he couldn't afford to be found walkin' *away* from the bungalow. So he put a bold face on it, got a little way away, and then walked back to it. And of course it was him who'd pinched the parcel of pods. I knew that, and I went round to the boardin'-house, hopin' I'd get a chance to search his room. But he and Miss Prees and Moon were all havin' supper there. So I made out I'd done a search of Moon's room instead; I made a lot of mess in there and left a note tellin' them all just what I'd been searchin' for, and then I made a nice, noisy get-away. So of course Weedon knew someone was after the pods, and that probably his room'd be next. Sure enough, down he came presently with a parcel, and after he'd rung up Vanedden and made an appointment to see him in the mornin', he went out and planted the parcel in Vanedden's motor-boat. Thought he'd worked it all out pretty nicely, I expect, but he oughtn't never to have tried on a thing like that with a man like Vanedden. Vanedden wasn't goin' to have anyone sittin' over him, bleedin' him – he hit out with a heavy piece of rock. Didn't do him much good, of course, because I'd put Dan Moon on to swimmin' after him – that was *his* mistake. Ah, well. . . . You know, Tobe, these criminals, they do keep one humble. They remind one that the best of us do make mistakes.'

'George! . . .' There was a short silence. Then Toby began again: 'George, did Moon know all this when you sent him swimming after Vanedden?'

'Not him. I told you. Tobe, I'd never give you away to anybody. I'm your friend. No, he believes your explanation of things just like the gospel. There's only the three of us know.'

'The three of us? Did you say – *three* of us?'

'Why, yes, old man Tingey knows all about it, Tobe. He knew it all along. He says he was sure it was Weedon from the moment Miss Prees went and poked her finger into the wax. But, you see, he was put off like you by Weedon's havin' saved the old man's life the night before; he couldn't find a motive.'

'But he thought Joanna herself was guilty!'

'Not him, Tobe. He told me afterwards – we were havin' a game of darts, and he's quite human over a game of darts – he told me it was you kept sayin' he thought Miss Prees was guilty. He says he never said so himself. He says he was trying to get her to explain the truth about the wax, but he says he never even thought of her bein' guilty. He only thought she'd been up there and that she'd seen Weedon; he thought when she put her finger in the wax she was droppin' him a hint. That was *his* mistake.'

'But why did he let everything drop then? Why did he let my version of things get by?'

'Ah, well, Weedon was dead, Vanedden was dead, Tingey'd put his finger on the drug-business, which was what he was really most interested in all along, and there wasn't any ten thousand pounds for the insurance company to be swindled out of. So he thought it'd be best for the people remainin' if the thing was just hushed up. He thought Miss Prees had been through enough already. He'd a soft spot for Miss Prees, you know; he told me while we was playin' darts that she was really just the sort of girl he'd like Irene Dawn to grow up into.'

Toby gave a cackle of laughter.

'And that's *your* mistake, George. I don't believe there *is* an Irene Dawn. In fact, I'm certain there isn't an Irene Dawn. Tingey found she came in useful whenever he didn't want to answer questions. Irene Dawn is just an official myth.'